Halfkinds Volume 4: North

by Andrew Vu

4
NORTH

Table of Contents

Need to catch up on plot, characters, or other information in the Halfkinds world?

Just head over to the online encyclopedia for all your needs:

http://halfkinds.wikia.com

Chapter 1 – Don Leons

Marks

September 10, 3071 7:12 PM

Seven in the evening and I'm still in the office. I got in earlier this morning, and I've been doing clerical work all day. Data quality checks here, datacube filing there, even refilled the coffee machines. It's hardly as exciting as what I used to do, and not a day goes by when I don't think of the positions I held in the Alliance. I was at the top, a supervisor of missions, and now I'm at the bottom, a cockroach that has been stepped on repeatedly. I work hard doing menial tasks.

It's a Sunday, for crying out loud, and I'm in the office, a small, one-room building that stores a bunch of compcubes. The walls are grey, the air is cool, and it's depressing as hell. Basically, the perfect place for guys like me.

It seems so long ago when I felt invincible. As a young man, I slowly climbed the ranks of the Alliance. First, I was a part-time investigator. Then I became a field weapons manager, and then I became an intelligence officer. I took many different jobs with the Alliance, but the trend was always upward. Each new position I took was better than the last, and I gradually was promoted to the higher ranks within the infrastructure. I rose and rose and rose; nothing was going to stop me.

By the time I was a middle-aged man in my sixties, I had reached what now became the peak of my career. I was a field mission supervisor. Correction, I was one of the top field missions supervisors out there. My job was to take on assignments, organize teams to execute them, give intel and provide equipment, and monitor the operations to ensure they were completed successfully. Essentially, I was a military coordinator.

It was an important role but also an easy one. I never had to go into the field or engage in combat. All my work was done in the comfort of my planning room. I would send communications via communicators and gather any outside resources that the action team might have needed.

At first, I worked on small missions. But as I became more and more successful in my supervising, I was given missions with higher prestige. Soon, I was commanding top-secret operations ordered from the top of the Alliance's military. Even the great General Rox put me in charge of some of his jobs. It seems crazy that I even interacted with the legendary dog now, but back then, it was all real.

I didn't exactly have the best reputation. A lot of folks weren't fond of my style. They thought I was lazy, pompous, arrogant, manipulative, and a plain jerk. But I didn't care; those people were jealous. None of that mattered. The only thing that mattered was that I got the job done. I never failed a mission.

That is until Operation Halfkinds. It was a search-and-destroy mission. The marks were a bunch of genetic freaks that the Alliance wanted to be done with. Genetic experimentation laws were as strict as they are today, so it was vital that such monsters be destroyed. I gathered a team, individuals selected by both my superiors and me. They were supposed to be the best, able to get the job done quickly and efficiently. Instead, things turned out to be a mess.

By the end of it all, two teleportation stations were leveled and five of my team members were killed. But all the halfkinds were reported dead. I was relieved. While it wasn't a perfect execution, the mission was successful. And as a bonus, one of my team members, Fenrir Snow, survived.

Yet, I was wrong. The ending wasn't happy.

That damn wolf. He lied to me. He said the mission was over, the freaks were dead. I believed him. I guess I should've done some extra homework, you know, sent an inspection team to make sure the job was through. But then again, I had no reason to believe he was a liar. He was a soldier, a damn good one, and I had no idea the head case that lay underneath. That's why I thought the deed was done.

It wasn't. A halfkind still lived, and the two of them disappeared from the Earth. The only one left to take the fall was me. And boy did I fall hard. I was stripped of my duties and demoted halfway to hell. I guess I should be grateful I wasn't fired or sent to a prison pod. Or maybe I shouldn't. I lost everything I loved. My power, my job, my money, it all went away with one order.

A few years later, I was involved with another halfkind mission, this time to take down their creators, a human supremacist group known as HORUS. But I was no longer in charge. I was simply an admin sent there to do some quick prep work for the assigned team. The guy who was the leader was handpicked by General Rox.

I tried my best at that job to learn the full scope of the operation. I wanted to make sure my prep was thorough. Turns out, the guy didn't even need me. He already knew all the answers. He was a jerk and called me out on my failures. He even questioned my role in his mission. How unprofessional is that?

Yet that asshole turned out to be the savior of the Alliance's military branch. Not only did he complete his mission, but he did so with flying colors. I heard he obtained some secret blueprints from HORUS and they were used to create a technological boom not only in military advances, but also medical ones. They were called implants, and they made the body stronger, more resistant to disease and harm, and heightened certain senses. An array of devices and enhancements were developed from that work. General Rox and his boy reaped all the glory, while I continued to slide.

I'm pretty sure that asshole, Brock West, put in a few bad words for me, and once again, I was demoted. The opposite started to happen. Instead of my career going up and up, it was going down and down. Now I'm at my all-time low. This poor soul is nothing but an old, broken man working some filler job out in the Pacific Northwest.

My daily routine consists of nothing more than maintenance and admin work. It's nothing of substance, nothing like what I used to do. Hell, a drone could do it. The hours are long, the pay sucks, and I often find myself thinking about leaving. Yet I can't. I've been a long-time employee of the Alliance. It's in my blood to be of service. And in a way, I suppose this job is their way of repaying me for my years of service. It's better for me to do something than nothing. I could have been kicked to the streets.

But it saddens me. I'm approaching retirement, and when I finally decide to hang it up, it won't be with dignity. It'll be with shame. I'll be filled with regret, thinking about what could've happened and where things went wrong. I'm a shell of what I used to be.

It's almost quitting time, and there's no one else in the office but me. The emptiness is a sight I often see. I feel like I don't know anyone else but myself. And after this, I'll drive home, prepare a bath, rest, and do it all over again. And I'll be alone, like every other day. What a life I'm living.

I walk around and start to shut down the compcubes. They'll need one final inspection before I leave. I kneel beside one of them, and that's when I hear a large clang burst from the other side of the room. I jump to my feet and clutch my chest. It feels like I'm having a heart attack. I calm myself down and rest my nerves. It's probably nothing.

But then I think about it. Like I said, I'm the only one here. Noise like that doesn't come from nowhere. It comes from a source, from a *someone*, from a living creature. Is someone else here? Highly unlikely. This administration center is far away from any major city, tucked way out in the wilderness. And we only have four active employees that work on rotational shifts. They'd be the only ones around, and they're all off today. It's only me and has been only me all day.

Still, I better check it out.

I get up and slowly approach the only door, which is at the north end of the room. I nervously set aside chairs that block my path. That includes a box of wires and some metal connector rods. My left hand shakes a little as I make my way there, while my right hand starts to feel clammy. My eyes get bigger and I breathe in deeper and faster. I don't know what's got me so jittery, but the sudden rush of fear is too hard to control.

I now stand in front of the chrome-colored door. Next to it is a retina scanner, so I lean forward and let it do its work. A smaller laser emits and shoots into my iris.

"Scanning complete," the computer says.

Locks and gears shift behind the door. I hold my breath for one last moment before it slides open. My fists clench, my teeth grind, and my heart beats. I impatiently tap my right foot. Here we go.

The door glides and I take a cautious peak outside. I exhale and relax. Nothing. Nothing is out there. I breathe a sigh of relief.

"Guess it was just my mind playing tricks on me," I say.

But then I notice something at my feet. It's a long piece of electrical wire, like the one I stowed away earlier.

"How'd this get here?" I ask myself.

Suddenly, the wire starts moving on its own! It quickly wraps my leg, coiling around it like a snake. I watch it, both amazed and stupefied by how it has suddenly sprung to life before my very eyes.

"What the fuck?" I say slowly in an awed tone.

Right after those words, the wire yanks. My leg goes with it. My face smacks the ground with a thud and I temporarily get knocked out. But I quickly recover and become conscious again. The first thing I do is spit out some blood. My tongue probes around a bit to discover that a couple of my teeth have been lodged loose. The pain shoots through my jaw like a drill hitting the gums.

That's when I remember the cord is still tied to my leg. I swiftly roll around so I'm lying on my back and hastily do a sit-up so I can detach it from me, but before my hands reach it, the cord tugs again. I stumble over, back slamming against the ground, and feel the friction as I get dragged across the room. I struggle for a bit, but after some effort, I'm able to lift my head to see who is pulling me. Yet, to my surprise, no one is there. The culprit to my towing appears to be invisible.

Then I look farther out of view and I do see something in the distance at the end of the room. It's a shadowy figure, dressed all in black. It's hooded and appears to be wearing some shiny armor. Its face is covered with a mask that's completely onyx except for some intricate vine-like designs etched in white.

The creature is bipedal and has arms and fingers, but I'm not sure if it's human. Its posture looks kind of… funny. I don't have much time to analyze it because the creature has already dragged me clear across the room. The cord stops its pull, and I'm left looking up at the dark figure.

"Stand," the creature says. Its voice isn't human, nor does it sound like any other animal I've heard of. It sounds like a computer. Could this thing be robotic?

I continue to lie there, disobeying its command. I don't know what this being wants and personally, I'm scared stiff. Even if I wanted to rise, I'd be too frozen to do so.

"Stand!" it says again. Once again, I balk. "Very well."

It extends its arm perpendicular to its body and spreads its palms out open toward a chair. Within a few seconds, the object begins to vibrate and, magically, it hovers in the air. Then the creature swiftly moves its arm forward to me, and the chair simultaneously flies in unison. It comes crashing my way, but right before it makes contact, the being closes its open palm into a fist, and the chair drops stiffly next to me.

"Sit," the creature says, pointing at the chair. "And you better do as I say this time unless you want to face the consequences."

Stunned and afraid by the events that have just transpired, I cautiously obey the order. I feel I have no choice.

"So, um, who are you?" I awkwardly say.

"I am a being known as The Collector," it responds.

"And, uh, what are you exactly? You don't look human."

"I am not, but it's not really your concern. What you should be concerned about is your life. Do what I say and you'll be spared."

"And what is it you want me to do?"

"Close your eyes."

"Excuse me?"

"I do not want to repeat myself. Close them."

I hesitate. Instead of following the order, I catch a glimpse of my surroundings. There's a communicator on a desk nearby. If I get to it, I can call the Alliance authorities. All I need is one good lunge. I look back at The Collector. The creature is intimidating, but this is my only shot. I have to take it.

One… two…

…shit.

Before I can even jump out, the wire that dragged me comes alive once more and wraps around me in circles. I'm strapped to the chair, tied like a prisoner.

"Precautions," The Collector says. "Now be so kind and close those eyes."

Guess I have no choice. I follow the order and the only thing I see is darkness.

"Now what?" I ask. The Collector doesn't respond. Instead, the chair starts to move, and I go with it. I feel lighter, like I'm off the ground. It must be the work of the creature. It's moving me somehow with its mind.

In fact, now that I have time to think about it, how is the being doing this? It could be some high-class tech, but I've never heard of any weapon that allows the user to hover things so delicately. Artificial telekinesis is clunky at best, and The Collector controls this power like a surgeon. Even the underground markets don't have anything so advanced. This is the work of something else, something I've never seen.

A sudden drop snaps me out of my thoughts. My butt bounces on the chair cushion and my arms clash on the rests. A loud bang echoes through the room, and I feel my shoes touching the ground.

"Now open them," The Collector says.

"Why?" I ask defiantly.

"Open them, or I will open them for you. And you do not want to experience that."

Yikes, that sounds grim. My eyes open and in front of me is a red light. It's no more than a few centimeters away.

"What is this?" I ask demandingly.

"Just stay still," The Collector says.

The red light blinks and a laser emits from it. Now I know what it is.

"Welcome, Don Leons," the artificial intelligence says. "Security check cleared. You may now access your workstation."

"That's all you needed me for? You just wanted my clearance?" I ask in a stupefied tone. "You could have just asked me for it."

"I know," The Collector says. "But I prefer my methods."

"What happens now? Are you going to let me go?"

"No."

The Collector raises its cloak, and a rod, no more than two feet long, is revealed from underneath. I look closer and see that it's sharpened at one end. Immediately, my mind thinks of the worse.

"Whoa, whoa, whoa… wait a minute here. Is this what I think it is?" I ask.

"It is," the being says.

"Wait, you don't have to do this! I… I can help you. If you're looking for something, information, a location, I can find it for you."

"No, there is nothing else you can possibly help me with."

The Collector spreads its palms, and the spear gets closer to me, inching toward my heart.

"Please don't," I beg. "I don't even know who you are."

The Collector stops its movement. I've gotten its attention. It bows its head and looks straight into my eyes.

"I am a ghost from your past, coming back to get what is mine: retribution. You are the first from whom I will collect."

My heart races. I'm confused. What is it talking about? But it doesn't matter. The Collector rises once more, as does the spear.

"Wait, no!" I yell.

It's too late. With a mighty plunge, the spear impales me right through my heart. Pain explodes from its location, dulling every other sense I have. I look down and only see its end sticking out of my chest.

I try hard to breathe in the air, but nothing comes in. My vision fades, hearing disappears, and the pain that comes from my chest becomes numb. And finally, I feel nothing.

Chapter 2 – Iris Lawton

List

September 10, 3071 7:30 PM

I move my hand back and my metal spear pulls out of the man's lifeless body. He struggled a bit when the rod took the plunge, but now he sits there motionless, cold as my feelings to him and all his scummy Alliance brothers. Don Leons is a dead man, and the world is better for it.

Surveillance has been scrubbed out thanks to some scramblers Lucy equipped me with. No one will know who killed this man.

I lean my body forward, down to his corpse, and lower my head to his level. His dead eyes meet mine.

"I know you were in charge of that mission those many years ago," I say. "Fenrir told me. You're the one who ruined my life. I wonder how things would have turned out if it weren't for you."

I think about that all the time. I can look into alternate futures, but not the past, not what could have been. What's done is done and the only thing I can really do is imagine it. I'd like to think if it weren't for this man and the mission he conducted, I'd still be living my life in seclusion with the rest of my family members. Maybe we'd be gone from Primm. Maybe we'd make it somewhere else. We could have worked out our differences and survived. It's not so farfetched.

Sure, when our mother died, our foundations had already started to crack, but at the same time, Operation Halfkinds is what pushed us over the edge. It expedited our breakdown, caused Tiago to turn on us, pit us against a team of highly trained officials. That mission was the end for us.

Yet, ironically, if it weren't for that mission, I wouldn't have met the love of my life, Fenrir. And perhaps things would have turned out the way they did anyway, regardless of Operation Halfkinds or not. Without our mother, we'd probably be lost. Tiago's "survive at all costs" attitude would have made him eventually abandon or betray us. Oscar would have clashed with him, and the family would have split apart. And my weaker brothers and sisters just wouldn't make it. Fate finds a way of making sure things that are supposed to happen will happen even if the paths are different. So perhaps the man I just killed isn't entirely responsible for the way things have turned out.

Yet he's still part of the problem. No one individual can be blamed for a series of unfortunate events. It's the sum that's the cause. Don Leons, the team that took out HORUS, Two Van Faye, the creators of the Alphas, they have all been the cause of so much pain in my life. They are part of the reason my family is forced to hide in the shadows like rats. Their time is coming. I've been at this for ten years, and I'm just getting started.

Patience is the key to revenge, to freedom. It is my greatest trait, and I will wait and wait until the moment is right, until I can lead the ones I love to victory. The road will be arduous, but I have the skills, the power, to take on these challenges. I have my plan, and in the next few days, I'll be executing a few steps in a long list of tasks. My goal is simple: to resurrect my kind, the hybrid species, and fight our way to freedom. The existence of the hybrid has long been kept in the dark. We've been decimated to the point of extinction, but with my vision, my leadership, that will change. Lucy, my daughter, and I have started the steps to rebuild, and it will only be a matter of time until we're strong enough to take this world head on. The days of living in darkness will be gone.

Lionel Changer tried to do it, but he was mad. He created us for human dominance. I do it for different reasons. I do it because we've been used, manipulated, hunted, and murdered for reasons I can't even comprehend. All we want is to be free, yet the powers that be, the Alliance, they deny it. They can do it because they're a powerhouse. That is why, for now, we hide. I have powers, Ivy has powers, but we aren't strong enough yet. Precognition and telekinesis help, but war is a long game. We don't have the numbers to fight back, not yet anyway. Even if we did, we still can't take on the world.

We need an edge, and I'll be looking for that edge during these next few days. I've consulted my visions, and I've seen this future. I know what I must do in order for my dreams to be realized.

I didn't kill Don Leons only out of spite. I actually have a specific purpose in coming here. Despite his fall from grace within the Alliance, Don Leons still had access to some pertinent information on Alliance personnel. He was a data admin after all. Thus, using his profile, I could gather some simple intelligence on particular targets I have my eye on. That's what the retinal scan was for, so I could get into the network.

I go to the station where the scan was performed and turn on the compcube. A holographic display pops open with a big alert that says, "Welcome, Don Leons." Looks like I'm in. I navigate to the Alliance directory database and run a test search. Looks like I can obtain a variety of info on Alliance personnel—position, species, physical description—but what I'm really interested in is contact information.

Lucy and I have been forming a list of candidates I want to pay a "special" visit to. This list is comprised of animals who have helped develop a secret government project, and I'm very interested in getting my hands on the blueprints for this project. And in particular, of those individuals, I'd like to pay a visit to one personally.

Time to call Lucy. I activate my communicator and there she is as a hologram.

"Iris Lawton," she says in her monotone voice.

"Hello, Lucy," I say.

"Assume things going well. Don Leons taken care of?"

Over the years, I've gotten used to her way of talking. Though, I must give her credit. Her grammar continues to improve as time passes. I think it's because of my influence.

"Yes, he's dead," I respond. "I got what I needed from him, and now I'm in the Alliance network. This is where I need your help, old friend. Do you have the list?"

"Affirmative," she says. "Not complete though. Could only find a few names associated to the GTS project. Encountered security walls during hacking phase. Had to back out of program before trail became too hot."

"That's okay. So whose information did you get?"

"Total of four names. Two humans, one female named Jennifer Kim, other male named Tony Angelo. Humans worked on initial design phase of the GTS and that is all. Clearance levels low. Most likely does not have the complete schematics you wish to obtain. Other personnel was Swin McClain, male gorilla. Created individual parts of GTS, but did not oversee production. Only has knowledge of specific areas of the GTS. Doubtful if Swin understands full functionality of device."

The news is disappointing, but I didn't care about any of those names. As long as Lucy can confirm one particular individual on the GTS team, then I can start the chase.

"Those creatures don't concern me," I say in a harsh tone. "You know who I'm interested in."

Lucy's eyes narrow and she looks at me with concern.

"Um, yes, I know," she says. "Eli Winde, former scientific head of the military branch of the Alliance. Recently retired. Current replacement unknown. Also participant in Operation HORUS. Rumored to have helped with the Project Alpha."

"Yes, him. I know all about him," I say. "Can you confirm he was in command during the development of the GTS project?"

"He was."

"Then that's who I will go after. I've had my eye on Winde for quite some time."

Lucy shakes her head. It appears she disagrees with my decision.

"Target high profile," she says in an upset tone. "Highly dangerous to pursue. Suggest different target."

"As a head in the Alliance's scientific arms division, Eli Winde may be the only one who may have the schematics for the GTS. He's our only lead. I don't even know who replaced him. If I don't obtain those blueprints, we won't be able to recreate the device. And getting a working GTS is critical to our long-term plans."

Lucy looks saddened, ashamed almost. I wonder if I'm being too hard on her. Still, it's reassuring. Years ago, she would never display such emotions. Now it's different. It's a true sign that I can call her my friend.

"Don't worry, Lucy. This isn't a knock on you," I say. "You're probably the smartest creature I know, but the Alliance will always have the edge on certain developments. They have more resources to work with. We need to get those documents so the edge is in our hands."

"Not worried about ego," she says. "Am worried about your safety."

"Have more confidence, Lucy," I say. "I'll get it done. I've seen it with my own eyes."

"Precognition is perfect. But you are not."

"I've been training."

I'm confident in my abilities, physical and mental. No more mistakes. I follow every single vision down to a tee.

"Now that I have the confirmation, I'll be checking the directory with my newfound access," I say. "All I need to know is a location. If I can find out where Winde is at the moment, I can consult my visions and figure out my plan of attack."

"Why not consult visions in first place to find out Winde's location?" Lucy asks.

"I can only see the future. I'm not omniscient. I can't find information at my command. What I can do is figure out how to find that information and what actions to take in order to obtain it."

"Ah, yes. Sometimes forget nature of powers."

"It's okay, Lucy. Sometimes it can be confusing."

I laugh to myself, and I see Lucy smile. It's nice to have these small moments of levity before heading into the storm.

"I'm going to continue my information gathering on Winde," I say. "You continue your work with Ivy. She is with you, correct?"

"Correct," Lucy says. "Currently taking break, but has been alert and eager to learn as we continue our research and work on hybrid creation. Splicing trials continue to improve, and results no longer equate to the brutes status."

"How is my daughter holding up? She seems a little down the past few days."

"Yes, have noticed too. Will try to engage conversation about it."

"Thank you, Lucy. I'm signing off now."

"Wait, have one last question."

"Go for it."

She pauses before she says anything. Her eyes look shaky, and I sense the apprehension radiating from her face.

"What is it?" I ask.

"Why did you come to confront Don Leons personally?" she asks. "Could have asked me to hack into personnel database. Confronting Leons was unnecessary."

"From a logical standpoint, yes, it was unnecessary. But from an emotional standpoint, it was."

19

"So this goes beyond doing sensible thing?"

"Yes. Nothing is logical when the reasons are personal. Don Leons is the first name on a list of Alliance scum and enemies that have not only ruined my life, but every hybrids'. From me, you, and Ivy to my dead family in Primm to the friends you had in HORUS. Creatures like him are a detriment. I have a list, and I was planning to get to Leons eventually. It's my own agenda. But I also have a larger scheme at play, getting my hands on those schematics. At first, the two objectives were separate, but now it appears they're converging. Let's just say by visiting Leons personally, I'm killing two birds with one stone."

"Ah, old human idiom. I understand. However, Lawton must understand while personal and larger goals can be completed in unison, one must not trump the other. Must be focused. Must keep eye on prize."

"Yes, Lucy, I know. We'll get the GTS soon."

"Am confident we will."

With that last phrase, Lucy shuts down her communicator, and I disable mine. I go back to the compcube and open the Alliance directory. Time to get to work.

Chapter 3 – Ivy Lawton

Nyx

September 10, 3071 7:51 PM

The vitals look good and the spliced specimens are
stable. We began this wave of fertilization a few
months ago, and each has been progressing quite well.
They're not ready to be released from their stasis, but at
the rate they're going, they'll be free soon enough. We
haven't lost a single sample yet, and soon we'll be mass
producing them in bunches. It feels weird using that
term, talking about the next wave of hybrids as if they
were drones being built in an assembly line, but it's the
truth. We have to produce fast if our species is to
survive.

Aunt Lucy is the architect and my mother is the
director. I guess that makes me the assistant. It's not
an insult or anything. I like my role. I'm here to
support. There's only three of us, and Aunt Lucy and
my mom need as much help as they can get. And I'm
learning a ton from both. Aunt Lucy teaches me the
skills that will be needed to cultivate a generation of
hybrids, and my mom is my mom. Without her, I'd
never be able to harness my telekinesis. She's the
expert and I am her student. It's been a strange, hard
road so far, but I wouldn't trade it for anything in the
world, not when I have them.

Aunt Lucy shuts down her communicator. She was talking to mom, but the conversation is over. Her attention turns back to me.

"How do monitors look?" Lucy asks. "Vitals stable?"

"Yes, they are," I say. I double-check them to make sure. The job is easy, but I'm distracted. I can't focus knowing what's going on with my mother.

Lucy senses my concern. She's getting better at detecting emotions.

"Iris Lawton is fine," she says.

That's a sigh of relief. When she told me of the mission she planned to embark on, I was worried. True, my mother is capable of holding her own against anyone. That doesn't mean she's invincible, and with the tasks she's outlined for herself, she's going to face some tough battles.

But my mom is a warrior. It's what I've known for the twenty-five years I've been alive. I'm an adult, but I'll always look up to her like a kid. My mother is magnificent.

It's been a strange trip ever since we left that island. My father, Bastion, is nothing more than a painful memory I'd rather not recall. Sometimes I forget I had a father at all. No, my only parents have been Mom and Aunt Lucy.

When Mom and I made our official move from Lionel Changer's backup facility to the base on the moon, I thought it'd be a tough adjustment. But it hasn't been tough at all. The new location didn't really mean much because we're still living the same way we did before—underground. But this place feels more like home, more like a place where I belong. Perhaps it's because Bastion isn't here to act like a dictator.

Maybe it's because with just Lucy, Mom, and me around, we've worked hard to build everything on our own. We even gave our moon base a name—Nyx.

Mom and Lucy were able to gather those shady contractors that built HORUS and the island to do the same construction on the moon. Mom did this all under the disguise of her "Collector" persona. Thus, we've been able to prosper discreetly.

Our telekinetic powers have also made construction easier. No need for heavy machinery when we can lift large objects with our minds.

The moon is also an interesting place to live. Well, not really. It's just like Earth. There's water, plants, sun, pretty much anything you can find on the mainland. And it's not like I really get to explore the above world anyway.

To a certain extent, it reminds me of the island. The area we built under is undeveloped, like most areas on the moon. The only things that populate it are trees, dirt, some water, and maybe a few unintelligent animals. The moon was terraformed during the Age of the Human, right before the Event happened. They changed the atmosphere to make it livable, introducing oxygen, carbon, and other essentials to the terrestrial body. Gravity machines were also applied to hold the atmosphere so it would be sustained. That's just one of the steps they went through on a long list. I don't know exactly how the humans were able to do it, but in the end, they had the knowhow.

Eventually, they finished their goal and modeled the moon after the Earth. Thus, there was water, plantlife, and everything to emulate that Earth experience.

They were ready to move in. Plans for cities and research centers circulated. The humans had grand ideas. Then the Event went down, and the moon was an afterthought. There was no time for anything else but war.

Since then, the animals have been fighting for their share of what has been nicknamed "The Great North." Some meccas have been built, but for the most part, development has been slow. Thus, most of the moon is uncharted territory. What a waste.

I should be happy. It's worked out for us. Maybe it'll end up as a hybrid sanctuary. With the progress the three of us have made, it could go that way.

I've called this place home for ten years. I can't believe time has flown by so fast. Seems like yesterday I was a teenager, watching streams, feeling depressed and worried about my uncertain future. Now I'm not afraid. I'm confident in the direction my mother leads us.

She's planning things, a way for us to fight back, a way for us to be free. That's what the last ten years have been about.

And honestly, even though we're not free yet, it's been a blast so far. The relationships I have with both my aunt and mom are stellar. We have normal family meals, bonding time. It's been a real family-first environment.

We even go on vacations. Of course not to big cities, but we have our little adventures in the world. Hiking, camping, visiting natural wonders. Mom uses her powers to foresee danger, to make sure our travels are safe. Once she confirms it, a simple personal porter trip is all we need to enjoy Earth and Great North in all its wonder.

Other days, when we aren't secretly traveling across the world, we entertain ourselves here. It's like living back on the island. Streams, games, nice beds, and plenty of entertainment to keep my mind occupied, even distracted. It could be a lot worse. I could be locked in a basement like Mom was when she was growing up.

And unlike the island, I have free will. Mom and Lucy respect my wants and make sure I live the fullest life I can, given our tough circumstances. I mean, it's always been that way living under Mom's roof, but I guess the change in scenery really reinforced the idea. Perhaps the move has helped me in more ways than I know.

These are the kinds of things I never experienced under Bastion's rule. I will always find it irksome that my mother killed my father, but that's what she had to do. He held us back, prevented us from living full lives. It's that taste of freedom that he withheld. It's that feeling of family that was missing. Bastion was my father, but he was never really my family.

Sometimes I look back and wonder why things are so simple. My life has been anything but that, yet the dynamic I have with Mom and Lucy has never been complicated. I suspect it's because we are upfront with each other. We share everything and rarely hide our secrets. It's this bond that has kept me sane throughout the years. I'm not a paranoid mess like Bastion. I'm in the arms of those who truly love me.

I feel alive again, not trapped in a broken home. I'm happy. And if this is what is in store for us after Mom is done with her plans, then I can't wait.

We're going to fight for our freedom. That's what all these years have been about. We only have two objectives: breed a new wave of hybrids in order to survive and be free, and build our underground empire so when the time is right, we can unleash upon the world our fury and take what is rightfully ours.

"Hey, Aunt Lucy, I'm going to take a break. I've been at it all day. Is that okay?" I ask her.

"Of course," she says. "Will complete rest of tasks. Mind setting up dinner?"

"Sure."

I walk out of the lab into a short hall. On the other side is a door and I enter through it. In front of me are various teleporters, each with different labels on top of them. They are labeled "kitchen," "barracks," "training room," and so on. I walk to the kitchen one and activate it. The light from the porter glows and I march through it. I end up on the other side of a porter labeled "research facility." I am now in a room that is identical to the first one, except now I'm in the kitchen pod.

That's how Nyx is laid out. When I said it was like the island, I meant it. There are several pods, one thousand square-foot quarters, scattered underground on the moon. Each one serves a different purpose. And the only way they are connected is by teleporters. There's no physical link, no bridge, no tunnels, nothing. Hell, the pods don't even have a lift to the surface. The only way you can get from one pod to the next is by teleportation.

We do have a general entrance of sorts that is a small pod filled with a bunch of teleporters. In there is a teleporter that is linked to our personal porters, meaning it's the gateway when we transport in from far destinations.

The reason they're set up this way is for security. If someone stumbles upon a pod, whether an excavation crew, the Alliance, whomever, that'll be the only one they breach. They won't have any idea where the other pods are because of the lack of physical connections. And to make it safer, each pod is built far apart from each other, making them scattered underground and hard to find. It's like looking for needles in a gigantic haystack.

There are quite a lot of pods, and we're continuing expansion. As years pass, more and more pods get built. The eventual goal is to build a city of sorts where you can get from one destination by teleporting around. We'll need to think big if we're going to house a generation of hybrids. Construction is never-ending, but it's easier when we have a constant cache of resources to work with. Lucy still has access to all of Lionel Changer's accounts, and we're still using them. Lucy has also created fake accounts and processed transactions in the markets. Credits aren't an issue for us. We've also been using Changer's contractors. Only my mother deals with them, and she's always in her "Collector" persona. We keep it as tight lipped as possible.

I walk through a corridor and continue my quest for dinner. I wonder what Lucy feels like eating today. I feel like something meaty.

The kitchen pod is one of the smaller pods. I mean, how big can a kitchen be really? There's the cooking area and a cafeteria. We plan to expand it once we get some more hybrids in. I imagine it will look like a dining hall after our operation gets bigger.

That's how all these pods will evolve over time. We'll need to expand and expand. However, these pods can only get so much bigger. Iris and Lucy have plans for what they call megapods. Essentially, they'll take the concept of a pod and make it huge enough to house an entire city underground. It'll kind of be like a below-surface biodome, complete with buildings, an energy source, and everything else that can be found in the above world.

These megapods will be the centerpiece of our underground civilizations. It's the only way for our society to progress, to move forward. It may be a dream now, but we have our plans, and I'm excited to get to the day when they will be a reality. The three of us are on the forefront of history, not only for our kind, but for all intelligent species. We will rise up from the shadows just like they did.

Iris doesn't like to use the term, but that's what we're essentially building, an army. We'll need one if we want to take on the Alliance. It's a numbers game, and the more we have on our side, the better our chances are. The three of us can't do it alone.

I'm now at the cooking station and need to see what we have in storage. I turn on a nearby compcube and do a quick inventory check. Lucy usually likes her food spicy, so I'll put in some peppers. We also have chicken in refrigeration and some fish. I'll fry some up. I could make one of the pre-programmed meals, but I want to work on my own cooking skills.

I dial up my ingredients. They're not held in the kitchen; they're located in our storage pod, which is a miniature supply depot. My order is confirmed and they are ported into the local insta-item.

I already have a recipe in mind, so I get to work on it. I think I'll be at it on my own, but a voice surprises me from behind.

"Need help?" Lucy asks.

"No, I can handle it. We'll be having chicken and fish if that's okay," I respond.

"Is fine."

Lucy sits down at a nearby table and pulls out a tablet to review her notes.

"Excellent work today," she says. "Iris will be pleased when arrives back from mission."

Ah, the mission. I was so focused on dinner, I had almost forgotten about it.

"So did she get the information she needed from that Leons fellow?" I ask Lucy.

"Yes," Lucy responds. "On her way to finding schematics for GTS."

About a year ago, Lucy dug up some data on a device that would be a game changer in the upcoming war against the Alliance. She wasn't completely sure what it did at first, but as she researched more and more, she assured us that if she could get her hands on the prints and build it herself, it would tip the scales in our favor. She explained to my mother what it did, and Mom agreed.

I've been kept in the dark for the most part, but my mother has told me that I'll know what it does once she completes her mission. Even the details of her operation have been kept only between Lucy and herself. All I know is that she'll be visiting the right creatures, gathering information and leads on her quest to find the plans of this GTS device.

I normally don't like being out of the loop, but I trust her judgment. If she feels I need to wait, then I will wait.

Still, I'm worried. I hope she doesn't run into any danger, but it sounds like it'll be unavoidable. Lucy stares at me, sensing my concern, as I avoid eye contact with her.

"Dinner is almost ready," I tell Lucy.

"Good. Hungry. But before eat, must show you something," Lucy says. "Put food on warmer. Will return to eat."

"Okay."

I set aside the meal I've made and follow Lucy back out to the teleporters. She walks through the one labeled "incubation" and I follow.

When I get to the other side, Lucy is waiting for me. I'm a bit puzzled why she has brought me here.

"What're you doing?" I ask her.

"Follow me," she says, avoiding my question.

We walk into a room that's on the west end of the pod. It's dark, but I've been here a million times.

Lucy turns on the lights.

"Why are we here?" I ask her.

"Sense you are worried. Needed to calm you," she says.

"But this place isn't exactly the calmest room in Nyx."

"Disagree. This is result of fruits of labor. Not awed by what have created?"

I take a look around and think to myself. She is right. We've toiled night and day in order to see the sight I see.

"I suppose so," I say. "But this isn't making me any less worried about Mom."

"Understand," Lucy says. "But must also understand this. Before you is what you and self have worked hard on. Has taken much blood and sweat, mistakes and frustrations. But in end, completed our work, and now know path. Iris Lawton is doing same thing. Has a mission to carry. Dangerous, will require much endurance and self-sacrifice. But in end, mission will help bring us to next step. Just as you look at this room and know struggle worth it, Iris Lawton does same every day. She struggles for us. She struggles because it is worth it. Knows you are worried, but she wants you to know that to get to goals, worries part of process. Only then will you become stronger."

It's strange to hear the words come from my Aunt Lucy. She's usually so stoic. Yet I know underneath it all, she has an emotional core that is hard to reach. Her knowledge goes beyond science. She taps at her soul. And that is why I appreciate her company.

"Thank you, Lucy," I say. "I understand and will try to have more faith."

"Welcome, Ivy," she says. "Let's eat."

We walk away from the room, but not before I have one last glance. Before me lies hundreds of hybrids in development, incubating in tubes.

"To the next generation," I say to myself.

I then turn off the lights and leave.

Chapter 4 – Falena Snow

Stray

September 13, 3071 9:20 AM

Did you know that Fang Snow had a daughter? Yes, I'm talking about the Fang Snow of the infamous Snows of the Wolf's Den. They were a once proud and honorable military family that lasted for generations until their quick fall from the top. The Snows used to be a name that was admirable; now it is only associated with treachery. Any good grace with my name had disappeared a long time ago.

I am the last of them, both by birth and by choice. I am the daughter of Fang Snow.

My mother was a great mother. I didn't have much time with her, but from what I remember, I was her world. She raised me as a cub and a few months later, when I could walk and talk, she taught me the ways of this world.

My mother was rough and fierce to others. She ordered my uncles around with ferocious veracity, being the blunt instrument that kept them together. She had to. They often challenged her, but she stayed tough in order to prove her worth. I always admired her strength.

Despite her rugged and ready ways with her brothers, she was gentle with me. I was a frightened little child, scared of this and that, and my mother did her best to let me know things were okay, that the world was a place to love, not one to fear. She protected me from those dangers and inspired me to be more confident. She told me the only thing to be afraid of was my own lack of assurance.

In the early years, my mom would go on missions. I didn't understand the nature of her job, but when she got home from her arduous operations, she always had a smile. She was happy to see me, and I was to see her. She'd drop her gear, nudge me with her nose, and ask me how the days had been.

Sometimes it'd be late, and I would be sleeping. I'm a light sleeper so I knew when she came back, but I'd pretend I was dozing away. She'd walk in, look at me with pride, and tuck in any loose blankets with her teeth. All the while, my eyes would remain closed, but I could feel her warmth, her gentle embrace and affection, as she licked my nose and sent me off good night. It was only after that when I could get a full rest.

And then, the next morning, I would wake up to crisp-smelling chicken. The food would already be in my bowl, and there would be my mom with hers, ready to start the day with a hearty breakfast.

Then we'd figure out the rest of the agenda. Where would we be going? What sites would we be seeing? What games would we play? It didn't matter; all that mattered was our bond. Me and her, her and me, those were the best days of my life.

I never knew who my father was. He left a long time ago when I was a youngling. But I didn't care. My only guardian was her, and my young, precocious mind was set.

And then, one day, she was gone. My mother went on a mission. It was the last time I ever saw her.

I wasn't even sure if she was dead. There was no body recovered, no explanation. I was told by my relatives that she was simply missing in action, along with all of my uncles.

It was very suspicious. I was fairly young at the time, so I asked questions just as any young one would. I asked where did she go, what happened to my relatives, everything. And all the time, I was greeted with short answers and dodged responses. My other family members shut me out. Thus, as a young, impressionable one, I had no choice but to accept that things were the way they were. My mother died on the battlefield and that was that. Nothing else to talk about.

But still, the yearning for truth harbored within me as I grew through my childhood. After my mother vanished, I was sent to live with a distant uncle. He was not a Snow by name. He was a Fallow. And thus I became Falena Fallow. I hated that name. I wished my uncle were a true Snow.

Even if he were one, he might have followed the lead of my other relatives. Left and right, my cousins, uncles, and aunts were changing their names. Some took the surname Howl, others Sleet, but all of them didn't want to be associated with the Snows.

Any links to the military quickly vanished. The Snows came from a long line of warriors, generals, soldiers, and officials, but you wouldn't have known it the way things played out. My relatives never referred to the past, only the present and future. Any images or streams of our history were deleted and destroyed. Artifacts, antiques, and heirlooms were sold. Dwellings were put on the market; new ones were bought. All the ties we had within the Brotherhood were also severed. The Snows were extinct.

I never understood why the sudden change. It confused my young mind. I had grown up idolizing my mom and the Snow lineage. They were heroes, brave fighters who did anything for their proud wolf heritage. They served the Brotherhood well. A family legacy doesn't vanish like that for no reason. The abruptness of it all was peculiar.

Then, when I was old enough, I was told the truth. My mother and her brothers were responsible for the downfall of the Snows.

It all started when Uncle Fenrir aided in the escape of a fugitive, these genetically engineered creatures called halfkinds. His failure was one of the reasons Alliance and Brotherhood relations became strained. All the other species were players in the Alliance, and the wolves were losing their place. They became the outsiders, and Uncle Fenrir's failure solidified this.

Fenrir was in hiding, and the Brotherhood punished the remaining Snows, including my mother. Those missions she went on were really mercenary jobs. My mother and my uncles had become the shame of the family.

Everything was Fenrir's fault. He had to pay for what he did. That's when she decided to hunt down Uncle Fenrir to restore honor for our family. But that was the last mission. That was when I never saw her again.

My family only knows that she and my uncles went on the hunt. But they don't know if she was able to successfully track down Uncle Fenrir or what became of their confrontation. They don't know whether she failed. Hell, they don't even know to where she traveled. All they know is that one day, the four of them, my mother, Uncle Raymus, Uncle Patrice, and

Uncle Danzel, left to pursue my outlawed uncle, never to return.

The Snow name had been dragged through the mud, and the rest of my relatives saw fit to abandon it. Yet, even after I was told what happened, I refused. I changed my name back to Snow. My mother was a hero, she deserved better than to be forgotten. The Snow name was the only thing I had left to honor her memory. As I grew older, I started to forget what she was like. It made me sad. But her name will always help me remember. Falena Snow would stay.

I eventually lived through an uneventful adolescence, went to university with a degree in infospace programming, and got a mundane job as an analyst for some middling compcube advancement company. I now settle in a sleepy, quiet town called Orf, located around the edge of civilization within the Wolf's Den. Quite a different life compared to that of my mother.

But I like my job. I get paid decently and get good benefits. I can't compare it to going on top-secret missions or teleporting around the world to exotic locations, but it's an honest living. I think my mother would have been proud.

I always have her in my mind. The fact that they never recovered a body from this so-called mission has kept the desire. The powers that be are hiding something from all of us. I lost my childhood, the moments I should've had with her. It was robbed from me, and I want to know how, why. It's the only way I'll find a bit of peace. I need to know what happened to her.

I've had a bit of a side hobby. A very illegal side hobby. When my mother disappeared, I always suspected it was the work of the Brotherhood or the Alliance. You don't work in the military and die mysteriously if it hadn't been a cover-up. Thus, using the skills I've gained over the year, I've done a little hacking into some very secure, very classified databases.

My first target was the Brotherhood servers. They were the ones who were hush-hush about everything, and they were the ones that the Snows had worked under for years. If any group was responsible for my mother's fate, it had to be our own government.

It took quite some time to improve my skills to a point where I was good enough to hack into the Brotherhood's secure files. A few off-market hacking companies helped me set up private test servers that emulated the protocols the Brotherhood used. I then spent hours every day after work attacking them, figuring out their tricks and weaknesses. This went on for days, weeks, and years. Finally, three years later, I was ready to dive into the real thing.

And I was successful. I was worried my hacking code would be traced back to me, but I was smart and applied several masks. They never even knew I was there. Mountains upon mountains of Brotherhood files were at my paws.

It took another year to sort through all the mess. I was looking for anything specific on Fang Snow and her death.

What I found was… very little. The only thing there about my mother was stuff I already knew—her military history, official missions, and so on. There was one small thing about her demise, that it was inconclusive. Nothing new there. The Brotherhood's files had zero to offer.

I was stuck, but an idea came to my head. The mission my Uncle Fenrir failed, the one that caused everything to fall apart, wasn't a Brotherhood mission. It was an Alliance one. Perhaps I was looking in the wrong place. If I wanted to find out what happened to Mom, I'd have to take on the big boys. I'd have to hack into the Alliance.

I was weary. Breaking into Brotherhood files was one thing, but tackling the all-powerful United Species Alliance was another. I used the same process, but I had to be extra careful. The Alliance is notorious for being able to track hackers down and taking the means necessary to eliminate such nuisances. They don't mess around, but if the reward was finding out my mother's fate, I had no choice but to take the risk.

After I had some practice in another test area that I set up, and after some self-convincing, I dove headfirst into Alliance servers. It took a few months, but I gained access to their classified documents. It was time to start digging.

It actually was easier looking through Alliance records compared to Brotherhood ones because my mother had limited dealings with the Alliance. Thus, there was less gutter information to sift through. Within a few weeks, I had stumbled onto a report with the details of something called Operation HORUS.

I first read the background regarding the mission. A bunch of commandos were sent to infiltrate some mad human's underground facility. It wasn't anything out of the ordinary. The human was doing genetic work, and the Alliance shuts that stuff down fast. But what caught my eye was what he was actually creating.

I had heard of halfkinds from what my relatives knew regarding Operation Halfkinds. They were half-man, half-animal creatures. Apparently this man, Lionel Changer, was the father of these creatures and planned to create an army of sorts. According to the documents, Operation HORUS shut that down quickly.

The initial information I read was interesting, but I was discouraged. What did Operation HORUS have to do with my mother? Why did it show up in my search results?

I continued my reading. Toward the end, I read a small section in the HORUS report that had something about wolves. And that's when I saw the connection.

This footnote detailed the finding of five wolf bodies within lower quarters of HORUS. From what I read, Lionel Changer was a notorious humanist, so I thought it was odd that wolves would be found in his domain.

It was only when I read further I found out the horrible truth.

"No," I said to myself.

The five bodies belonged to five members of the Snow family: Raymus, Danzel, Patrice, Fenrir, and sadly, Fang. This is where my mother ended up. For one reason or another, the Snow conflict was resolved in HORUS's walls.

Or so it seemed. There was more to the report. Only three perished. Two remained alive. They were comatose and severely injured, but they lived. The last part of the report states that the two survivors were sent to the United Species Alliance Science Division for further study.

One of the survivors was Fenrir Snow. The other was Fang Snow. My mother was still alive! I was excited, gleeful of the possibility. But then I realized Operation HORUS happened almost thirty years ago.

And according to the report, my mom was in bad shape. The chances she was still on Earth were slim.

There had to be more information about her, but that's all the report stated. I couldn't find anything else within the Operation HORUS files that further divulged my mother's fate. My search had hit a dead end.

I took a break to try to think of what else I could look for. What would the United Species Alliance Science Division want with her and my uncle anyway? I scoured the file for any other relevant information.

That's when I saw something about biotic implants. The report stated they harvested some schematics from HORUS. I recalled there was also a big boom in the industry during this time. Seems like it was more of a coincidence. But I wondered why this would be included in a report that mentioned my mother.

It was a long shot, but I investigated if there was a connection between the two. I did a cross-reference search between both Fang and Fenrir Snow and biotic implant development, hoping it would lead me somewhere.

As usual, the results were bountiful, and I had to go through each and every one of them if I wanted to make sure. That meant reading the results inside and out, ensuring that no fact was ignored. I spent many sleepless nights toiling away. Awakeners and stimulants were my diet. I did it because I had a feeling this time, the search would lead me somewhere. It was only a feeling, but I had never been so certain about anything in my entire life.

It took weeks, but I've finally reached a reward to my arduous search. Hidden deep within the encrypted personal files of an Alliance dog, General Rox, the creator of the HORUS report, is something called

Project Alpha. I haven't started my review of the files, but from the summary, it seems very promising. What I find here may lead me to discovering what happened to my mother. Then, at last, I can get some closure.

I will find out the truth.

Chapter 5 – General Rox

Ops

September 13, 3071 10:40 AM

"Quick, efficient, and no collateral damage. I'm very pleased. I've read the details of his mission and will report them to my superiors. Tell Bains that she did an excellent job, and I will touch base with her soon," I say to Jo, my secretary.

"Yes, sir, General Rox," she says. "You also have a meeting regarding future biotic plans with the United Species Alliance Science Division later this afternoon. Will you still be conferencing in?"

"Of course, but I can't stay too long. The meeting must be brief. I have a lot of work to do today."

"I will notify them. The work you are referring to is the security leak you discovered this morning?"

"Indeed."

She pauses before responding.

"Shall I schedule an additional meeting with a member of your operations crew?" she asks hesitantly.

"No, not yet. I'd like to personally pick who to send on the job," I say. "Thank you for your concern though. That is all for now."

"Yes, of course."

She walks out and the door closes behind her. Jo Su is an excellent secretary. She's a hog, a pig, whatever you want to call it, but she breaks the stereotypes.

She's patient, organized, and thorough. She knows how to deflect beings for me and is diplomatic in her cancellations. Both my superiors and my operations team like her.

She's just one of the many perks I've been able to afford over the past years. Biotic development continues to improve, but it's far from where I would like it to be. For now, I have to accept what it is.

My goal has always been to create a super-powered army of implant soldiers. I needed to convince the Alliance that I knew what I was doing and could deliver. I created an extremely detailed report based on our prototypes, the Alphas. The Alliance was impressed with their capabilities and durability, but the need simply wasn't there.

The world had entered a peace state. The biotic boom that I helped launch with Operation HORUS was transforming health care. We were approaching the state of what once was, the era before the Event, the era of prosperity. Implants were being created that helped immune systems, repaired damaged limbs, and increased lifespan past the worldwide average. It was a biotechnological revolution.

However, that led to an increased peace and decreased military intervention. I find it ironic that a military operation was what helped propel the world to this state, yet my superiors don't want to pay the foundations back. They turn a blind eye to the destruction and carnage that helped pave the way here, and continue to do so.

Yet they did throw a proverbial bone to this dog. I was given a small development team to improve biotic military application. The goal still was to enhance my soldiers, but it was done on a much smaller scale than I intended. Despite that, I was promoted within the ranks.

But I interpreted all this as a formality and nothing else. The Alliance wanted me off their back, so they sent me on this side project, hoping I would be too infatuated with my devices to push my agenda. And I decided to play their game. If the Alliance didn't want to take me seriously, I would form a group that would capture their attention. I had a development team to work with, and I would morph my unit to produce so my superiors would beg for my services once more.

I had a vision. If I couldn't produce an army of my creations, I would create a unit, a black ops team, if you will. They would be unstoppable, elite soldiers that I could send on the dirtiest missions that the Alliance would never admit they needed.

The first step to all of this was to continue where we left off with Project Alpha. Eli Winde and a newly paroled Mark Allen, the chimp and the human, were still under my command, so they would be my development leads. Those two were the ones that transformed those vermin wolves into the fighting machines that started it all.

With my funding, I gave them everything they needed to move to the next step. But credits and equipment weren't the issues. Getting test specimens was.

We needed to create a few more of our prototypes to validate the first runs and ensure we could produce more implanted soldiers on a regular basis. Since our prototypes were built on wolves, we only had design plans based on their anatomy. Thus, for the phase following the original Project Alpha, we needed more wolf donors.

To get new subjects, we posted fake mercenary missions on the Brotherhood of Wolves's military boards. We wanted current or ex-soldiers as our bases, wolves with fighting experience, because that's what the Snows were. Once they responded to our postings, I had my team meet and sedate them. If their families inquired their fates, the explanation was always that they died on the mission. In actuality, they would be transformed into new models of implant soldiers while they dreamed away for eternity.

My methods had to be done in secrecy. If the Brotherhood found out what I was doing under Alliance jurisdiction, it would be an international incident. They might be foolish enough to go to war. And the Alliance did not want anything to threaten their precious peacetime.

The Alliance themselves never intruded on my operations. They simply turned a blind eye. One must remember I was black ops, and while the Alliance disagreed with what I was doing, they didn't stop me because they understood such sacrifices needed to be made for progress. As far as the world is concerned, my activity was classified.

Winde and Allen's team produced several upgraded versions of Blackwolf and Silverwolf. They were given names similar to their predecessors. There was Goldwolf, Steelwolf, Diamondwolf, and so on. They were the Alpha Twos. Every one we created was sent to the field for testing, and they were always successful.

A few years had passed and the Alpha Twos were thriving. All those who knew about it were impressed. The Alliance was pleased. I was pleased. Winde and Allen had made great strides in the military biotic implant field. They understood their product inside and out, and now had the knowledge to be more flexible with their application. It was time to move on.

During the ongoing Alpha Two Initiative, Winde and Allen had started development on modified biotics for use on other species. The Alpha Twos had finished their usefulness and were going to be decommissioned. In the upcoming year, they would be disassembled and their bodies disposed of.

That's when it was time to make the switch from comatose subjects to live volunteers. I had my eye on personal picks. All I needed to do was persuade my targets.

Most of them actually stepped up on their own. These soldiers were ones that I have worked with. They came in a variety of species. Humans, gorillas, bears, rhinos, eagles, chimps, cows, pigs, a whole sampling of the animal kingdom. Winde and Allen had developed biotics for all of them. I knew their loyalty would be unquestioned. If I came asking, they would answer.

Also, the modified biotics that Winde and Allen created were designed with consciousness in mind. The new subjects wouldn't be mindless drones as the Alphas were. They would be in complete control of their body. Essentially, they were super soldiers. Their strength, endurance, and durability would be amplified far beyond what their mortal bodies could do. With rewards like that, it was hard to find soldiers who didn't want to sign up. They came begging to be inducted into the newly created Implant Program.

The terms for an applicant were simple. In exchange for enhanced attributes and near invulnerability, they would be at my service, under my supervision, and engage in any black ops operation I choose. There would be no resistance to anything I asked. They'd do as they're told and nothing else.

The implants were installed, and my new subordinates adapted to their gifts. We sent them to the training room and marveled as they accomplished feats of strength, speed, even mental sharpness. Tons were lifted above their heads. Speed records were broken for their respective species. They could engage in physical combat for hours while simultaneously solving difficult puzzles in minutes that would take the average animal hours to do. These volunteers were the perfect soldiers

And over the years, I have gained a collection of them, ready to engage in any mission I choose. They are suited for assassinations, bombings, enforcement, espionage, and even extortion if I deem it necessary. Everything is done for the greater good of the United Species Alliance. Though they don't want to admit it, they are grateful for my efforts.

The mission has always been the priority, and I have one that needs completing post haste.

My tech crew has informed me of a security leak from my encrypted files. Some brilliant hacker has found their way through my data walls and into my most confidential documents.

It seems I wasn't the only target. I had my boys analyze the hacker's pattern, and it appears he or she has been all over the grid. Some of my colleagues also noticed their systems had been intruded upon. However, I'm the only target that had his files tampered with.

This hacker was looking for something particular, information only I had. She looked at my final report on Project Alpha and nothing else. There were tons of other classified documents for the taking. She could've stolen the data, but she only wanted that.

For almost the past thirty years, there has only been one thing that has defined my career: biotics. That's what the hacker was after, that's why she only cared about the Alphas. She wanted to dive into my work and perhaps sell my schematics to some renegade faction. The information alone could be worth a fortune. The hacker was out to make a profit.

At least that's what I first thought until my tech crew identified the perp. Turns out the hacker is the daughter of Blackwolf, the daughter of Fang Snow. Her name is Falena. She's a smart one. She had enough skill to break into the Alliance network. And she was careful too, just not careful enough.

I know why she did it. It wasn't for the credits. Her mother disappeared without warning. I imagine Falena wonders what happened to her. Things like these are always personal and such emptiness can be the strongest of motivators.

So Miss Snow, it seems you aren't in the business of trading secrets. Unfortunately for you, the data you stumbled upon goes beyond petty individual desires. It contains a lot more than just what happened to your mother. The data you have is enough to start wars. A simple leak of that report and my entire operation would be exposed. And there are certain parties that would object to what I did, mainly the use of wolves as test subjects. With that data in your possession, you have become dangerous. You have become a high-priority target.

It may be personal to you, but it's not to me. It's simply good politics.

I log on to my communicator.

"Jo," I say, "that meeting with the United Species Alliance Science Division may run even shorter."

"That's fine," she says. "I'll notify them at once. May I ask why you're cutting the time?"

"I have a last-minute operation I need to organize, and any additional seconds could aid me greatly. The Science Division will understand."

"I see."

"In fact, make sure I'm not bothered at all this afternoon unless it's necessary. I have an important task that needs to be executed, and I know the right man for the job."

I'm about to disconnect when Jo brings up one more thing.

"Also, sir, it appears an Alliance employee was killed in North America on Alliance property," she says.

"What did he do?" I ask.

"Well, he was just some low-level filler job employee. The property he was killed on was a data center."

"And this concerns me how?"

"Apparently you worked with him."

"Really? What was his name?"

"Don Leons."

It sounds familiar. I jog through my memories and try to picture someone. Nothing comes to.

"Sorry, Jo, I don't know who that is," I say.

"He used to be involved in some Alliance authorized missions. One was Operation Halfkinds, another Operation Horus," she says.

Now I remember that loser.

"Oh, yes, Leons," I say. "Have they identified a culprit?"

"No, sir," she says. "Surveillance was disabled, even the atmosphere scanners. No video or holographic images could be processed."

"Sounds suspect. Yet, then again, Don Leons was a nobody and this is just a data center. If there's some update, let me know, but I don't think this concerns me."

"Very well. Have a good day, sir."

"You too."

I disconnect and get back to my main task. Time to contact the man who will track down Falena Snow.

Chapter 6 – Ivy Lawton

Brutes

September 15, 3071 8:01 AM

It's past early morning. That means only one thing: it's feeding time. With a bag packed full of leftovers, bread, processed chicken, dried vegetables, fruits, sandwiches, and water, I make my way to the young ones.

I go through the teleporter and enter the pod. It's a long hallway down to a single-room barrack area, but I'm excited. The time away from my mother has been refreshing. I admit I miss her around Nyx, but at the same time, it's nice to get some time to myself. God knows I could use it with all the stuff going on right now.

Sometimes Mom can be a bit judgmental. She certainly wouldn't approve how I'm spending this morning. She'd tell me not to get too attached, that I should be concentrating my energy on other things. She doesn't go as far as to say she hates the young ones, but I know she does. She's told me they are imperfects, liabilities, creatures that are temporary. Sometimes she is so harsh.

But I know she does this because she's trying to teach me a lesson. Never get too involved. I understand.

And I am worried about Mom. I hope her mission goes well. I hope she doesn't encounter too much danger. I pray she comes back alive, safe and sound.

Crap, what am I doing? I can't think of these things right now. They make me sad and scared. The only thing I should be thinking about is happy thoughts, like the quality time I'll have with the outcasts.

I'm outside the barracks where they reside. The door is closed. I stand on the other end, waiting to go in. A deep breath in, deep breath out, the door opens and I walk through. The room is dark and cool. It's also quiet. The only sounds I hear are snoring.

But once I turn on the light, they wake up. They take a few moments to adjust, but the second they see me, they are ecstatic. They run to me. Though I use the term young ones, we generally refer to them as the brutes.

They are hybrids like Lucy, like my mother, like myself. There are ten total. Two cats, three tigers, three lions, one gator, and one elephant. Half of their makeup is their respective species, the other half is human. However, they look more like their non-human counterparts.

Their skeletal structure is similar to a human. They are bipedal, have feet, legs, arms, and hands. They also have toes and fingers, five on each appendage like a human. They have necks and backs, stomachs, and shoulders.

Yet on the outside, they are very animal-like. Their heads match their animal counterparts. Their skin has fur or scales, depending on which brute you look at. Some have tails, others have claws on their hands. They are a mishmash of human and other.

And it's not a smooth combination. Their appearance isn't as transitioned as Lucy or my mother and me. No, they are deformed. Bumps and pieces of bone protrude from their bodies. Just a list of some of the facial deformities: misaligned eyes, teeth that grow out of the mouth, and drooped and unnaturally curved lips.

I do my best to take care of them, to make them look complete, but all ten of them are simply too malformed to make appealing. One word comes to mind with them: monsters.

The creatures are also huge. Each brute towers over me, standing above eight or nine feet. They weigh five hundred to six hundred pounds apiece

With such size comes great power. They are behemoth-like. We've run tests on them and watched them level doors, knock down tress, lift hovercars with little effort whatsoever. Lucy has measured their lifting ability to over one thousand pounds.

All of this is done without training or the aid of implants. I've seen them match my mother in terms of physicality. And this is with her body modifications and years of training. The brutes have nothing but raw power built within their bodies.

My mother is not fond of them. She has seen the carnage they are capable of and fears them. She warns me they are an untamed force that cannot be trusted. Mom is calculating and precise, the brutes are wild and unpredictable. To her, such beings serve little purpose in her grand plan.

But even then, there's a truer reason Mom dislikes these creatures. The brutes are called brutes because, essentially, that's what they are. They lack the key thing that has allowed so many rising species to survive and thrive. They lack intelligence.

They are functional, but their cognitive development only goes as far as infancy. They know simple words, react to stimuli, but can't think for themselves. They rely on their instincts and cannot process logical thoughts.

Yet I know they are not monsters. Despite their animalistic ferocity and grotesque appearance, they are kind in nature. I say they have the intelligence of infants because that's what they are. There's an innocence to them. Their minds don't have to process the complexities of this world. All they know are their raw emotions. They can react in anger, but they also have feelings of love, of loyalty, of childlike wonder at the simplest things.

This is why I am so fond of them. They take me away from this hate-filled world and make me realize in the end, when we are broken down to our emotions, that bigotry and prejudice don't matter, only those fleeting feelings of raw passion.

They look up to me as a provider, a mother, and it's nice to know I could create something that is abandoned of hatred. Lucy and my mother see nothing but uselessness and liability when they look at them. I see creatures with souls, just like the rest of us. How hypocritical is it that we have been exiled from society, yet here we are doing the same thing?

I suppose their loathing is because the brutes' creation was not supposed to be. It's been a source of controversy, anguish, regret, and disappointment ever since they came into this world.

It all started after Mom and I moved in, away from the island, to these pods within the moon. After we settled in and got Nyx running, the first initiative was to start the splicing program. There were a million reasons we went this route instead of the birthing route, and Mom was adamant on getting production ready as soon as possible. I was Lucy's assistant, and together, we crafted a method.

The first task Lucy embarked on was the development of two things: a genetic recombination device and an accelerated incubator. It would be the key to our plans. On a high level, the genetic recombinator was a machine that could take two samples and splice DNA to result in the formation of a fetus. Then once that was formed, we put the sample in an accelerated incubator that could rapidly grow our creations.

We had harvested plenty of samples from other species to work with, so doing this method wasn't that difficult once we had the tools. We decided to stick with hybrids for now, humans and other species, because we didn't want too many variations. My mother's plan was to grow an army, and an army is vastly difficult to control if it's not uniform. However, we saw the need to branch out from other species and not make them simply feline hybrids because each species had their own unique gifts that would be useful.

Our planning continued after birth. Once the hybrids were formed and stable enough, we would release them from the incubators. There were already plenty of childrearing drones out in the market, each catered to different species. All we had to do was reprogram them to rear our children, our generation of hybrids. Then it would be on to childhood development with more drones that would help us manage. They would teach the waves of hybrids common knowledge and lessons that all children need to learn. They would be the educators. Eventually, with wave after wave of hybrids coming, a society would be formed.

That was the process we outlined. Recombinate, incubate, and nurture. Simple, right? But we learned there was a reason Lionel Changer decided not to pursue this path. The genetic recombinator was quite difficult to create, even with Lucy's super-genius intellect. There couldn't be a flaw in her design or calculations because the results would be extremely off target. We learned that the hard way.

When that first wave of hybrids came out, the ten of them, we knew something had gone wrong. They were unbelievably huge out the gate. Their faces and bodies had the deformities they have today.

And their lack of intelligence showed as the initial months passed. They made noises, but they were slow and sauntered, never uttering words. They couldn't complete the simplest cognitive tasks that other animal counterparts their age could do. They were dumb, and it showed.

When we realized what they were, the three of us had a decision to make: would they live or would they be counted as failures and scrapped up for disposal? Lucy was for the latter. It was the first time we disagreed on something.

She argued that allowing their existence in a world not suited for them would prolong their suffering. They'd be out of place in the society we were set to create.

I argued that doing so would make us no better than those who were hunting us. We viewed them as abominations, creatures that shouldn't be, yet we are seen the same way by our pursuers. It would be a sin to cast them off, considering we understood their pain.

Lucy countered this by saying our case is different. Logically, we fit in the world's society. We are functional, intelligent, and can contribute as productive members. The only reason we are hunted is because of our roots in genetic experimentation, something outlawed by the Alliance. These creatures were not the same as us. These brutes would be detrimental to the effort for our freedom. They would be liabilities, more mouths to feed. They weren't wanted examples and would always be viewed as outcasts, not because of what they were, but because of what they couldn't do.

My mother was the tiebreaker. I knew she agreed with both sides. She wanted to let Lucy have her way because, as a leader, Lucy was right. These brutes had nothing to offer. The only thing they could do was offer some muscle, which was not needed thanks to Lucy's implants.

But as a mother, she sided with me. My mom has had to make tough decisions, cold ones sometimes, but she simply couldn't do it. She couldn't destroy creatures that had no say in their creation. We made them, we were responsible for them. It wasn't in her nature to turn away the helpless.

So we agreed to spare them and that they would be my responsibility. We've set up this little pod for them to live. They don't need much because of their mental state. All they need is food, some area to exercise and roam free, and some companionship. I've even given them names. The two cat hybrids are Carrie and Carl, the three tiger hybrids are Terry, Tuner, and Tonga, the three lion hybrids are Larry, Lucia, and Leo, the reptilian hybrid is Croc, and the elephant hybrid is Elle.

In a way, as twisted as it sounds, they're almost like our pets.

Well, at least to me they are. Lucy has little affection for them, and Mother tends to keep her distance regarding the brutes. She allows me to do my thing and entrusts their lives with me, but deep down I know she will never consider them her children the way the next generation will be. Mother doesn't want to get too attached.

Lucy has restructured her recombinator and has guaranteed that the next wave of hybrids, the ones that are in incubation as I speak, will not turn out like the brutes. In her words, they'll be like us—smart, capable, perfect. That's not fair. After spending time with the brutes, I wonder what the meaning of perfection is. Is it simply the ability to be proficient? Even at the cost of morals? Sometimes, I don't know.

I start taking out the food and they rush to me. I put my hand out and motion them to stop, and all ten of them halt. Even though they aren't intelligent, they can still be trained, and I've been working with them to execute simple commands.

I place the food in front, and the ten of them look at me eagerly. It's not just the food, they're happy to see me. They don't have to smile. Their body language tells the story. They stand in uniform, but all have anxious twitches that show their excitement.

"Hello, my little ones," I say. "Are you all hungry?"

I hold a sandwich in the air, and all of their eyes follow it. I move my arm left and right, up and down, and their heads shake and bobble. I then toss it to Leo. He gobbles it up without hesitation.

The others look at me, perplexed, as if they want to know why him. But I have all the sandwiches set up, ready to eat. I test them, waiting to see if any will go without command. They do not.

"Good job, my young ones!" I exclaim. "Go! Eat!"

The delight shines on their faces. Each of them hastily grabs their sandwiches and start devouring it. I then start setting up the trough, ensuring they have plenty to drink.

They all look so happy, without a care in the world. And they're so well behaved. It's taken a lot of patience to get them this far, but I am proud of them, much like a mother would be.

Chapter 7 – Iris Lawton

Itinerary

September 18, 3071 8:01 PM

New Westport, the city where I'll find my next target. It's a small town in the western area of New Zealand. Many retirees are found here. But I'm looking for one in particular.

I stand on a cliff, huddled in shrubbery and beneath the covering of a large tree, equipped in full Collector garb. My black armor reflects the azure-shaded beams from the moon. It's the only source of light around. The main city is far away, and above me is a canopy of stars. They look like diamonds in a celestial ocean of darkness.

The air is cool and the wind howls, but my face can barely feel it under my mask. I can feel the force pushing me ever so slightly and it keeps me light on my feet. I need to stay alert if my plan is going to be successful. He's right in front of me, my target, my mission.

A hundred yards on another cliff lies Eli Winde's compound. I use the zoom lens on my mask to get a closer look at my target's fortress. It's a mansion that overlooks the sea.

It was Winde who helped guide the development of the Alphas. It was Winde who had a hand in turning Fenrir into a monster. And it was Winde who has been one of the leading voices of the Alliance's military implant program. Then he handed the keys over and quit. The Alliance gave him a huge package as a result of his service in the science division. Must be nice to retire in a palace. From my vantage point, I don't see the chimp anywhere. But I know he's there, resting up while living off the profits he made with his Alliance blood credits. They pay a high salary for murder.

I scope around to see if there's any watchdog drones guarding the area. Both Lucy and my visions have confirmed there won't be, but I can't be too careful. One slipup can send me on an alternate path that I don't want. But a quick scan affirms the information I received. It's just me and him, one on one.

After I was done scouring the information found at Don Leons's office, I synced up with Lucy to determine exactly where Eli Winde could be found. She did some research and I did some research, and through our work, we came upon his compound in New Zealand. I did a quick scan of my visions to see if he would be there anytime soon, and low and behold, on September eighteenth, he would be there. Thus, once I knew his location for sure, I planned my attack.

I already had Lucy upgrade my implants a few months ago. Her craftsmanship has evolved over the years. The biotic implants she develops today make her work with HORUS look like a child's toy. The ones within me aren't really implants, per say. They feel more like an extension of my body. Lucy has made them fully integrated aspects of my physiology, like a new muscle or organ.

Sometimes I forget my strength, agility, and enhanced mental capabilities are a result of the work

Lucy has done. It feels so natural, like it's always been there. I suppose that was always her goal, to make it free flowing. She has succeeded beyond both of our wildest expectations.

Yet I must give credit where it's due. We have the Alliance to thank for the sudden boom in our technology. After the whole Shogun operation was finished, Lucy and I had inherited an unexpected reward: the body of Fang Snow, or actually, Blackwolf. Her armor was fully intact when I ended her life with a metal rod, and Lucy had something new to dissect. We both identified it as a source of possibility. The Alliance had spent over fifteen years creating something like the Alphas, and with a working copy, Lucy could find ways to exploit the technology. Blackwolf was full of implants and upgrades. Lucy was determined to learn from it so she could apply the same biotics to us.

The focus was always on splicing hybrids, so this was more of a hobby for Lucy. It wasn't high priority. Still, she made remarkable progress with the limited resources and time. Lucy was able to first disassemble Blackwolf for study. After she removed the armor and dissected Blackwolf's construction, she analyzed the individual pieces. There were hundreds of tiny implants in Blackwolf, and Lucy figured out each one.

Lucy then began designing prototypes based off her study in order to replicate and reverse engineer the technology. Blackwolf was loaded with pieces designed to enhance her strength and agility. Even more peculiar were some mental implants found in her cerebrum. Lucy explained they were there so a user could command Blackwolf verbally. Lucy hypothesized there was a way to modify them so they could amplify my own mental powers. Obviously, I was very interested.

Years had passed and Lucy had slowly made progress on her free time. She eventually finished her analysis and started to work on modifying the technology she replicated for our own personal use. Ivy and I were stronger than ever, both physically and with our powers.

Funny that in creating the ultimate weapon, the Alliance has helped us create our own. I don't think they would have ever known what we'd be capable of once we got a copy of the plans. Blackwolf allowed this. In fact, they probably don't think we exist anymore. I'm sure the Alliance assumes they got the job done at HORUS. They didn't.

Lucy's even been able to upgrade the armor I wear as the Collector. It's based off the very armor that adorned Fang Snow's charred body. The Alphas were incredibly durable, being able to take in the carnage I threw at it. Now the exterior that protects me is just as strong. It's even integrated into my cloak so it's tough enough to deflect blaster fire. I wanted myself to have this power in case the need arose. Lucy delivered.

After we were done with Blackwolf, we discarded her body and that was that. Fang Snow gave us the opportunity to learn, and I thank her for that.

We still had Silverwolf though. Lucy asked if I wanted to apply the same process to my love, and I immediately rejected the idea. I was not going to tear apart Fenrir like an experiment. He deserved so much more than the fate he was handed, and I wanted to honor that legacy.

Instead, we carefully removed his armor and cremated him. It was my own private ceremony, my personal way to let go of the years of anguish I suffered without him. When he died, a part of me did as well.

The only thing I have of Fenrir is my recording, the last moments of his life, the last moments I had with him. It is one of my most cherished possessions, a reminder that even though he was turned into a monster, a part of the wolf I loved resided within his hollow mind. I watch it from time to time so I can remember the joy I felt when I was with him.

Eli Winde was part of the team that transformed him into a steel beast. Though I am here to extract information from him, a small part of me is also here for revenge. When I end his life, I will feel no remorse, no mercy. I will feel enjoyment. He should burn in hell for the things he's done to my love.

And he is certainly living off the profits of his dastardly work. Eli Winde is currently on a temporary retirement, and it appears he has no desire to go back to action anytime soon. From the looks of the luxury he has, why would he?

While he lives lavishly, he and his kind's work have caused creatures like me to be pushed underground, hiding like maggots in the dirt. No more. Once I have my army and acquire this weapon, this GTS, fate will be on my side. I haven't seen it yet—my powers don't go so far—but I am certain my hard work will pay off once and for all.

But for now, I have a task to do. I've seen my visions and know what must be done to get to the GTS. I've seen the conversation where Winde spills the beans. Hell, I even know the exact words I must say in order for him to fess up.

Even though I know where to go, I cannot act on it until I complete the steps to get this information. No miniscule detail can be overlooked, the future might alter in ways I cannot see. It is a flaw in my gifts. I can see much, know much from my visions, but it'll be worthless if I don't do what's necessary to obtain such knowledge.

And I must execute it perfectly. There's a theory called the butterfly effect that proposes even a flapping of a butterfly's wings is enough to divert timelines into different directions. The same is here. I know how the future will play out but only if all the conditions are met. If one thing is off, it may lead to something else, something unwanted. Thus, I must be extra careful in my execution.

I've gotten better at what I call "on the fly" precognition, where I can immediately determine the effects of an incorrect action. But I don't like using it because it doesn't allow time for analysis. It's a quick look and nothing else. It's impossible for me to understand all the consequences if I don't have time to look at each one.

Luckily for me, I don't think I'll have to worry about it on this particular mission. My battle plan is straightforward and Winde's security is surprisingly light. I guess he didn't want to make his home a fortress. Or he's just arrogant.

I know the only security I'll have to face are two surveillance drones that hover around the perimeter. They have a few basic functions such as thermal scanning and X-ray mode. It helps them detect any intruders.

Yet their top speed is fifty miles an hour, and if I use my telekinesis quick enough, I'll be able to knock them out of the air with my spear or a rock. It doesn't matter what I use, the plan won't be altered. Then, once they're grounded, I simply rip out their power cores before the alarms sound. It'll be a clear entry.

Winde does have a full security grid on his actual premises, but it's only used when he's away from home. Since he's inside his compound, it will be disabled, and I won't have to bypass anything. A simple slip through the backdoor will do.

The key thing to keep in mind is stealth. Though his strength is his technological and bioengineering knowhow, Winde is still a trained soldier with years of experience. He'll be able to detect an intruder with as the sound of a pin dropping. Thus, I have to be light on my feet, or not on my feet at all.

I won't be on the ground. Instead, I'll make my way through using my powers. Some call it flying, and I suppose in essence it is. But what I'm really doing is using my telekinesis on my armor to lift my body. I still can't use it on a living organism, or else I'd simply rip my enemies apart limb from limb. No, I need to be creative to use my powers effectively.

At that point, he'll be in his living area, busily occupied with some light reading. That's when I strike. I need to focus on surprise. He'll need to be caught completely off guard. If he has even a second to react, he could get away and the plan will go awry.

Ultimately, my goal is to fire some energy whips, my weapon of choice, to restrain him, and the questioning will go from there. I'll say what I need to say, he'll say what I expect him to, and then I'll get what I came for: the confession. He'll tell me all about where I can find the GTS, and then once I've gotten what I needed, well, I suppose he won't be of much use after that.

That's the checklist, the itinerary of my battle plan. My execution must be flawless. I can only make so many mistakes until the future is altered to one I don't desire. And I can't afford to change course. I need things to work out the way I have planned. I've faced this dilemma many times ever since I inherited my power. Precision is the key.

And then it'll be on to the next stop, and the next, until I acquire what Lucy describes as a game changer. I will get my hands on the GTS schematics. Once I do, the puzzle will be complete and I'll be closer to that goal of freedom.

I don't know exactly what will lie years from now, but I have a gut feeling what I'm doing will guide me the right way. If I can't rely on my precognition, I'll have to rely on faith.

The attack will commence in an hour. If I'm patient, the prize will be worth it.

Chapter 8 – Falena Snow

Discovery

September 18, 3071 8:22 PM

My god, what have I just read? Wolf automation? Living weapons? Underground explosions? Alliance conspiracies? This is the stuff science fiction, not reality, is made of.

Getting through the report was difficult. I had to read, in graphic detail, how they debased my mother's body. Every cut, every shock, every maiming was vividly described during their implant process. Tears flowed as I read in horror the atrocities. And it was written so dryly, without empathy. It was like I was reading about a procedure in a textbook. My mother wasn't an individual to the Alliance, she was a test subject.

And as I read more and more, the facts hit me like punches to the face. Each paragraph was brutal. One recalled how they had to cut certain sections of skin off to regraft it. Others detailed how they implanted cannons directly into my mother's torso. All the while, they kept her alive. They needed her brainpower and natural functions intact to keep the implants running.

It was also the only way they could ensure her instincts were still there, the natural wolf ones that kept her alive on the battlefield. They acknowledged my mother's merits as a warrior and wanted to preserve them. But was it really necessary? Did they need it that badly? Couldn't they just let her and my uncle rest in peace? They deserved better.

The Alliance took the comatose bodies of my family members and turned them into living weapons. All the implant ideas they obtained from HORUS went into them. The Alliance took what was left of my mother and made her soulless. She was a destroyer. My childhood, the hope I had that she was still out there, has become extinguished.

I am a puddle of emotions, utterly speechless. I'm filled with anger, rage, and fury. Yet I'm also filled with sadness, despair, and hopelessness. Is this all that awaits for the Snow legacy? Nothing but a bunch of bullshit and bleakness. My family has no future, and now it has no past.

I've spent years searching for something, anything, that could lead me to my mother's fate. My nights were restless, my search was arduous, but I pushed forward, clinging onto hope. I knew if I did find an answer, I would most likely be disappointed, but I pushed on with determination and denial. I ignored that side of me that told me to abandon my quest, because I had to know.

And now I've made it. I have my answer, and it saddens me greatly. I should've followed my instincts and stopped my pursuit. The answer was always there. She's been gone for decades, any trace of her vanished from this planet. No body was found, not even a strand of DNA. She was missing because she was dead. I should have known that, but no, I needed to find out more. I chased down the white rabbit until the bitter end, and now I'm left feeling ultra-ambivalent.

I could feel her pain. I think about what my mother went through during the process. The report states they found both my uncle and my mother engulfed in a grenade blast. After their bodies were extracted, they were kept alive. During this time, the Alliance created implants and inserted them into my mother and uncle. Their goal was to test out implant development on these so-called subjects.

I wonder if my mother was aware of anything at all during this time. She was stated to be comatose, but we know so little about what happens to a creature when they're out like that. Was she off in her own little world while her body lay dormant? Did she feel the dissection, the pain, the mutilation the Alliance forced upon her?

Did she think of me? Did she wonder where I was, how I would live as an orphan? Or was her mind gone a long time ago?

I will never know the answers to these questions. I will only live thinking about the "what ifs." I wish I knew her fate sooner. I wouldn't have to lament the possibilities now. It seems my hunt for the truth has created more questions.

But I'm glad the search is over. I won't have those confused thoughts anymore. My mind will no longer feel the need to look for something elusive and secret. I have a little closure. I know what happened to my mother, Fang Snow. She died long ago, not when her body was destroyed, but when her soul was. The only thing that remains is what I remember of her.

The end to her story is far from over, though. It's only begun. Though she may be long gone, the real question remains: what to do from here? What the Alliance did is unforgivable. They broke so many ethical laws. They ban the world from playing god, yet

I have the evidence they've been doing the same for decades. They're hypocrites to the highest degree.

It blows my mind that they've been doing it for years all while the public lives in the shadows. If this were a fair world, they would pay for their crimes against my mother.

Project Alpha is an atrocity, not only to my family, but all of wolfkind. I am certain the Brotherhood of Wolves has no idea what's been going on. If they did, they'd be as angry as I am. Any species, not only wolves, would be in an uproar and demand justice for the evils waged upon their brothers. Yet this is news to me. I haven't heard anything from the Brotherhood. I'm sure my findings would be news to them too.

There's no doubt the Alliance is keeping them in the dark. Tensions are high between the Brotherhood and the Alliance. They have been for a long time. The Brotherhood is just looking for a reason to rebel. The information I have on my hands could incite that rebellion.

Wolves are prideful creatures. We are proud of our heritage, of our ability to survive. It's what we've done for centuries. When the lands were divided and we were given the cold wasteland of the north, we persevered. We found ways to adapt to our surroundings, to thrive in an area that is frozen. And we did it on our own. Wolves never needed the Alliance to help us. We only join them begrudgingly because of the fear of being outnumbered. But inside, the Brotherhood is looking for a reason to fight.

This could be the motivation. Even if the odds are against the Brotherhood, with a leak of Project Alpha, war would begin. The crimes against wolves must be paid for.

The Brotherhood would first order a breakaway, a succession from the Alliance. All relations between wolves and their peers would cease. Trading, resources, and public records wouldn't be shared. The Alliance needs the wolves for valuable minerals harvested in the north. Wolves are also the source of a large chunk of taxes doled out by the Alliance. Without this capital, the United Species Alliance would take a huge hit.

That would lead to an assault by the combined forces of the Alliance into the Wolf's Den. The Alliance is comprised of the major governments of all the intelligent species. The High Human Council, the High Dog Council, the Gorilla Government, and the others would unite to make the Brotherhood of Wolves bend down to their will. It would be an attack on all fronts. No one would ally with us. They have nothing to gain. We'd have everything to lose. The Alliance controls all, and if they crush this hypothetical rebellion, it would serve as a lesson to the other governments who would be tempted to do the same thing.

I start to see the chaos of this rebellion in my mind. The first shot would be a huge explosion in the form of a bomb. They'd burn and blast whatever they could to test my kind's will. Thousands would die. Yet the steely determination wolves possess would disallow any surrender.

That's when the Alliance would continue the massacre. After the first attack comes the second wave. Wolf's Den towns getting bombed by air assaults of the avian intelligent species. Bears, rhinos, and other "tank builds" would be serving as small armored destroyers. I can already see them fire their plasma rockets and high-powered explosives as wolf cities get blasted to smithereens.

The humans, dogs, and cats would be in the war room, planning out their stratagem. The Wolf's Den would be their playground as they send their troops in to decimate what remains of the north. It will be set afire. The streets will be crowded with a cadre of species, all looking for wolves to terminate, all willing to dish out the punishment for an uprising.

The wolves would do their best to maintain their ground. We'd enter combat with purpose, defend our homeland at whatever cost. Yet no matter how ferocious our attitude, we simply cannot beat the numbers. With the combined powers of all the species, wolves would be outnumbered one hundred to one. There'd be too many enemies to fight on too many battlefields. Our kind would be slaughtered, our rebellion squashed. And in the end, the only accomplishment our struggle will have would be the decimation of our government and the possible extinction of the wolves.

Thus, I have a dilemma. I have been granted the power of knowledge. It is worth more than any jewel on this planet. It's enough to make governments go to war with each other.

And it's information that will grant justice. It will name those responsible for the horrors that have been plagued on my kind. The world will know the cruelty and sins committed by the Alliance. Whether they want to act on it and ally with the victims is their choice, but at least creatures will know who was wronged by their leaders.

Most importantly, it will return my mother's name back to glory, have her legacy vindicated and out in the open after years of secrecy and disgrace. That's my real motivation. My mother has been viewed with dishonor by my family, by the Brotherhood, by everyone. But it's unfair. She didn't want to be a mercenary. She didn't want to be excommunicated by the government. Her life was misunderstood. The only wolf who understood it was me.

She was my mother, kind, brave, assertive. She did everything she could for me. This is the side few have seen. She was a hero for her kind, an all-star agent of the Brotherhood, and she deserved to be remembered as one.

If I release this report to the general public, my mother will be a martyr. She'll be seen as the purpose of the cause, the one that showed the world the truth that had been hiding from them. The pain she went through, the sacrifice she endured, it will not be forgotten. We'll rally the troops, and when they go out fighting, it will be her name they will shout. She will not be a disgrace, she will be a victim to the Alliance scum that have oppressed us for so long. Then, finally, I will be at peace.

But on the other hand, I know what the outcome will be. I don't need to be a fortuneteller to see the events that will come. Releasing the horrible truth will set the course for destruction, a monumental struggle that the Brotherhood will not win.

War versus doing the noble thing. Do I risk an entire nation by divulging the evidence that may drive them to their destruction? Is it worth risking for the sake of a lost justice? I don't know.

Whatever decision I make, it cannot be rash. I must think this through. There's a weight on my back that I wasn't prepared to handle. My body and my mind need some rest.

Time is my friend right now. There's a lot on the line, so I will have to sleep on it. However, I may find it difficult to rest with this burden hanging over my weary head.

Chapter 9 – Iris Lawton

Intrusion

September 18, 3071 9:16 PM

Like mindless sentinels, the two security drones hover in the air. They're round, about eight feet in diameter, and weigh in at two hundred pounds apiece. The moonlight reflects off their hardened exterior, and I eye them carefully, observing the targets as I prepare for the attack.

They're both Kolo Tech S-45s, preprogrammed with standard security routines. S-45s are higher-end models, plated with synthetic metal armor. They also have weapon capabilities with two high-caliber energy blasters on the bottom of their bases. However, their flaw is in their hover system. It's uncovered, and a precise shot could destroy it and send them crashing to the ground.

That's what I have my eye on right now. I spend a few good minutes staring at the hover booster on both drones. Precision is the top priority, so I need to focus so I don't make a mistake. I have my metal rods with spear tips, each two feet in length. They will be my ammunition.

I have to hit both drones simultaneously. If I attack separately, the remaining drone would signal the alarm and all hell would break loose. The reserve sentinels would emerge and it'd be a one-versus-ten situation. I know. I've seen it.

I also have to make sure I rip out their power cores immediately before they can sound the alarms. My attack will damage them badly, but they'll still have access to their alert system while grounded. If they go off, I foresee another situation where I'm outnumbered. Swiftness is the key.

After they're out, I'll simply have to mow down a blaster turret Winde has hidden underground. It's one of many. They're run by weight-detecting sensors, so no matter where I step, they'll sense me. But I have a few spears under my cloak. A few thrusts into the blasters and I'll be fine.

Lucy has often inquired why I use these spears instead of energy blasters. It's about practicality. Energy blasters make noise and use up the battery in their power cores. Thus, ammunition is limited. With my spears and telekinesis, ammo is unlimited. All I have to do is drive them into an opponent and take them out.

They're also small and discrete, the perfect tool for the stealth missions I often engage in. And they're made from some of the hardest material around, sharpened with high-impact light cutters. They'll pierce through anything, even the expensive coating that plates Winde's drones.

More importantly, my spears are precise. I don't like using energy blasters because I have to aim, and quite frankly, it isn't that great. And since a lot of my tasks require fine execution, I'd rather control the trajectory of my ammunition myself. It helps cut any mistakes.

The drones finish their first sweep around the perimeter and now head back in my direction. They're in position. It's show time.

I detach two of my weapons from my cloak and levitate them in the air. My hands guide them so they're aimed outward, away from me and at the machines.

I look back at the drones. Both come from different directions, but both are also closing in on one point. My eyes search through their casings, looking for their weaknesses. I see the hovering systems exposed on the bottom and hone in. I have a clear shot.

My eyes take a final glance at both. It's now or never.

I spread my hands open and the spears go whizzing into the air. I focus with all my might on the rods' paths, closing my eyes and visualizing their flight. I hear two small crackles burst from the drones, followed by light swooshing. Then, finally, a small thud comes from the floor.

I open my eyes and see the two drones shaking helplessly on the ground. A few sparks fly as they uselessly try to get back to the air. Their flight capability has been disabled. I clench my hand into a fist and pull back my arm. My two rods fly back from the remains and in front of me. I quickly snatch them and sprint to the drones.

A few seconds later, I stop right in front of them. I have to act quickly before the alarms sound, so I locate their power cores and extend my arms. My left palm faces one drone while my right palm faces the other. I shake them violently, focusing on the cores. They don't budge. They must be secured tightly.

I start to get nervous. If I don't hurry, the drones will still send out their signal and the alarms will go off. I'll be screwed. I concentrate harder and my arms shake more violently. I start to think about their precise location and imagine them getting ripped from their sockets. That's it. That's what I need to picture. I pull my hands back promptly and I hear a tear from within the drones.

The lights that adorn them dim, and their shaking ceases. Any motors and moving parts stop. I am successful. The power cores have been taken out, the drones are disabled. They won't be sending any alert signals anytime soon.

"Drones are done for. Winde is sitting cozily in his compound, while his security system is turned off. Perfect. It's an easy entry. Time to slip through the back," I say to myself.

I walk around the remains of the drones to Winde's backdoor. I have time to observe the perimeter. Several of the lights are off in his house, though there are a few rooms that are lighted. The outside of his house is pretty luxurious. Some bushes are placed against the wall. The plant life looks exotic and well-maintained. Rumor has it that Winde is a big gardening freak, and it certainly shows.

The compound itself is large and painted in a beige color. I'm guessing there are fifteen to twenty rooms. The previous owner was a human, and from what I've read, Winde liked the extra space even though the house wasn't suited for his smaller chimp body. Still, he made the modifications necessary and ended up with a palace to retire in. As far as I know, Winde is living alone, though I'm sure he uses the space to throw large parties.

Suddenly, a turret rises from the ground. I must have stepped on a sensor. The gun uncurls and its barrel is aimed straight at my head. But, without even looking at it, I simply lift a spear from my cloak and jam it right through the blaster. I then pull my hand back, and the metal rod returns to my cloak. Threat neutralized.

I reach the backdoor and, unsurprisingly, it's locked. There's no physical handle. It's automated and requires a bioscan to get in. If I place my hand on the door, and it will send out a pulse that scans my body and looks for a match to Winde, thus granting him or her access inside.

Obviously, I can't mimic Winde's biological structure to get access, but I do have a handy device that Lucy integrated into my armor. It's a decryption program that allows my suit to access the World Wide Health Department's database and upload by touch the information into the door's security function. Once the door gets the data, it'll recognize the user as Eli Winde and let me in.

I activate my armor to do its work and obtain Winde's information. A minute or two later it beeps and lets me know it's ready. Then I place my hand on the door and a faint light emits at contact. I stand nervously waiting for the door to be unlocked. If it fails, the alarms may go off.

"Welcome, Eli Winde," the computer says.

My anxiety is lifted. It worked! Once again, Lucy saves the day.

Through the backdoor I go, and on the other side is a large living room with a single door at the end. And through that door is a maze of hallways that will lead me to where Eli Winde currently is. According to my vision, he should be nice and comfortable on his couch, relaxing the day away, totally unaware that an intruder has broken in.

I have some time to kill before Winde is in place, so I look around. Winde's house is clean and nicely decorated. As I walk through the halls, I see a variety of artwork and pictures as well as souvenirs and trinkets. There's quite a few antiques from a lot of places around the world. Some look like they're from South Asia while others originate from across the world in South America. They appear to be mementos from his days in the field as a soldier. This along with the gardening hobby tells me Winde must be quite the connoisseur of cultural refinement.

I walk into the next hallway, which is filled with holo-images of his war days. I stroll by and observe renderings of him and his teammates. Even though I don't recognize anyone, I'm awed by the sheer amount of tours he's been on. There are several images with different teams. Each is comprised with a diverse cast of animals. Winde has done tours with gorillas, dogs, cats, humans, even elephants, eagles, and pigs. I've done my research of Winde, but I mainly focused on his scientific achievements. I was never aware he had as decorated of a military career as this.

I'm about to exit the hallway, a mere few rooms away from where Winde sits, when one last rendering catches my eyes. It's a holo-image of a group of soldiers. Normally, I wouldn't even notice the hologram, but something about this group looks familiar. The caption reads: "Company Manticore, First Mission."

Manticore... Then it hits me. I see a bear in this group. I believe Clipper was his name. Fenrir and

Bastion killed him during our escape. This was the team that raided HORUS, the team that killed all the hybrids.

This hologram brings out a rage in me. It makes me remember that night, HORUS, and the day my happy life with Fenrir was demolished by Alliance scum. They forced me into living underground all my life. All of them are murderers. Eli Winde was one of them long before he experimented on Fenrir. It's bound in his blood to be a destroyer, and now I am itching at a chance to end his life.

I now stand at the door that leads to the living room. It's an old style, meaning I can manually move it, so I open it slightly and take a look beyond. The room is nicely lit and decorated with swanky-looking furniture and shelves. Good. On the roof hangs an expensive-looking chandelier. The room has a classic feel that matches the look of the rest of the compound.

Just as I had predicted, there sits Winde on a couch, back facing me. I've timed everything perfectly and now he's right where I want him. All I have to do is slink up behind and ambush him. I'll strap my whips, get the information I need, and end the primate. Simple, quick, and effective is what I do.

But I shouldn't be too confident. Sneaking up on him won't be easy, especially now that I've seen the military experience he has. He's not doing anything distracting, just reading. Even at my lightest, if I go on foot, he may hear me. That's why I have to levitate my way over.

I carefully open the door all the way, and with a thought, I use my telekinesis to lift myself in the air. I do it slowly, trying to be as cautious as possible. Once I'm fully suspended, I gently float my way over to

Winde, making sure to avoid any mirrors or reflections that would give away my advantage.

My glide is successful. I drift stealthily as I zone into where Winde is sitting. He's still slouched on his couch, reading some article on his light-tablet. Yet little does he know the impending danger that lurks behind him.

I'm now a few feet away. His back is still facing me. It's time to strike. I prep my energy whips. They're primed. Once I have him tied down, I'll start my interrogation.

The opening is clear. I pull the trigger. The coils of light fly from my wrists right to Winde's body. I can see them latching to his waist and slamming him to the ground, pinning him helplessly while I swoop in to securely restrain him.

But none of that happens. Instead, he rolls forward and dodges my whips. The coils bounce uselessly off his couch. It's a miss.

The chimp immediately recovers from his roll, gets back on his feet, and greets me with an energy pistol in hand. He fires a few shots. I'm so stunned at the change in events that I'm barely able to react fast enough, but luckily, I turn my body around swiftly and the shots hit my cloak. The armored cape protects me from any damage.

I turn back around and stand face to face with Eli Winde. The chimp rises up and measures me with an expression of curiosity mixed with amazement.

"The Collector," he says. "I knew I would meet you one day."

"You are correct," I say.

"What do you want?"

His voice doesn't tremble, nor do I detect any fear. He's confident and defiant as we confront each other for the first time.

"Information," I say.

"Of course," he responds. "Come to attack a retired intelligence officer. Hoping to steal some Alliance secrets? Like I haven't encountered your lot before. I've defeated many who have tried to extract information from me. I'll kill you and solve a mystery that has been plaguing Rox and I for years. Who are you?"

I stand silent.

"No answer? No matter," he says. "You made the mistake of breaking into my house. Rox will pay a nice bonus for your head."

"How did you know I was coming?" I ask, ignoring his threats. "Your security system was off."

I need to know how my powers failed. My vision told me the sneak attack would work and Winde would be disabled. Where did I go wrong?

"It's true it was off, but I still had it on standby," Winde responds. "There are pressurized sensors on the ground. I have them placed around the house in random patterns. You must have stepped on one in my trophy hall. When they're activated, a holoscreen instantly pops up in front of me and gives me a video feed of the intruder. Thus, I saw you the moment you triggered it. After that, I simply waited for you to get close enough so I could go on the attack. But since I didn't kill you, it seems we're at a standstill."

I knew I should have been more careful. In my vision, I saw myself going through the hallway in precise movements. I went forward, left, right, back forward again, basically walking in zigzags. I did so because walking in those steps must have helped me avoid any sensors, or else I would have seen the result in the vision.

However, when I walked through the hall a few minutes ago, I must have made a mistake. Instead of going left, I went right, instead of taking long strides, I might have taken shorter ones. All these small alterations that differed from the vision of success lead to failure. I mistakenly stepped on a sensor and now I've gone on a different timeline that I did not anticipate. And I can't look at my visions now to see this newer future, not when Eli Winde has a gun pointed at me.

Yet as long as I complete my goal, I'll be okay. All I need to do is get Winde pinned down. But, man, do I hate improvising.

"Good job," I say. "Few have ever had the drop on me. I'm the one who usually has the drop on them. However, it's too late for you."

"What?" Winde says.

He doesn't understand what I'm talking about, and that's when I strike. I flick my right hand outward, and a telekinetically controlled spear goes careening in his direction. But he's a shifty chimp and leaps out of the way before it impales him. He's shocked by the cheap shot, but now he's focused.

He lifts up his energy blaster and starts firing. I instantly turn my back and shield my body with my cloak. The gunfire bounces off, safely protecting me while Winde continues with his assault. One blast, two blasts, three, and he keeps going. There's no pause or stopping, just an onslaught of ammunition that doesn't do anything.

I can't sit here and be a turtle, though. I need to act. From the corner of my eye, I see a heavy-looking shelf about fifteen feet from Winde. I spread my palms to it and lift it with my mind. It floats in the air a brief second until I swing my arm toward Winde. The shelf goes with it and flies in the direction of the chimp. He sees this, stops his assault, and jumps high in the air to avoid the collision.

Winde latches onto the fancy chandelier, hanging from it with one hand while the other is still holding his gun. He points it downward and fires another hail of ammo. This time, I'm not fast enough, and one brazenly hits my shoulder. Lucky for me, my armor stops it from doing any damage, but the force still knocks me off my feet and on my ass.

The chimp sees me in a vulnerable position, swings the chandelier, and lets go. He comes crashing down to the floor, right above me. Winde is probably hoping to land on my body to stomp and crush my stomach and pin me down.

I look around for something I can use and see a small table six feet to me right. That will do. I point my hand to it and pull my arm back. The table jerks off the ground and leaps toward me. Then, right before Winde can land, I recklessly force the table to drop right above me with the legs barely crushing my own. Now I'm completely under it and the table acts as a barrier between Winde and me.

Winde lands on top and I hear a hard thud on the other side. I don't think he was expecting that. Maybe he landed awkwardly and broke a leg or two. I wish. Instead, I hear a clicking noise. It's the energy gun. I better do something quick before he blasts me while I'm under here.

I lift a spear from my cloak and shoot it upward from below, through the table, straight to the wall. It makes a clear pierce as it rips through the top and onto the ceiling. I don't hear a yell, though, not even a scream. Instead, I hear some thumping traveling across. He must have avoided my shot.

Hiding under the table is useless if I can't see my target, so I lift both my hands and concentrate on the opposite sides of the desk. It starts to rumble and a crack splits open from where my spear made the hole. I concentrate harder, and in the blink of an eye, the entire table shatters into large chunks as I spread my arms fully. The table is now in pieces and Winde has nowhere to hide.

He falls off the top to the right of me and goes tumbling to the floor. He continues to roll right back onto his feet and instantaneously fires some more shots. I lift up a piece of the table and shield myself from the gunfire.

Pieces of tabletop go flying from my safeguard and Winde continues to fire. Unbeknownst to him, I detach another spear from my cloak and look slightly beyond my makeshift shield to get a clear shot. I have it. I lift the spear and chuck it right at him.

It shoots straight at Winde, but once again, he dodges it. Damn, he's quick. The spear instead hits one of the chimp's fancy paintings on the wall.

"You need to learn some new moves," Winde says tauntingly.

"Perhaps I do," I say. "Or perhaps I already have."

"What?"

With my mind still controlling my spear, I pull the rod back and the painting it pierced comes with it. The frame is large, much bigger than Winde. It rips off the wall and smacks the back of his head hard. He falls forward like a stiff board. The chimp is dazed and in pain.

No time for mercy. I lift up two heavy-looking pieces of the broken tabletop and they levitate in front of me. Then I get into a boxing stance. Though my fists are clenched, they won't be hitting anything. The debris I have in the air will.

I launch a left jab, and the left piece of tabletop goes in the same motion, smacking Winde in the face. I then launch a right hook, my fists hitting nothing but air. But the right piece lands a blow on Winde. I use the two chunks like boxing gloves. My arms throw the punches, but the debris makes all the contact.

I throw another jab and the piece smashes Winde's face. I throw a straight and Winde gets pummeled by debris. Another jab, another straight, and finally a hook. Three more devastating blows crush Winde. He falls to the ground, blood oozing from cuts, face swollen like a balloon.

He struggles to get back to his feet, but he can barely even move. Nonetheless, he's still alive and alert. I'm glad. I need my information after all.

His gun has fallen to the ground, and I pick it up and throw it out of his reach. I squat down and lift him up to a sitting position. One of his eyes is closed shut, but the other one looks at me with a defeated gaze. He breathes in hard, wheezing and gasping for air.

"Now, about what I need," I say.

"After all this, you still think I'm going to tell you anything?" he asks despondently.

"Of course, unless you want to make things worse."

I lift up another piece of the broken table, a sharp jagged portion, and aim it at Winde. It floats in front of his face coyly. I taunt him with the hint of what's to come and the chimp gazes at it nervously.

"What do you want to know?" he asks.

"I need the schematics of the GTS," I say.

He looks at me wild-eyed at first. Winde is bewildered with the question, surprised I would even know what that is. But then his senses come back to him and he starts laughing at my face.

"Like I have that," he says with a disturbing chuckle. Looks like our battle hasn't changed the script my vision outlined.

"Don't lie to me," I say. "You were the head of the Alliance's covert science team. The GTS was one of your many projects. Why wouldn't you have the plans for it?"

"You think they let me take my work home with me? I'm retired. Anything I designed stays with the Alliance. I don't have it. Hell, they even extracted the information from my brain to make sure it was a clean wipe."

This was the answer I was expecting. I just need him to spill the beans on who in order to fulfill the steps of my visions. It'll ensure that what happens next will actually happen.

"So where do I go to get it?" I say.

"I'm not telling you," he says defiantly.

I push the jagged splinter closer to his face and Winde stares at it fretfully.

"You sure about that?" I ask. I move the pointed debris even closer.

"Okay… you win," he says in a cowardly tone.

"Good. So if you don't have the GTS schematics, who does?"

"My successor. The guy who's leading Rox's covert development team: Mark Allen."

"The same Mark Allen you worked with on Operation Alphas?"

"Yes."

"Excellent."

I move the splintered piece even closer to him, aimed right at his chest. He instantly recognizes I was lying.

"No, you said…!" he screams.

"I said nothing," I respond. "This goes beyond business. This has always been personal. I hope you see your creations in hell."

"Wait!"

His pleas are futile. I ram the broken tabletop right into his heart and he lets out a loud shriek. He grasps at the piece, now in his body, trying to pry it out. But I push harder, making his attempts useless.

Blood oozes out and his body becomes weak. His hands no longer cling around the fragment. Instead, they limply fall to his sides. His pupils gradually retreat to the back of his eyes. It only takes a few more seconds until he's dead.

The deed is done. Eli Winde lies in front of me, lifeless, and I get Lucy on my communicator. Her face pops up on my holo-screen.

"Iris Lawton," she says in greeting. "Expecting call. Surprised. Later than scheduled."

"I ran into a bit of trouble. Plans altered and I had to act on the fly. As a result, Winde and I had a small battle. But don't worry, I got the better of him. He's dead," I say.

"Future altered?"

I close my eyes and dive into my visions. Nothing has changed.

"No, we're still on track," I say.

"Now you can tell me identity of holder to GTS schematics?" Lucy asks.

Even though I knew who when I saw my first visions, I had to wait to tell Lucy. Things always need to pan out accordingly.

"Yes. The target is Mark Allen," I say.

"Not surprised," she says. "Will start digging information on current whereabouts."

"Good. Get back to me when you're done."

"What will Lawton do until then?"

"I need to clean this place up. A top Alliance agent just died."

"Understood."

She's about to hang up the communicator but hesitates.

"What is it, Lucy?" I ask.

"Sure that future has not been altered as result of confrontation with Winde?" she asks.

"I took a quick look, and so far, so good. I'm still scheduled to make my way to Mark Allen's location, provided that you'll be able to provide me where the Alliance his hiding him. And I know you will. I've seen it."

"See no differences than before?"

"Not yet, but I only took a quick glance. Once I'm done here, I'll have time to concentrate and take a more detailed look. But don't worry so much, Lucy. The important thing is the big picture is still there."

"Okay."

"Do your job. I have to do mine now. Iris out."

The communicator closes and I look down at the mess that's been made. I'll need to stage the scene and remove any evidence that I was involved.

Then it'll be on to my next target.

Chapter 10 – Maya Lawton

Gifts

<u>February 13, 3025 1:00 PM</u>

I can't believe it's been more than a year since I left that place. Escaping HORUS's clutches was no easy task. It was like breaking out of a prison. Granted, it wasn't heavily guarded with soldiers or anything, but there were the drones. Good thing drones are easy to disable, even for someone who isn't tech savvy. I also had some inside help.

His name was, is, Cid Heartily. He's one of the security admins at HORUS and a very nice guy. He's always helpful to everyone and had a good heart. That's why he agreed to help me.

After I had Iris, I was told that she was special, whatever that means. Lionel Changer never disclosed to me what was so special about her, and even now, more than a year later, I still have no clue. All I know is that whatever she is, whatever power or potential Changer sees in her, it makes her a target.

Changer and that chimp freak that follows him around wanted to experiment on her, see what makes her tick. She's only an infant, but the only thing they can think about is dissecting and prodding her. Disgusting. I would never let them do that to any of my children. I don't care if Iris has the power to change the world. She is my child, and I refused to let that maniac get his hands on her. I can only imagine the horrors he'd expose her to. That's why I needed to leave, that's why I had to make my escape.

Cid heard of my plight and was equally revolted by the schemes that Lionel Changer and his crew were up to. He believed in Changer's cause, but he also drew the line at child endangerment. I was pregnant at the time, and he wondered if my unborn child, Leonard, would also be on the list. The only way I could be protected from such madness was to leave.

Cid was in charge with the security operations of the HORUS facility. That meant he monitored who came in and who came out. He also operated the drone schedule. So if he were to find a window where I could come in and come out while he temporarily disabled the drone security routines, I could technically make a relatively easy escape. I wouldn't be leaving unnoticed, but the only person who would be watching would be the guy who was helping me out. It was as sure of a shot I'd ever get.

Thus, we worked out the fine details, and a few weeks later, we were ready to start our action plan. With a group of my halfkind children holding my hands, I led them out through HORUS's gates. Cid had set up everything, and all we had to do was walk out while everyone was resting. It was quick, it was quiet, and it was surprisingly easy. I have Cid Heartily to thank and I'll be forever in his debt. He saved my life, and he saved Iris's life.

Cid also did more than just help us leave HORUS, he helped me and my family find a place to live in. Cid had contacts outside of HORUS. He knew some real estate buddies that fixed me up with a home. According to Cid, there was a small house on the outskirts of a town in Nevada. It was isolated from the rest of the community and the land was cheap. He also hooked me up with some contractors that could help make some, um, underground adjustments that would accommodate my family.

Of course none of this was free, but I had plenty saved up from my days as a prostitute and was paid handsomely for my work at HORUS. Lionel Changer was a madman, but he did have money to spare. I was willing to pay anything to not only find a place that was safe for me, but also one that was safe for my children.

1523 Chakming Drive was the address, located in some dumpy town called Primm. That dumpy town is the city I now call home.

I owe everything to Cid, but after it was all done and I had settled in, we stopped communication. Well actually, he stopped communication. I wonder if he was found out by Lionel Changer. I'm not really sure, because I would have been caught by now. I just hope Cid is okay, and I hope one day we'll meet again.

In the meantime, it's been a real adventure raising all these kids. I had Leonard shortly after arriving here, and he's been quite the handful. He's only an infant, but even for a newborn, he's awful clingy. He cries constantly and always wants me around. I suppose that's just how it goes with babies.

Curtis is kind of an enigma. He's a quiet little boy and always seems so sad. I'm scared he's going to be an outcast among outcasts. His scales and teeth don't help. But there's also this loyalty about him. He tries to fit in, and even though he doesn't run with a particular crowd, you can tell he cares for all of his siblings.

Candy is my little genius. She's so smart. I hope the world can catch wind of her potential and look past the exterior to see the true genius that lies inside.

Oscar is so kind. I'm proud of him. He's strong and noble, and he's only six years old. My little cub is always sticking up for his more timid brothers and sisters like Maddie and Lombardi. And boy does he have his work cut out from him.

The world is full of bullies, and this family is no exception. Ace and Alex are that. I guess they're a little older, so I never had time to really care for them. They're kind of mean to the others, and definitely hard to control. Boys will be boys.

I can't blame them. They look up to their oldest brother so much. If there was ever a leader among my children, Tiago would be it. He's charismatic and strong. At the same time, I worry what kind of influence he has. He's rash and sometimes cruel. Yet, there's this drive in him, a determination that I don't see in the others. That's a good thing, right?

Finally, there are my twins, Iris and Isaac. They're so young, yet so beautiful. Isaac and Iris are a pair, twins birthed from a miracle.

And Iris, well she's the reason we're here I guess. Special. It's the word that's been used to describe her so many times. I have no idea what is so special about her. I guess all my children are special in a way, but she's different. I don't know how to explain it. I just sense something wonderful about her, like she's destined to be someone great. All parents think that of their children, but with Iris, it goes beyond that. It's her destiny.

Lionel Changer was a smart man. Crazy yes, but also a genius. He's much more intelligent than me.

And he saw something hidden in Iris. I guess that's why she's special.

Only time will tell what the future will bring for all my little ones. I'm worried that something will happen, I'm always worried. Every day brings a new fear, a new danger that could knock on our door. But it's better now that my children have had a taste of freedom instead of living in captivity at HORUS. Their lives are theirs and no one else's. That's the greatest gift a mother can give.

Chapter 11 – Mark Allen

Promotion

September 20, 3071 9:34 AM

"How are Rod Traynor's vitals?" I ask one of my surgeons.

There's a soldier on the operating table. Part of his arm is opened up, a mix of blood, muscles, and electronic bits. He's currently sedated, and I'm overseeing a team of three that's working on the installation.

"They're steady," he responds. "Arm implantation almost complete. After that, we'll move on to the legs. Overall, everything is going according to schedule, Mr. Allen."

"Good job. I need to go back to my office and study the results of the other patients. I'll trust you with the rest of the procedure."

"Yes, sir."

I exit the operating room and make my way through the halls of the Sector Six facility to my office. It's been a pretty quiet day so far. I haven't received any communication from Rox, nor has there been any fire drills. I kind of like it. Sometimes things get so hectic that I barely have time to soak in what I've done and how far I've gotten.

We're located on the outskirts of Allied City, in a top-secret location that's camouflaged by a chameleon field. The only creatures who know that this place exists are top-ranking Alliance officials like General Rox.

This building has been my workplace for the last ten years. After the success of Project Alphas, I was immediately granted parole at the request of General Rox. He was the dog that lobbied for my release, stating that my scientific aptitude had far exceeded his expectations. They were skeptical at first, but they were impressed by how well crafted the first prototypes, Blackwolf and Silverwolf, were. I was given a long interview where I detailed my work, though Rox told me to not elaborate on where the donors for Project Alphas came from. After much discussion and meetings, the leaders approved Rox's request, and I was a free man.

Well, technically, I wasn't completely free. Rox was still my warden, and I was only granted a conditional parole. In order to be out of prison, I had to work under General Rox. The plan was to continue developing technology for him so he could use it on the battlefield, and I had a particular focus on biotic implant crafting. I wasn't going to be alone, though, as Eli Winde would remain my mentor. We would work as a team, much like we did during the course of Project Alphas.

And I couldn't really complain. Life had changed so much for the better that I could only be grateful for all that happened. I went from the frigid Siberian wasteland of Arkady and sent to sunnier shores of Allied City near the lakes of Michigan. Allied City is one of the largest cities in the world and the unofficial capital of the Alliance. It holds all things Alliance. Every species has their own embassy here and there's the United Delegation Building downtown. It's where all the leaders of each respective species meet and conduct meetings and where the Alliance council creates their laws and rules for all species under the Alliance umbrella.

As part of the conditions of working for Rox, I was granted several benefits along with my parole. I was given a nice loft in Allied City and a stipend to pay for living expenses. I also get free meals thanks to the cafeteria they have in Sector Six. Hell, they even have a gym too. I probably spend more time here than at home, but it's nice to know I have a good bed to sleep on. General Rox has treated me very well.

Our little team has grown over the years. First it was just me, Winde, and a few of the lab techs that we worked with back in Arkady. They made the move to Allied City as well, and we started the next phase, which was Project Beta. We were still using wolf bases to do our developing. General Rox supplied them. We improved the original design from Project Alpha, making the implants more seamless and the armor even stronger.

Since we already had the schematics from Project Alpha, our small team was able to progress through Project Beta much faster. It didn't take more than a decade this time. We finished it within a span of two years.

Rox was even more impressed with Project Beta than Project Alphas. Testing and live missions proved to be successful compared to the Alphas, who failed their field test.

At the end of the period, the Betas were hitting the ceiling. It was time to go to the next phase, the final phase of the implant story. Rox had commissioned us to start work on the Implant Program: live installation on working soldiers. Eli Winde was put in charge. He had retired from his military career and focused on his scientific pursuits.

I was second-in-command. We were quite the team. I consider Eli a good friend. You don't spend over twenty years working together and not share a bond. He started out as my enemy, a chimp that was on the team that apprehended me from HORUS. But in the end, our bond over technological progress broke down any barriers. I suppose I'm also thankful that he saw potential in me and guided me during those first few years in Arkady. Without his backing, I'm not sure if Rox would have had much patience when I was studying Lionel Changer's notes. Winde was always my first supporter and encouraged Rox to wait things out while I gained more experience.

Together we spearheaded the Implant Program and ensured Rox that his dream of a super soldier would be fulfilled. First things first, this was more demanding and complex, so we increased our staff count. We still retained our old team, but we promoted them to supervise the technicians we would hire.

Applicants came in all sizes and species. Dogs, cats, gorillas, pigs—all of them were recruited, and each one was personally screened by both Eli Winde and myself. We hired about thirty new members. Each brought their own unique skillsets and it was a pleasure to gain such a diverse team.

We started work right away on the recruits that Rox sent. It was a challenge at first, because Winde and I had only crafted our biotic implants on wolf subjects during Project Beta. Now we were forced to draw up and create implants for humans, eagles, crocs, gorillas, and a bunch of other species. Rox brought in soldiers of all shapes and sizes. Winde and I had our work cut out for us.

We made a few mistakes along the way. We've had a few failed subjects. Winde and I had to learn from our mistakes and strived for improvement. That's why I'm proud to say after years of work, the Implant Program has grown strong and is the crown jewel in all of the underground work Rox has commissioned.

Looking back, I can say I've accomplished many great achievements. I've personally overseen hundreds of successful installations on all sorts of animals. With each passing year, the soldiers are getting more powerful.

Eli Winde retired from the team a few years ago, and the reins to lead the project have been handed down to me. I was ready to take over then, and I'm still going strong now. I've gained a lifetime of experience and have learned managerial skills that the meeker, younger me never could. My staff has increased, and my duties have become more important. Team members actually look up to me and go to me for guidance. And I'm happy to instruct. I've grown both as a scientist and a leader.

In turn, Rox gets more and more weapons to use for his black ops assignments. There is a part of me that worries about the moral ramifications of my work. I've never been one hundred percent concerning Rox's illegal methods in procuring subjects during Project Beta. And though I'm not directly involved, I am aware of some of the less noble goals of Rox's operations that he sends my creations on. Yet I know in the end this work is done in the name of the Alliance, and everything they do is for the greater good. My work may not be altruistic, but it has its own merits and does more positive than negative.

And I must admit, there are some days when I miss my comrade Winde. You forget co-workers when they leave, but you don't forget mentors. He taught me everything, not just about the technology, but about the games that are played in the Alliance. I was never good at politics, but Winde showed me what to say to Rox, how to say it, and how to handle situations when they become drastic. It's only thanks to him that I am Rox's personal project manager.

I've been given several additional benefits. I'm still technically on parole, but Rox always approves sabbaticals when needed. I can travel anywhere I want and take vacation anytime I want as long as the general approves it and it fits within schedule. I've never really had a problem, as most of the times it does.

My stipend has also increased and I'm the recipient of several tax deductions on any major purchases. I've gotten to meet some very interesting and influential leaders thanks to my close relationship with both Winde and Rox. And most importantly, I've been given access to work on the most cutting-edge military projects thanks to Rox's funding.

I've been branching out recently, away from the biotic implant field. Rox believes for now, we've reached the limits of what biotic implants can do. He said there needs to be a shift on focus, to expand what technology we can create so it'll help him with his goal of being the military hammer in an ever-changing world.

This has been the most exciting time. I really get to test my imagination and creativity. I've been working on implants for so long that some diversity will be welcome. I've already created a few prototypes, some real world-changing stuff. None of it has been commissioned yet, but Rox has reviewed some of my devices and is looking into getting a few mandated. He's been pretty impressed with how out of the box I've been. Rox has always thought I was just an implant jockey, but this new period of creative freedom has allowed me to demonstrate how much I've learned over the past years.

And the best part is I am one of the few that hold all the secrets. All the undisclosed projects I've been working on are classified only to me, Rox, and some of his superiors. They trust me that much. I guess that's why Rox makes sure to treat me so well. I have no intention of committing treason.

I've been gifted with my own biotic implants, as they store my memories into an artificial database implanted in my brain. I'm able to access the information internally, and it's impossible to hack. The only way anyone could ever gain access is by hacking my mind.

It's a precaution the Alliance installs into all their high-level scientists. Winde had the same procedure done as well. And when he retired, they simply ran him through a painless, targeted data wipe to ensure no information would be leaked out. That's how it will be for me. And personally, I don't mind. I'll still remember my work here, still remember my accomplishments, but the details behind it, the stuff stored on file, will be Alliance property.

But perhaps I'm thinking too far into the future now. I've reached my office, and it's time to get back to work. My compcube activates the moment I step in, and my artificial intelligence welcomes me back to my office.

"Hello, Mark Allen," it says.

"Hello," I respond. "Subject Rod Traynor is almost complete. Please files the status report when the operator is finished with the installation."

"Affirmative."

"Also, please display the final report from last week's subject, Dan Ewald."

"Will display, but first, you received communication from Alliance personnel."

A holo image flashes in front of me and displays the sender.

"General Rox," I say. "Please get him on the line right away."

"Affirmative."

Rox receives his communication and I'm chatting face to face with my boss and warden.

"Allen, you called just in time," he says.

"Hello, General," I respond. "What is going on?"

"When I got on my communicator, I wanted to link up with you to discuss how the last month's recruits have been responding to the implants. However, that will have to be put on hold. There's been an incident involving Eli Winde."

"Incident?"

"Yes, it happened last night, but I'm just getting some of the details."

"Is he okay?"

"Like I said, I'm just getting the details now. I'll brief you on a full report once I know exactly what happened. You can expect something later this afternoon."

"Okay."

"Just continue your work. I believe you're on Traynor now, correct?"

"Yes. We're finishing up on him right now."

"Good."

"Please update me on what happened with Winde as soon as you can, General."

"Will do. This is Rox, out."

Our conversations tend to be brief like that. I hope everything is okay with Winde. The general was being awful terse about it. No matter, I'm sure I'll hear the news from him later today. Until then, it's back to shop.

Chapter 12 – General Rox

Precautions

September 19, 3071 1:01 PM
"So you're ready to give me your final report of the crime scene?" I ask my contact out in New Zealand.

I'm currently in my home's study room as images and holograms of Winde's decimated compound take up the air space. I was going to go to the Alliance headquarters in downtown Bath, but I didn't have time with the hubbub going on this morning. My former lead science officer is dead.

"Correct," she says through the holoscreen. We're both currently linked up with communicators.

Her name is Amy Lind, a pig and senior investigator out in New Zealand. She's a little over forty and her appearance is rather standard. She's a pig, and to me they all look the same, so there's nothing else to elaborate on.

I met her a decade ago when I was doing a tour overseas. I knew she was a star detective and wanted to work with me, so I recruited her, and she's become a valuable resource since. When I heard Winde had retired out in the down under, I asked Lind to keep tabs on him for me. I wanted to make sure Winde still fell into Alliance line, even after service. I trust my soldiers, I really do, but you can never be too careful. And sadly, when Lind came with news, it was the unfortunate kind. She currently stands in the middle of Winde's compound, surrounded by the destruction from last night.

"Okay then, proceed with your findings," I command.

"Of course," she responds promptly. "At around half past nine yesterday night, an intruder entered Eli Winde's compound through the back. The perpetrator took down two security drones on the way there, disabling their flight system and disconnecting their power cores."

"And there was no trace of ammunition you say? No model weapon to match the damage that was unleashed on the drones?"

"Correct."

"I see. Continue."

"The intruder worked its way to Eli Winde, traveling quietly through his hallways. Winde was located in the living area. After the trespasser arrived and found Winde, it attacked. However, there were no footprints found leading to where Winde was sitting, so we're unsure how the assault was initiated."

I flash Amy a skeptical look.

"I find it hard to believe you didn't find anything about that," I say.

"It could be possible the creature was using a self-hover device," the pig responds.

"What makes you say that?"

"Um... you'll see once you review the footage."

"Okay. Continue, then."

"Right. At that point, we suspect Winde had detected the invader's presence and initiated battle. As you can see from the damage, the fight was quite chaotic."

"Load up a rendering of the room."

"Certainly."

Lind activates her communicator's landscaper, and a rendering of Winde's living room pops up. I see broken tables, smashed shelves, and toppled pieces of art. In the corner of the hologram lies Winde's now dead body, limped over and head down.

"One thing to note is that everything appears to still be here," Lind says.

"All of Winde's valuables are still around?" I ask surprisingly. "I remember he was quite a collector. There were several expensive paintings and artifacts strewn across his property. I'm astonished all of those things remain intact."

"That appears to be the case. There's no sign of anything valuable being taken. The perpetrator was not a thief. It was a targeted attack."

"What about information? Was any of that stolen?"

"From what the tech boys have gathered, that's a no also. There wasn't much data in his brain to extract anyway. Yet I'm a bit perplexed. With someone as high ranking as Winde, I would have expected at least an attempt to harvest some of his knowledge. He probably had a boatload of Alliance secrets locked away in his memories."

"Well, maybe he did at one point, but after he quit, we took it back."

Lind shoots me a confused look.

"General?" she says.

"That's precisely why we did those mind wipes. I never could be too careful with all the sensitive information we entrusted into Winde," I explain. "When he left, we took it all away from his memory banks. He understood why we did it, and it seems this situation is exactly why we took those precautions."

Amy Lind looks slightly disturbed by my display of callousness.

"Forget what I said. Just know the intruder didn't steal anything, physical or intangible," I say confidently.

"Um, okay," Lind says, still puzzled by my rambling.

I observe the holographic rendering of the crime scene in its current state and deduce that there's nothing else to see. However, Lind also has more substantial pieces of evidence.

"So the footage of the attack," I say. "Were you able to identify the suspect?"

"No, but perhaps you might," Lind says timidly. "From what I saw in the reel, I think this one might be out of my jurisdiction."

Lind uploads the security system's feed to my communicator and I start to watch.

"The footage started to record the moment the silent sensor was activated by the perpetrator," Lind adds. "This occurred in Winde's trophy hallway. After it was triggered, Winde was aware of the intruder but played possum."

At first I only see Winde sitting there silently on his couch. Nothing seems out of the ordinary. But then, an entity comes into view right behind him, floating in the air. Everything hits me. The black cloak, the armor, the telekinetic powers. I've seen this all before. It happened ten years ago, but I remember it like yesterday.

"The Collector!" I exclaim. "The creature has resurfaced."

"So you recognize the suspect?" Lind asks.

"Yes, I do, though it's been quite a while since I've actually seen it in action. We tried to apprehend The Collector about ten years ago but failed. The creature escaped. Since then, I've been on the lookout for it, but the trail got cold. I figured either the creature was lying low, or it vanished off the earth. And now it seems it's back."

Lind doesn't respond. I'm stunned by the reappearance of this foe. It's been such a long time, and we spent so many years looking without a single shred of evidence to find. Watching the creature do its work is like seeing the ghost of a sworn enemy reappear in front of you.

I keep observing the feed. I watch as The Collector completely thrashes around Winde, like a toy. The chimp puts up a valiant fight, but I've seen this cloaked menace in action, and I already knew once the battle started how this scene would play out.

"The suspect is quite powerful," Lind says casually.

"You don't even know the half of it," I say. "But why is The Collector showing up now? And why did he attack Winde?"

"Keep watching and you'll find your answer."

Winde is barely able to move, and it is at this point in the feed The Collector starts to question him. The creature gets straight to the point and asks about the GTS. Ah, so that's what The Collector wants. As we all know, though, Winde doesn't have the detailed schematics, so The Collector asks who does. That's when Winde spills the beans.

"Mark Allen!" I say. "That's who The Collector is going after."

"So you know this Allen character?" Lind asks.

"Yes, very well actually. This is critical. I need to talk to him right away. Send me the rest of the details of your report after we close communication. Understood?"

"Yes."

I shut down our link and Amy Lind disappears from my holoscreen. I immediately dial up my communicator to contact Mark Allen. He should be expecting me anyway. And there is he, on a holoscreen.

"Glad to see you're still alive," I say.

"Excuse me, General?" he says in a perplexed manner.

"Eli Winde is dead."

Right away, the confused look on his face turns to grief and sorrow.

"I... I kind of expected that," he says. "When we talked earlier, it sounded like something bad had happened to him. But... to hear the actual words come from your mouth, it's devastating."

The two of them were close. I give him a few moments to sort out his emotions, but that's all I give. There are much more important things to talk about, and now isn't the time to stir up feelings of weakness.

"Chin up," I say. "Right now there are much more pressing matters. I called because your life is in danger."

"Sir?" Allen says, with an astonished tone.

"Our old friend The Collector is back," I say. "The creature was the one who killed Winde, and you are next on the list."

"Me? Why?"

"It's looking for information on the GTS project."

Allen tilts his head back and puts his hands on his head. The mere mention of the GTS causes him to be a little anxious.

"The GTS? Of all things, it wants that? Not the biotics schematics?" Allen says.

"That seems to be the case," I respond bluntly.

"But why? We don't even have a working copy of it. It was simply a side project that got lost along the way."

"Well, considering what the GTS is hypothetically capable of doing, I'd say there are plenty of reasons The Collector might be after it."

"But like I said, we don't have a working prototype. The information is useless if there's no one to make sense of it."

"Well, maybe The Collector can. Or maybe it's going to extract the data and sell it on the black market. We can't underestimate the creature."

"When you say extract the data from me, what do you mean?"

"You know what I mean, Allen. The information isn't on some server nor encrypted compcube. The only place it's stored is inside your head. How else will The Collector get it?"

Allen lets out an audible gulp.

"So are you going to send someone to protect me?" he asks.

"I'll send someone to get The Collector. I want the perpetrator captured, interrogated, and killed. We're ten years late on this. Time to make up for lost time," I say.

"I see. Well, who are you going to send? The top agent you always clamor about?"

"Unfortunately, no. He's already out on a mission, hunting down some wolf spy who hacked into my files and obtained some classified information. But I do know someone who is just as skilled a warrior. She'll find The Collector before The Collector finds you, Allen."

"Um, okay."

My declaration puts little confidence in him. I flash him a narrow frown.

"Don't be so pessimistic," I say. "We have this under control. The Collector will be found. Just continue your work. Stay in Sector Six for now. Don't go home."

"Yes… yes, sir," he says sheepishly.

"This is Rox, out."

The communicator shuts off. I have one last call to make. Hopefully, it'll be the last for now. I send out the link and wait for the response. It's established and up pops up the recipient.

"Two Van Faye," I say. "I hope you've been well."

"General Rox, what brings you to my neck of the woods?" she answers grudgingly.

We're not the best of friends. The Elephant Queen of Crime and I have a complicated history. The only thing we can do is tolerate one another's presence. She should be more grateful, though. If it weren't for me, she'd still be earning pennies in Shogun. I made her Fan Zui Bin Empire possible.

"I need the help of your bodyguard," I say.

"Ash Han? Why? What for?" she says.

"Something's come up, and it'll require the expertise of someone like Han. I require an expert tracker and warrior. Han fits the bill."

"Why don't you just ask one of your own cronies instead of requesting mine?"

"Well, this is as dark of an operation as it gets. I'd like to keep it off the books so to speak, so I'll need to reach out to other resources. And besides, I only trust one of my soldiers with this job, and he's busy. Compared to the rest, Ash Han is much more qualified."

Van Faye looks at me, a little bewildered by the statement.

"Oh, really," she says. "And who exactly are you hunting down?"

"The Collector," I say calmly.

Her jaw drops, and her trunk straightens out. My simple utterance of the statement causes her to be shocked to the core.

"Are you certain Ash Han is the right candidate for this job?" Van Faye says.

"Yes," I say. "After all, she's built with all the biotic implants we supplied to you. The only other person I know who has such hardware is my top agent. I've seen her do your dirty work. She's capable enough for me."

Van Faye sways her trunk a little and thinks about the situation. She's extremely hesitant. But she knows I have her in a bind.

"Okay then, Rox, you'll get her." She yields. "I owe you that much. And personally, I'd like to see The Collector brought down. This grudge match has lasted for ten years. The creature will pay for the loss of Sai."

"Good," I say.

"So what is the battle plan?"

"Right now, The Collector is looking for the head of my science division in covert affairs. It wants to extract some information. I'll need you to send Ash Han to Allied City for protection services. It is extremely important that The Collector doesn't get to my guy. Keeping him safe is top priority."

Van Faye appears intrigued by my briefing.

"And what is this man's name?" she asks. "It is a human, correct?"

"Yes," I respond. "His name is Mark Allen. I will send you his home address and where he's currently hiding, an Alliance facility called Sector Six. Please keep in mind all of this is classified."

"Of course."

"Make sure to tell Ash Han what The Collector is capable of. I will send you what information I have on the creature, but you know more than I do how dangerous The Collector is. If your assassin plans to take it down, she'll need to be prepared."

"Naturally."

"Good. Once she gets to Allied City, I'll update her on the situation. That's all for now. I'm closing communication."

"Okay. It's always a pleasure, Rox."

I put away my communicator and reflect on what's happened. It's been a busy day, but I'm excited. I'm hoping to get some closure on a case that should have been closed ten years ago.

Chapter 13 – Two Van Faye

Expansion

<u>September 19, 3071 4:02 PM</u>
Damn that General Rox. He thinks he can just call me up like a servant and demand things on a whim? That dog has been overstepping his boundaries ever since we made our first deal those many years ago. He was a tyrant then, and he's a tyrant now. Things never change.

Doesn't he know who he talks to? I am the Elephant Queen of Crime. My reign expanded throughout the decade. I now employ top-notch soldiers and rule every corner of Fan Zui Bin. No more is this crime country divided between hundreds of bosses. The only boss is me. I am the unofficial ruler of all Fan Zui Bin. I have conquered the wildest of states, a place made of thieves, crooks, and schemers. My rise in power is unparalleled.

Yet I know my arrogance is shallow. No matter how powerful I grow, I cannot match up to the Alliance, and I certainly am not foolish enough to take on Rox and his black ops division. He works in secret, but everyone who is anyone knows to fear the black-and-brown dog. I resent answering to him. Despite my boisterousness, I know he is still the boss. It doesn't matter who you are or who you have working for you. The underworld knows if you dare go toe to toe with the general, it will end with the loss of your life. His power is great, even greater than mine, the ruler of Fan Zui Bin.

The funny thing is if it weren't for the general, I never would have been able to expand my empire outside the city of Shogun. The Van Faye family had a legacy back then, but it was only limited to one city, one small region. I had greater ambitions. I wanted to be the leader of the whole damn state. Yet Fan Zui Bin had been ruled independently for years. Each family had their own stake. I didn't have the pull or manpower to tackle every crime syndicate. If I wanted to shoot for the stars, I needed an edge, something that could strengthen my claim.

That edge came in the form of Alliance power. The general and I had a working relationship. The dog that has become my warden was originally my greatest resource. Weird how things have turned out.

It started when I agreed to help him apprehend a dangerous individual known as The Collector. The creature was one of my clients in the trafficking business. I supplied The Collector with a host of animals. I never knew what the being did with my captives, but I didn't care. The Collector paid well. Unfortunately, Rox paid greater. He wanted The Collector brought in, and after some hesitation, I agreed.

Our mission was a failure. We never caught the creature, but I continued to work with Rox. I suppose he saw me as a valuable asset, and I saw him as the individual who would help me rise to be the boss of bosses in Fan Zui Bin.

It was a simple partnership. I supplied Rox with information about Fan Zui Bin, stuff only a boss and not some hoodrat informant would know. Whether it was rumors about what the other bosses were doing or evidence against my rivals, I delivered to the general. I helped him on his investigations and gave him the inside dirt he could never get on his own.

In return, he supplied me with firepower and soldiers. No more did my subordinates have to use crummy black market weapons. Instead, I was given the newest and greatest tech the Alliance had to offer. And I had professionally trained Alliance soldiers doing my dirty work. They were handpicked and sent by Rox himself, posed as my own subordinates, and exterminated any rivals that dared defied my growing empire.

But perhaps these gifts paled in comparison to what Rox truly offered: amnesty. Rox's influence caused the Alliance to turn a blind eye to all my activities as long as it was done on Fan Zui Bin soil. My industry included prostitution, gambling, extortion, drug trafficking, basically any crime that could turn a profit. I got away with everything. Thanks to Rox's help, I gained a foothold on my war, complete control, and absolute power. Legitimate and illegitimate blurred lines, but the only thing any citizen of Fan Zui Bin had to know was that I was the epicenter.

And there were no restrictions on my war. I was ruthless, cunning, brutal to all my adversaries, and the Alliance did nothing but observe. I was allowed free reign to do what was necessary to take the crime country for my own.

The secrets of Fan Zui Bin were once priceless, but with my status as an informant, the price was set. I owe everything I've gained to my partnership with Rox. My empire was built on Alliance foundations, and with it the Van Faye legacy will last eternities.

At the same time, though, I feel empty, incomplete. I'm on top of the world, so why do I feel so ambivalent? I ask a question, and I know an answer. Despite my status as the top lord of Fan Zui Bin, I don't feel like a top dog. Instead, I feel like a pawn, a drone, an attack dog sent to do the real top dog's work. I own Fan Zui Bin, but General Rox and his Alliance scum own me.

This is the truth ever since I extinguished my enemies. Secrets are running thin in Fan Zui Bin now that only one ruler commands the masses. The only information I can give Rox is about my own operations. And since I'm bound by my agreement, I must deliver. Either that, or I'll watch my power disappear like the fog.

Since I report information on my own operations to him, that doesn't make me a lord, it makes me a subordinate. General Rox is my boss. In my quest to obtain ultimate power, I have sold out and lost any chance to be the true leader. The Elephant Queen of Crime is simply a moniker, it doesn't mean anything anymore.

As the days pass, it becomes more apparent that this has always been his plan. He was probably rooting for me to succeed all along so he could instill a leader he could control.

For centuries, Fan Zui Bin had been untouchable to the Alliance. It was a land ruled by murderers and the untrustworthy. And there was no one true tyrant, simply smaller tyrants constantly fighting for a piece of the pie. The Alliance wanted nothing to do with it. We strived on isolation and lawlessness.

My rise to power meant the end of this era. I ratted out my comrades to the Alliance in order to get to the top. Heavy is the head that wears the crown. And Rox does control me. Sure, he lets me get away with my crimes, but at the same time, he monitors my deeds. I'm forced to inform him about my operations, and he has subtle influence over it.

At first, I was okay with it. I was so drunk with my supremacy that I simply didn't care. But then I started to realize my limits.

I'm told what I can do, what I can't do, always with the threat that his black ops force will be coming if I don't comply. He ignores the little stuff and lets me do my dirty deeds, but he makes sure it occurs within Fan Zui Bin's boundaries. My crimes can never leak outside to the real world.

And by controlling me, he controls all of Fan Zui Bin. This was his master stroke. His plan was never about helping me. His plan was always about helping the leaders of the world. I have power, yet at the same time I am powerless.

Rox himself is as dirty of a player as any of the former bosses of the FZB. He's sneaky, manipulative, and authoritative. He flaunts his crew of biologically altered lackeys like a giant sword and is willing to point it at anyone that gets in his way. His creations are his leverage. There have been times when I have voiced my dissent, and I've always received veiled threats from his direction.

I must be honest, though. I will always remember without Rox, I would be some penny snatcher dreaming big in the city of Shogun. I thought I was so mighty back then, but what I've obtained over the years has made my earnings during those days seem like chump change. And when I look back on it, I realize how far I've come. It's only because of my work with the Alliance that I was able to grab so much.

I can't go back to that life. I've always prided myself on being a contender, never a pretender. As much as I hate to say it, I was a pretender back then. I didn't have any real pull outside of Shogun. But now everything I own is absolute. Without a doubt, I am on top.

Many in Fan Zui Bin know of my Alliance connections. It's not exactly a secret, but it's not broadcasted on billboards either. I prefer it this way. The Alliance is feared not only in Fan Zui Bin, but throughout the world. Enemies think twice to mess with me, knowing who is backing me up. That is why I foresee my empire lasting ages.

And now the path has come full circle. I never thought I'd hear the name again. The Collector is back in business and I'm tasked with killing it.

Weird how things turn out. The Collector was one of my first major clients. I have to admit that the creature was an excellent partner. It delivered payments on time, not a credit missing, and was straightforward and more reliable than any of the deplorable scumbags I've had to work with over the years. If I had it my way, I'd still be working with The Collector.

But then the great general had to make me an offer I couldn't refuse. And when he showed up with those two mechanical beasts, I saw the future in biotic implants. I knew immediately I had to cut a deal with General Rox, not only to get Fan Zui Bin, but also to get a cut of the tech.

After the ordeal with The Collector was over, I quickly tried to convince Rox to get me a piece of his implant action. But the general refused to hear any of my pleas. The whole Implant Program was his baby, and I guess he didn't want the filth of Fan Zui Bin to get their grubby mitts on it. Rox could give me his weapons, he could give me his soldiers, but biotic implants were for him alone.

But then I reminded him that I lost one of my own during the showdown with The Collector. Sai, my rhino bodyguard, the best soldier I had, was killed by the being, his head crushed like a walnut. He was a feared beast among the residents of Shogun and a much needed asset if I were to expand my empire. Simply put, my bodyguard was irreplaceable.

I demanded a replacement and wanted Rox to pay for it. My new bodyguard had to be tough, durable, near indestructible like Sai. In addition, he or she needed to be just as skilled in weapons, strong, agile, basically everything that made a great warrior. My life was on the line after all. Bosses would be gunning for me, and I didn't want an expense spared if it meant my well-being.

The expectations I had for my new bodyguard could only be fulfilled by one thing: biotic implants. Naturally speaking, Sai was one of a kind. If I were to craft a new soldier for myself in his image, I needed some enhancements in the hopes that my warrior could measure up to his physicality. Rox had the goods, and he needed to deliver.

He was reluctant to hand over the keys. But I wasn't going to budge. I needed a replacement.

Thus, we cut a deal. One of my own, and only one, would be allowed access to Rox's Implant Program. If my candidate died, ran away, or stopped working for me, that would be it. I wouldn't get a second chance. I had to choose wisely.

I looked through my lot of schemers and underlings to find a suitable volunteer. And quite frankly, I found none. These subordinates could barely hold a candle to Sai, and all were deceptive. They were born and raised in Fan Zui Bin and were backstabbers and power hungry. The first thing they'd do with their newfound abilities would be to overthrow me. How could I trust my life with any of them? One turned back and I'd be dead.

No, if I wanted to find a replacement, I had to start from the ground up. I'd have to pick someone who didn't know such dishonesty. And most importantly, I needed to pick someone who was desperate, ready to fight teeth and claw for the good life. That meant I needed someone from the bottom, and the only species that were at the bottom in Fan Zui Bin were humans.

The world is a funny place. While humans are the most powerful species outside of the FZB, here they are a minority. It's the end result of their ousting in Fan Zui Bin. They were once on top and all the bosses were humans. Then, after the animals overthrew the lords and became lords themselves, humans fled in masses. Few wanted to live in a place where animals were their superiors. The few unfortunate ones that were left behind slowly fell into poverty, and that's how it works today. They are the bottom rung. But they're also the hungriest. Thus, a human, and only a human, would be the successor to Sai.

I went to the human orphanage to see my prospects. There were many children, each cute and charming with smiling faces. They knew who I was and acted out their adorableness so that the Elephant Queen of Crime could take them away from their depressed childhoods. Some were polite, others tried to act tough. Each had their own characteristics that made me consider taking them in.

The only problem was they all looked the same. I saw only mediocrity, until one stood out. She did not look happy. She did not greet me curiously. She didn't even attempt to play the part in the hopes that I would adopt her. Instead, her face was aloof, her expression apathetic. She looked dull and boring. She just didn't care.

But as I looked closer, I saw a fire in her eyes. Her indifferent appearance was an act. She was a fighter. It was subtle but noticeable. When I observed her playing with the other children, she would secretly take their toys while they put their attention on me. When I talked to her, she answered with short answers, but I could tell she was holding her tongue. She was a rebel, she just needed me to bring it out. Thus, this girl, Ash Han, was the perfect candidate.

I took her in, trained her, and shipped her to Rox for the Implant Program. She has grown into an indestructible soldier and bodyguard. And on occasion, she's an assassin.

That's who Rox is asking for. He wants Ash Han to eliminate The Collector. Yet we both know this is no ordinary target. I feel dread simply thinking about what The Collector can do. The creature trashed my penthouse, killed my bodyguard, laid waste to everything in a matter of seconds. Ash Han is my best warrior, but The Collector is a foe that she might be unprepared for.

I don't have time to think about it anymore. Ash has her gear and is equipped with weapons and armor.

"Do you remember your instructions," I say in a serious manner.

"Yes. I will rendezvous with an Alliance agent in Allied City and receive my orders," Ash Han says calmly.

"Correct. General Rox hasn't given me much info, but from what he tells me, he is currently keeping Mark Allen under safeguard. But he has reason to believe The Collector will no doubt be in the Alliance capital regardless."

"Yes, that's the target. As the details of the mission stated, my job is to eliminate The Collector. Allen is for the Alliance to worry about. My focus will completely be on The Collector."

"Good. The general and his contacts will update you further upon your arrival."

Ash Han and I have a complicated relationship. I trust her with my life, but at the same time, I sense no love lost between us. I had her trained from youth, bred to be a killer. It's no surprise we don't exactly share a mother-daughter relationship, more like a slave and master.

"Did you have a chance to review the information on The Collector I gave you? The messages we exchanged back when I trafficked animals for it?" I ask intensely.

"I did," she responds bluntly.

"And the report Rox supplied? Did you look over that?"

"Yes."

"What about the video from the battle in the penthouse?"

"I looked over those too."

"And?"

She looks at me with dead eyes. Her stare is cold, her mouth unwavering

"The Collector will be taken care of," she says in a nonchalant fashion.

"Don't be too arrogant. You haven't seen what this creature can do," I say.

Ash Han nods silently.

"Then good luck in Allied City," I say. "Send me your status throughout the day. Tell me everything you see and hear. And pay extra attention to General Rox. You can't trust that dog."

"Yes, master," she says.

She walks out of my office and leaves on her mission.

Chapter 14 – Falena Snow

Dreams

September 21, 3071 7:01 PM

I look around and see I'm in a meadow. The sun is out, the grass is green, there are trees and mountains surrounding me. The air is so crisp and fresh, and the wind blows against my fur, creating a relaxing, cool feeling that makes me smile. I don't know where I am or how I got here, but I feel serene, at peace.

I walk around to get a better glimpse of my surroundings. In the distance, snow caps the mountaintops and they glisten brightly under the illuminating sun. I see some deer prancing about, grazing on the plant life. I also hear birds chirping and watch the leaves rustle on evergreens that must stand at least a hundred feet tall. The sky is a bright blue, clear as an ocean, mesmerizing as a jewel.

I absorb everything around me, and that's when it hits me. The landscape, the noises and smells, they're very familiar. I've been here before. I didn't recognize it earlier, but now, as I see everything in front of me, I know where I am. This is the place where I grew up, my childhood retreat.

Well, not this exact field, but ten minutes away was my home, out in the Wolf's Den. Our neighborhood was settled right next to this open land, and often my mother and I would walk ten minutes from home to get to this field. We spent our free time here, enjoying picnics and appreciating the wonders of nature. Some days, we'd explore beyond the field and go into the woods. My mother took me here to show me my wolf roots, to remind me that there was a time when all wolves needed was the earth and we had little use for the technological wonders that consume our everyday lives.

I miss those days greatly. It's when she was still in my life, when we were happy. She was a hardened soldier, but she had a soft side. When she was stripped of her rank, that tenderness disappeared. But she still tried her hardest to be a good mother. Being in this field reminds me she wasn't always so obsessed with the job, that she also appreciated the beauty in simplicity.

Just thinking about her now makes me miss her so much. And then she appears, standing in front of me, coming from thin air.

"Falena," a familiar voice says.

"Mom?" I ask, half eager and half scared.

I blink my eyes a few times to make sure I'm not hallucinating. She's still there and looks at me, smiling and proud.

My mother looks young and radiant. Her coat has a healthy shine. Her posture is strong. Her eyes are sparkling yet piercing at the same time. My mom looks different from when I remembered her during my youth. She's full of life instead of despair.

"What are you doing here?" I ask her.

"Don't you remember?" she responds. "You asked me if we could spend the day in these woods."

"I did?"

"Yes, right after breakfast?"

"Breakfast?"

Her eyes narrow, head tilts, and confusion is shown on her face.

"Are you okay, Falena?" she says. "You sound sick."

I'm still stunned that she's in front of me, alive and speaking. I shake my head to try to get myself back to reality.

"Um, sorry, Mom," I say. "Guess it feels like I haven't seen you for such a long time."

"Silly one, you saw me this morning," she says comfortingly. "Now let's go."

She starts walking away from me, leading me through the meadow. I sprint forward to catch up to her, but as I get closer, I start to realize she's huge. In fact, she towers over me. I have to look up to greet her eyes. I'm perplexed.

"Why are you so big?" I ask her.

She looks down on me and laughs.

"Well, I eat a lot and I train to grow strong," she says. "One day you'll be as big as me too."

"What?" I ask, still puzzled. "One day?"

I didn't realize it before, but the grass of this meadow seems rather tall, as it almost touches my stomach. In fact, when I compare myself to my surroundings, it seems everything is much larger. The sky looks higher, the trees huge. Even the deer are the size of behemoths.

That's when I realize it. It's not that everything else is larger, it's that I am smaller. I now know where I am. Everything correlates to familiarity, and this place only feels familiar without being such. It's because I'm in a memory. I'm not an adult, but rather a child, a young pup still clinging onto my mother. I have yet to experience the hardships of age. Instead, I'm gifted with innocence. But when I see my mother standing in front of me, I know she isn't alive. What appears before me is simply what I remember of her.

My revelation makes me realize I will not be in this place long. Soon my mother will fade away just like all the other memories I have of her. I run to her and press my head against her body.

"I miss you," I say desperately.

"I miss you too," she says.

Her words echo through my mind. I take one final glance and close my eyes. When they open, I'm greeted with a view of my dark, cold room. My compcube is on, my airflow running. I've awakened from my dream, transported from my surreal meadow to the mundane existence of my home.

Something's off, though. I hear a beeping. I'm still trying to fully awake, and the noise is an ever-annoying presence. *What is that?*

Then I become fully aware and realize what it is. My security sensor has gone off. An intruder is in my home.

"Security feed enable," I say.

My home's artificial intelligence recognizes the command and several holoscreens quickly pop up in front of me. They each contain a live feed to the various rooms in my home. I scan through each one, inspecting the images. My kitchen is empty, my living room too. The bathrooms don't have a single soul in them. Even my study is clear.

That's when I see him, in the hallways. The trespasser is a human, male, and really, really big. The muscles on this guy bulge out of his skintight outfit. As I take a closer look, I realize it's not any old fabric he's wearing, it's a high-density stealth armor. The gear is a charcoal color. Coming from a military family, I know the kind of resistance garb like this has. It's a human manufactured armor. Thus, it'll take a lot of hits to protect their relatively fragile bodies. Though the muscles on this guy look like armor enough.

The man stands well over six feet, probably closer to seven. Not only is he ripped from head to toe, but he's also a bulky fella. His legs are as thick as tree trunks and his arms the size of bazookas.

He wears a ski mask that wraps his entire head. It's completely black, covering his mouth and nose. He also wears some dark-shaded goggles, most likely eyewear that will aid his stealth mission. They appear to be Wiselers and probably have a built-in interface unit that feeds him information. His glasses already surveyed the area. That's why he's able to navigate through my home so easily.

The gear and body frame make me think one thing: he's no ordinary burglar. The whole cut of his look screams professionalism. I'm assured he was hired for this job, yet what he wants from me remains a mystery. Why is he here? And why does he look so, um, military?

He approaches closer, making his way to my room. I don't have long to figure out this mystery. Is he from the Alliance? His appearance kind of indicates that. But what business do I have with them?

That's when I see the blaster in his hand. He's a killer. But why? Oh shit. The data. I think they may have figured out that I've been snooping around their classified information. And that means…

This guy has come to clean up the mess. He's come to kill me.

Why else would he be here? To negotiate? I highly doubt it, especially considering he's dressed to kill.

Crap, what do I do, what do I do, what do I do? I look around for an exit. The only door in my bedroom leads to the hallway. And other than that, there's a wall, a wall, a wall, and a...

Window.

I rush over and look at it. It's an old style window made out of glass, so I slide it open using the automated switch. I then peer out. Unfortunately, I'm on the second story. It's about a fifteen-foot drop below. I could make a graceful landing, but the height might be a little too much for my legs, as its nothing but solid concrete below. But then I see a full bush right below me. That could break my fall. It's risky, but I have no other choice.

I hear the footsteps getting close and closer. The assailant will be here any minute.

Before I make my jump, I need to get my compcube. The files on Operation Alpha aren't stored on a cloud or server. I didn't want to make it possible for the wrong hands, or the Alliance, to gain access to my stuff. Instead, it's only on that compcube. I can do a mind transfer later, but for now, if I lose that, I lose everything.

I go over and quickly program it to latch mode so I can carry it with me. Two hooks protrude from its surface and I kneel down on four legs right next to it. The compcube senses my presence and quickly fastens onto similar hooks that protrude from my clothing. The connection clicks and now the pocketsize compcube is securely fashioned to my body. Time to make my escape.

I approach the window and look down. The drop looks bigger than it actually is, and fear temporarily paralyzes me. But that only lasts a few seconds when I hear a sound coming from the door in my room.

Knock! Knock!

Fuck, he's here! I freeze in my position, anxiously looking out the window, then turn to see the door behind me.

"Who, who's there?" I say sheepishly.

No answer. My eyes continue to fixate on the door, wondering what's happening on the other side.

"Who's there?" I ask again.

Once more, there's no response.

"Answer… answer me!" I scream desperately.

A burst of energy explodes from my door, blowing a giant hole through it. Splinters and debris fly in my direction, hitting me in the face. I'm shell-shocked by the blast but unscathed. He answered all right, with his gun.

That's my cue to leave. I quickly do an about-face and look down at the bush. It's now or never. I close my eyes, take in a deep breath, and jump. The instant I go into the air, I hear another shot ring from my door.

It seems like an eternity, but a mere fraction of a second later, my front legs and face crash into the shrubbery. I feel leaves and twigs pierce through my fur and graze my skin. My body hits it with a thud, and it feels like I've been smacked by a log. I quickly open my eyes to recuperate. I'm a little dazed but conscious. The adrenaline takes over, and I start churning my legs, making my way outside the group of stems and branches.

I'm on my feet and glance back up to the window I just leapt from. There I see the man, mask and body armor still intact, looking in my direction. He takes off his goggles, and our eyes meet each other's.

And then, without hesitation, I turn the other direction and start running. I don't know where I'm going. I just know it needs to be away from here. The only chance I have to live is if I hide.

Yet I have a feeling I haven't seen the last of this pursuer.

Chapter 15 – Iris Lawton

Miscalculations

September 22, 3071 6:10 PM

Allied City sure is chilly during September. A few days have passed since my confrontation with Eli Winde. The next being on my hit list is Mark Allen, and I've journeyed from the island of New Zealand to North America to get to him. I had to move carefully, using my personal porter to get across the globe without being seen by the public.

All this secrecy and risk will be worth it once I get my hands on GTS device schematics. It's imperative to my future plans, and it seems only one man has it. Don Leons didn't have what I needed. Eli Winde didn't either. But Mark Allen does, for I've seen it in my vision.

At least I saw it in my original vision. I did make a mistake during my assault on Winde's compound. He caught my arrival when he wasn't supposed to. But things still played out correctly. I got Allen's information, and I speared him in the heart, just like I was supposed to. I don't see how one tiny miscalculation could drastically alter things so differently.

Lucy has advised me to take a look at my visions, just in case something has changed. She's always weary of the dependability of them because of how idiosyncratic time can be. Lucy states that there are literally thousands, maybe millions, of variables that could alter a timeline, that the smallest detail could change what I envisioned and set me off on a new course. That makes sense, but to look into each one is time consuming. Thousands of variables mean thousands of alternate futures I'd have to look at. If I had a few weeks to take a look, perhaps I could, but right now I don't have the time to investigate something so small. That, funny as it sounds, takes time.

Thus, I have to rely on my instincts to a certain degree. I can use my precognition to look into something quick, but a full analysis like the one Lucy pushes is out of the question right now. And since things went according to plan with Winde, for the most part, I have full trust that my original vision still stands. Mark Allen will be here, and I will get the information I need.

My vision shows me he'll be arriving back to his loft in about five minutes, back from a day of working under the Alliance. It's empty right now. I made my way in through his window. I first teleported to the roof and then used my telekinesis to guide myself down into his loft.

His accommodations are pretty nice for a former Alliance prisoner. There's a lot of space and several high-quality furnishings scattered about. He must have a cleaning drone employed here, as it's also relatively spotless. He doesn't seem to be a man who cares for leisure. I don't see a fancy entertainment system or anything of that sort.

As I walk around a bit more, I do see a busy workstation. It's in his study. There are several compcubes around, though they are currently shut down. I also see a slew of documents messily strewn on his desk. The fellow seems like a real scatterbrain. He reminds me of Lucy to a certain degree.

Lucy tells me before he was captured by the Alliance, Mark Allen spent some time at HORUS. He appears the type. However, Lucy said he was a new candidate, so she never had time to fully know the man. But it seems the Alliance has been able to extract whatever potential he had and used it for their benefit. He's been able to replicate Lionel Changer's biotic implant work and improve on it.

Lucy's work is still much more impressive, especially when you factor in the gap in resources between the two. If Lucy had access to even half the stuff Allen did and still does, then I wouldn't even need to scour for the GTS schematics. Lucy would already have it done. He may be the Alliance's golden boy, but he'll always be second rate compared to her.

Speaking of the devil, I hear someone coming. Outside in the hallway, the sound of footsteps approaches the front door. They come at a fast pace, in heavy cadence, and are getting closer and closer. And then the stomping stops right at the front door. I check the time and see it's almost a quarter past six. That must be him, right on schedule. Looks like my vision held up.

I quickly approach the door and arm my energy whips. They should pin him down like they've pinned down so many of my enemies. I don't want him dead, not yet. I need to find out where the schematics are being held first. Once I get that info, then he will die. He may not have been a monster like Leons or Winde, but he's a soldier in the ongoing war between the

Alliance and me. And he was responsible for turning Fenrir into a freak. He needs to die.

I'm ready to open the door when something unexpected happens. The footsteps that are on the other side start scampering away in another direction. They sound like they're fleeing. Is that Mark Allen escaping? Why is he running in the other direction? It's like he knows I'm here and is now making a break for it. This wasn't how it's supposed to go down.

My first instinct is to hurry outside and see what's going on. Yet I think about what Lucy has told me about time, how everything affects everything. This was never supposed to happen. Mark Allen was supposed to walk through the door with no worries, and I'd apprehend him. But now, things have changed, and if I do something even rasher, will the change continue to spiral out of control? Will these actions lead to another set of actions until I get a totally undesirable future that I can no longer grasp?

It's what I always must think about, and now I don't have the time to see how things play out. I could take a few seconds to look, but those few seconds might be the ones he needs to get away. And if he gets away, he'll run back to Alliance headquarters, out of my reach. The mission will fail. But without knowing what's going to happen, I run a big risk of stepping into an unknown future. Simply walking through a door could lead to big consequences.

Ah, screw it.

I open the door and enter the hallway. I look left and right, but I don't see a sign of him. I even look up at the ceiling to make sure there are no games being played. He's not there, he's not anywhere. It's like he vanished into the walls.

"Strange," I say to myself. "The timeline has been altered. I need to regroup."

I turn around, back to his loft, when out of nowhere, the force of a blast knocks me off my feet. I stumble backward, and my hands catch me before I'm on my back. I then quickly kneel down and look forward to see what happened.

In front of me stands a woman, a human. She's about five feet and two inches tall. She's covered head to toe in stealth armor. It shines a greenish shade as opposed to the usual black. It looks sturdy and high grade, like a modified Alliance unit.

She's also armed to the teeth. In one hand she has a blaster and in the other a long, spear-like weapon with its tip coated in light. My eyes fixate on the blaster. That's what knocked me down, and it's a good thing my armor absorbed it. I'm a little sore, but I'll live. I've taken worse.

The assailant's face is exposed, the only part of her body uncovered by armor. The woman looks young, and her features suggest someone of Asian human ancestry. Her eyes are sharp and focused. Her skin is clear and strands of black hair hang from under the triangle-shaped helmet that protects her head. Her features are sharp, yet at the same time, she looks delicate, soft almost. By human standards, she's stunningly beautiful.

Before I can continue my gaze, she lifts her arm and starts firing the blaster again. This time I react soon enough and shield myself with my cloak, much like I did when Winde fired his barrage of shots. They harmlessly deflect off my coat, but at the same time, my view is obscured.

It's because of this that I don't see the energy wraps she fires from her wrist. They hit me and quickly tangle around my body, pure, concentrated light that constricts and bounds my arms together. In a matter of seconds, I'm on my knees, tied up, helplessly looking straight at the woman.

Yet this woman should know no shackles can hold me down. Although it's physically impossible for me to get out of my binds, mentally, I'm more than capable. I concentrate on the wraps and create a mental image of them getting looser as I control it with my mind. Slowly they slacken, enough for me to expand my arms. Then with one mighty effort, I flex mind and body, and the wraps snap and disable. The light dissipates in the air, and I stand up, completely free. The woman is astonished by this and quickly gets in a battle stance.

We look at each other, and as I think about the last ten minutes, I'm consumed with shock. I wasn't expecting this at all. It's possible that Mark Allen got scared and ran away by something I did, but who the hell is this? She looks like an assassin. More importantly, she was expecting me. I've walked into a trap. I never walk into traps. I can see the future. If anything, I'm the one who creates traps.

I've been careless. I should have followed Lucy's advice. I could have seen this coming. What's the point of having precognition if you don't use it correctly? My arrogance prevented me from being extra careful and now I'm paying for it.

I'm staring at an opponent that I wasn't prepared to fight. I don't know what this enemy is capable of. She's human and probably has been sent here to protect Mark Allen. But she doesn't quite look like an official

Alliance soldier. Those cronies tend to appear a bit more professional. This one looks rough and ready. She's probably a mercenary or a contract killer.

Whatever the case, I'll have to dispose of her before I pursue Mark. I have the power to do it. Confidence may have made me fall into this trap, but now it's the only way I'll get out of it.

Chapter 16 — Ash Han

Showdown

September 22, 3071 6:20 PM
The Collector, my target, my mark, is in front of me. We stand silently, both anxious to do battle. I'm sizing up the creature, and it sizes me. Behind the cold mask is a human, or at least I think it is. It is bipedal, slim, has arms, a head, everything that would suggest it is human. But I don't know, something seems off. The way the creature stands, the way it's shaped, doesn't look natural. It's the small things. The hands appear thick, the calves are huge, the shoulders are slim. If this creature is human, then I'm guessing it was mutated somehow.

None of this matters, though. What matters is The Collector is my enemy, and I've been sworn to kill it. Ms. Van Faye is counting on me, and I will not fail. I'm not sure why I'm concerned with her opinion, really. But I want to succeed. I've been bred to be a killer since childhood. It's what I do best, and if I can't kill my target, I might as well not live.

I've seen the tapes. The Collector is powerful. Possible telekinesis, cat-like reflexes, strength, grace, agility, intelligence—it has all these things. I've taken down a lot of power junkies in the past, but The Collector is the cream of the crop, the challenge of challenges. I will win, and my victory will be my greatest achievement.

"You going to make a move first or should I?" I ask it.

The creature lets down its stance slightly. I find the move odd. I'm still on full alert, ready to strike at any moment. I'm not sure if this is a mind game The Collector is launching, but I won't fall for it.

"I won't make a move, not until I ask a few questions," The Collector says.

What is this creature up to?

"What questions?" I ask.

"First off, who do you work for?" The Collector asks. "Your gear doesn't suggest Alliance ties. You must be working for a private party."

"Very observant of you. Yes, I do work for a private party, but I will not be divulging who."

"Not even if your life is on the line?"

The threat scares me a little because it's delivered so calmly. But I continue to answer confidently. I can't show one shred of weakness.

"Trust me, my life is not on the line," I say, smirking. "I don't foresee my defeat at your hands, or whatever you have."

"I wasn't talking about death by me," it says. "I was talking about your employer. I'm guessing it's not your sense of loyalty that binds you to your boss, or even the credits. It's fear. You won't tell me because you're scared of who you're working for."

That was unexpected... and true. I've been Two Van Faye's slave since the moment I left the orphanage. She has raised me but under heartless ruling. I've killed hundreds, but I've done so because I'm afraid of my childhood terrorizer.

The Collector is astonishingly insightful. Perhaps I can use it against the creature.

"It's true," I say as I try my hardest to tell a sob story. "I was raised by my master, plucked from an orphanage. She's been my ruler, I am her slave. When I was young, she used to cane me every time I made a mistake. You see, I…"

I start to force some crocodile tears. The Collector's guard is down. I've gotten to the creature. Time to strike.

"I…" I sob once more.

That's when I attack. I quickly draw my blaster and aim directly at the creature's head. It's a perfect shot, but before it connects, The Collector ducks. I've missed.

The Collector swiftly crouches and covers itself in its cloak, taking the same defensive position it did before. It was able to withstand my previous swarm of gunfire, but how durable can a thin cape be? Time to find out.

I blast The Collector with everything I've got. Shot after shot lights Mark Allen's loft in flashes so intense my surroundings become completely illuminated. A chorus of rings echoes and bounces off the walls. I must have wasted at least a hundred bullets in the span of a minute.

After the room dims and silence spreads, I lower my weapon to see the damage I've done. The answer is nothing. Amazing. The cloak is still intact, not a single hole or dent. And The Collector sits there uninjured, perfectly healthy. I guess that cape is pretty durable after all.

Still, The Collector hasn't attacked, so maybe I shocked it into submission. Suddenly, I see a lamp fly my way. Guess I was wrong.

"Aww shit," I say helplessly.

It hits me square in the face. I feel the pain shoot from my skull to the rest of my body. The lamp feels like it weighs well over thirty pounds, and getting hit with it is like ramming my face straight into a steel wall. I stumble backward clumsily as my body reacts to the blow. My arms go limp, and my legs go weak. I drop the blaster in my hand to the floor. I fall backwards and the next thing I know, I'm lying on the ground, face up.

I feel dizzy and nauseous. My head is throbbing, and my forehead burns. My vision is hazy. Yet, despite my fazed state, I can still think clearly, and the first thought that comes to my mind is how the hell did The Collector throw that lamp at me? It was huddled underneath its cloak the whole time.

Then I see what's in front of my face: a sharp metal rod about two or three feet in length. It's not powered by energy, it's an old-fashioned weapon. And behind it The Collector floats in the air, one arm forward, palms outward. Then it hits me about the lamp.

Shit, telekinesis. How could I forget?

I jerk my head away and the instant I do, the spear thrusts in my direction. My reflexes save the day. The spear misses impaling my head. I do one more quick sidestep and hop to my feet.

The instant I'm up, the same spear thrusts again, aiming for my torso. This time I do a step to my right, and the spear hits air. I look up at The Collector. That's twice the creature has missed, and I'm sure it's frustrating.

The spear is still levitating above me as the creature waits for a moment to strike again. Perhaps it'll try a different tactic since this has failed twice.

I'm wrong. The Collector flashes its palms open, and another thrust comes at me. I step backward just in time, but before I can relax, another one comes. I jump behind once more, but right as I land, the spear shoots again. And again and again. I dodge each stab skillfully, quickly, and gracefully. The Collector moves forward and I move backward in a cadence, playing out this dangerous dance throughout Mark Allen's loft.

Then The Collector stops its pursuit. It sets its arm down and closes its fist. The creature attempted to impale me ten times, and each time I made like the wind. The weapons hit nothing but emptiness. I have bested the creature.

The Collector launches one more attempt, abruptly lifting its arm and spreading its palms. The spear jettisons my way, but this time I'm anticipating the attack. I swiftly clutch my own energized yari and do a full spin. When I complete my turn, I make eye contact with The Collector's needle and force a mighty swing. My yari connects with the spear and bats it away. I watch it harmlessly fly to the other side of the room.

The Collector watches it too, shifting its attention. The Collector's guard is down. It's the opening I've been waiting for, and I take it.

I leap at The Collector, driving my yari straight at it, but the creature is agile. It flies backward using its telekinesis to avoid the blow and opens its palms up to a small table nearby. With a swipe of its right arm, the table flies in my direction. I see it just in time and slam my yari through it, slicing the table like cheese. It cuts in two halves and falls limply to my sides.

The Collector mentally throws another piece of furniture, this time a chair, my way, but once again, I swing my yari and it gets slashed to pieces. The telekinesis simply is too slow. I see the startup and have enough time to react.

I believe The Collector has caught on. It stops its telekinetic barrage and clenches its hands into two fists. A loud sheathing sound comes from its wrists, and two blades protrude from it. Once again, there's no concentrated light involved. These are old-fashioned weapons made of synthetic metal.

The creature comes charging at me and unleashes a sturdy slash at my head. I duck under it just in time to see the other blade aiming for my torso. I'm forced to fall on my stomach in order to dodge it. And once I lie facedown on the floor, The Collector slams a blade to the ground. I roll to my left just in the nick of time.

I hop to my feet, but the moment I'm up, I get a boot to the stomach. I flail back, and before I can even recover, I see The Collector pointing its wrist at me. The blades are gone, retracted back to their hidden position. Instead, a burst of energy flies from The Collector's arm. I get shot in the shoulder and fall on my ass.

Damn, that hurts. It feels like I've been stabbed by a knife and the wound is twisted. The stinging spreads throughout my shoulder, and I clutch it to relieve the soreness. Yet, a few seconds later, the pain is gone. I look at the hand that I used to cover my wound, and there's not a trace of red.

I glance at my shoulder. Of course. My armor has saved me. That pain I felt was only from the shock of getting blasted, but I'm lucky. Thank God the Alliance upgraded it for me before I attacked.

I stare back in front of me, at The Collector. I need to think carefully about my next move. We've already thrown quite a bit at each other and we've only fought to a stalemate. I wonder how long we'll be fighting. Eventually one of us will make a mistake. Or maybe we'll just continue our battle until neither of us has the will to go on.

"At this rate, our showdown is going to last forever, so what do you want to do now?" I ask while breathing in heavily.

The Collector doesn't respond immediately. The creature looks at me curiously, but I hold my defensive stance.

"You ask what I'm going to do now?" it says with a synthesized voice. "End this."

The Collector spreads its arms apart, fists closed. Its cape opens up behind the creature, and spreads apart completely, flapping in the air. However, shiny objects on the cape flash in the light. They sparkle and shimmer, and I look closer to deduce what it is.

Crap. It's a bunch of those tiny needle-like spears, the same weapons The Collector was using a few minutes ago. Actually, it's more than a bunch. I'd say there are close to twenty.

Then The Collector spreads its palms open like I've seen so many times during our encounter. It's telekinesis time.

The spears spring out from the cape and take their positions, hovering above and around The Collector like a rainbow of blades. Each one of them slowly rotates until they all are pointed at me. I can bat one away, but I can't deflect all of these.

Or can I? I've been working on a trick that's perfect for this situation. I start rotating my wrist and twirl my yari like a propeller. It starts spinning faster and faster, and as it picks up traction, I spin it from left to right. My yari continues to rotate and increases in speed as the seconds pass. By the time I hit my stride, it's spinning so fast it looks like I'm holding a circular shield instead of a weapon.

Try and get your spears past this.

The Collector jerks both hands, and the rods fly at me in unison. Each and every one jets my way, and within a few milliseconds, they make contact, not with me, but my yari. I furiously swing my spinning weapon from left to right while eyeing each spear that flies my way.

Clang! I knock five out to the right

Clack! There go three to the left

Ding! Out go six to the right

Dong! I get the rest in one swoop.

Each rod soars in the opposite direction. I've batted all of them away without a single scratch. I stop my rotation, my wrists and arms tired from my effort. I shake them off to loosen my limbs.

The Collector stops its telekinetic hold. Its cape falls quietly and hugs its body.

"Impressive," it says. "Too impressive. That doesn't seem like something a human is capable of. Perhaps you've had some upgrades. Maybe an Alliance military implant or two."

"What?" I ask.

I'm completely shocked at what the creature has just said. How does it know about military grade implants?

I'm too stunned to follow up with a further response.

"Nothing to say, huh?" The Collector says. "No matter. This clash is over. I've encountered things I wasn't anticipating. I need to regroup. Until we meet again."

The Collector presses a button on its wrist and a blinding flash erupts from it. The light envelopes the creature, and I turn my head away because it burns my eyes. Yet it starts to disappear. The room darkens, and I open my eyes and face forward. The Collector is gone.

Damn, I was worried the creature would use that trick. I saw it in the briefings and knew it was a possibility. The creature is gone without a trace, and I'm left standing like an idiot. Now I have to deliver the bad news to my bosses.

I activate my communicator and link up with both Van Faye and General Rox. Both appear on separate holoscreens in front of me.

"Ash Han with a status update," I say to both of them.

"How did it go?" General Rox asks.

"You were correct. The Collector did indeed go directly for Mark Allen. It was a smart move keeping him at Sector Six. It appeared The Collector was expecting him here. I waited on the roof until our surveillance alerted me of The Collector's presence. I saw the creature come in through the windows, levitating in. At that point, I had one of your men act as a decoy, drawing The Collector away from the window, where I swooped in and engaged from behind."

"Yes, yes, enough with the details behind it. I want to know the results," Van Faye rudely interrupts. "Were you able to kill The Collector?"

I pause a bit. Delivering bad news is never easy, especially to the Elephant Queen of Crime.

"No, the creature escaped," I say softly.

Immediately, a rush of anger shoots through her face. She's furious.

"You incompetent idiot! How could this have happened? We trained you for these kinds of missions! You're supposed to be the best I have, but you can't even follow a simple assassination. What do I expect trusting a human?" she rants. She appears more on edge than normal.

"Calm down, Van Faye," Rox interjects. "We both knew The Collector would be a challenge. The creature is after Mark Allen. We'll have another chance to finish it off for good."

"Quiet, dog," she scolds. "I will talk to my subordinates however I like."

"Mind who you are talking to," Rox threatens.

Van Faye shoots Rox a spiteful look. I decide to stay quiet.

"What has you so shaken up anyway?" Rox asks. "I thought the Elephant Queen of Crime was supposed to be more composed."

"Don't you get it?" she says. "I'm vulnerable out here. The Collector is alive and killing high-profile targets. It's obvious I might be one of them. I did betray the creature after all. And I'm a sitting duck in Shogun without my top bodyguard to protect me."

"So you're worried about protection?" Rox says. "I'll send a couple of my best men out to Shogun to keep you safe."

"Your best men are not Ash Han," she says. "I don't trust them. I only trust my own, especially when my life is on the line."

"So what do you propose, then?" Rox says.

"I'm coming to Allied City."

Rox looks taken aback, and I myself am pretty astonished by the declaration.

"Absolutely not," Rox says. "I don't need a crime boss in Allied City, especially one of your clout. And right now we have The Collector figured out. Your presence may interfere with our mission."

"I don't give a shit about your mission," Van Faye says. "I'm not safe without Ash. If she is in Allied City, that's where I will be. If you refuse or attempt to block me, then Ash Han will no longer be at your service."

"Damnit, Van Faye, this is not the time!" Rox yells. "We have a plan to act out."

"This is the only time! I need to be near Han!" Van Faye screams.

Van Faye is on the edge of insanity. I have to say something to calm her down, even maybe try to change her mind.

"Excuse me, boss, but why would you want to come to Allied City?" I ask. "Why would you want to come closer to The Collector? Isn't it more dangerous out here, even with me, than it is out in Shogun? You're on the other side of the world. That's as far as you can get from the creature."

"Didn't you see the flashing light?" she says. "The Collector can show up anywhere in the world. Why, it could appear right behind me, right at this moment, to kill me. The creature has that ability. It doesn't matter where I am, The Collector can go anywhere. That's why I need to be near you."

Damnit, she has a point. And it appears she won't take no for an answer. What Two Van Faye wants, Two Van Faye gets.

"But boss," I say, trying another attempt at reasonableness.

"But nothing! Know your place, slave!" she screams.

"Van Faye, try to be reasonable," Rox says. "I'm not going to have your paranoia jeopardize this operation."

"You can't stop me, Rox! I'm coming to Allied City and that is that!"

She cuts off the link, and all Rox and I can do is look at each other in bewilderment. Looks like this hit has gotten a whole lot more interesting.

Chapter 17 – Ivy Lawton

Breach

September 22, 3071 7:36 PM

I'm currently in the lab with Lucy, going over the status of the newer wave of splicing subjects, when suddenly, a signal echoes through the room. It's a ring that both of us seldom hear, and we look at each other in mild shock.

"Perimeter signal sounding," Lucy says to me calmly.

"Yes. We don't hear it that often," I say. "That means someone is within two hundred yards of one of the quarters."

"Check which one."

I pull up the monitoring screen and the layout of our entire pod and teleportation network displays in front of me. It's a detailed, holographic representation of the base we set up, all interconnected by teleportation stations. I scan through the map to see where the signal is coming from.

"It's not the kitchen pod," I say.

"Barracks pod B also unaffected," Lucy observes.

"The brutes' quarters and the weapons depot also appear fine."

"As is food storage."

"Perhaps the main base nest is okay. We should look at the teleportation ring."

"Excellent idea."

The teleportation ring is the outermost areas our base extends to. It's literally a ring of scattered teleportation stations we use to allow entry via teleporters hidden above surface to our base. Think of it as a middle point between the outside world and ours.

We dim out the main living and storage pods from the hologram and focus on the transportation ones. Immediately, I see where the signal originates.

"It's one of the farther outer teleportation pods," I say. "Teleportation pod DZ."

"I see," Lucy says. "Bring up monitor screen to check surface level surveillance."

I follow her instruction and we get a live feed of what's going on up above. There's a lot of heavy-duty machinery scattered about. I see a laser driller and industrial-size suction shovel. I also see a few compactors and portable tech stations set up nearby. Looks like they're digging for something.

"Excavators?" I ask Lucy.

"Perhaps," she says. "Keep looking."

I also spot a few pigs working at the stations.

"Should I magnify the view?" I say, pointing to the workers.

"Yes," Lucy responds.

I optimize the view and zoom in, specifically on their clothing.

"Doesn't appear to have government affiliation," Lucy observes.

"You're right. I don't think these are Alliance pigs," I say, agreeing. "I don't think they're even members of the Pig Government. In fact, as I look at the whole group, they're not wearing standard uniforms. Perhaps they are a private company?"

"Negative. Unsanctioned excavation banned in area. Not allowed here. That is why Iris Lawton and I chose to set up here long ago. Alliance still facilitating with species' governments over ownership of land. Until then, should be dead zone."

"So you're saying that they're doing this illegally?"

"Correct."

"Who do you think it is?"

"Perhaps smugglers or dealers. Need new locations to run secret jobs. Moon as undeveloped as it gets. Perfect place to start and run an illegal operation, especially now that Fan Zui Bin has heavy Alliance influence."

What Lucy says is true. Since the moon is uncharted territory, a lot of the ousted bosses are trying to secretly claim parts of the area before the Alliance can officially stake their claim. Thus, they send their boys to start building.

"Do you think they'll make contact with one of the pods?" I ask.

"From observance, possible they are heading in that direction," Lucy says. "Would be surprised if made contact with pod. They will dig into outer synthetic wall of teleportation pod. Most likely they will desire to break in."

"And if they do, they'll know what they've discovered. The only thing in the teleportation pods are easy to recognize teleporters, and those allow teleportation to any of the pods in our base. They could get to the kitchen, our lab, even our living quarters."

"Yes. That is not good. Operation could be ruined."

I pause to think.

"The world doesn't know about us, do they?" I say.

"Correct. Only ones who do are key Alliance personnel. And even then, Alliance under assumption that hybrids have been exterminated due to Operation HORUS," she says. "Only thing world knows is The Collector exists, but no animals know who is behind mask."

I look at Lucy cautiously.

"So if this illegal crew stumbles upon us and officially leaks us out to the world, we're in big trouble, aren't we?" I ask.

"Understatement," Lucy says. "Everything we plan long term is built under notion of secrecy. Alliance must not know we are still around, rebuilding. We need this for element of surprise. Iris Lawton has stated that only way we can succeed, only way we can get freedom and claim our right as independent species, is by striking when least suspected. I agree. We have history to draw upon as evidence."

Lucy's voice then fades a little.

"And if Alliance finds out, then they will hunt us down, like at HORUS," she says softly. "Do not want to relive that experience."

"So we have to stop these humans and pigs from stumbling upon us at all costs?"

"All costs."

I give Lucy a skeptical look.

"All costs," I say. "What does that mean exactly?"

"You know what that means," she says ominously.

The room remains silent for a few seconds. Then Lucy continues.

"This won't be problem when development of our base progresses," she says. "Iris Lawton's goal is to have one, unified underground city instead of scattered underground base. Thus, with centralized area, defensive measures will be taken. No need for ring of teleportation pods that are easy to breach. Secrecy ensured. Just takes time."

"So until then, I'm on security duty?" I ask.

"Yes. Can't simply put turrets there. Must be sure handling of problem discreet and efficient. Iris Lawton not here, but you have power to do so. Can't trust task to artificial intelligence."

"Fantastic."

Sometimes I don't really know what my role is in the grand scheme of things. I'm not exactly calling the shots like Mom and Lucy are, and honestly, I don't really want to. I like my role as a loyal soldier to Mom. I'd do anything for my mother, so I don't mind being a follower.

Yet sometimes I disagree with her views and opinions. I'm not exactly comfortable with the way she treats the brutes. They've always seemed expendable to her and Lucy. It's just that she hasn't spent time with them like I have. And I'm not exactly crazy about her ruthlessness against other species. I don't know how she flips the switch from loving mom to cold killer so easily.

Overall, though, she's still a wonderful mother. She has always had my best interests in mind, even when I can't see it. I'm also glad I have the clarity to appreciate her efforts. And now, she needs me more than ever.

Another alarm rings through the room. It's not a security alert, it's a communication alarm. Speak of the devil, it's her.

"Mom!" I say excitedly.

The feeling is genuine. Knowing how dangerous her missions have been, I'm glad to see her safe and sound.

"Hello, Ivy, Lucy," she says in a greeting voice. "I'm glad to see you."

"How did Mark Allen mission go?" Lucy asks.

"Tough," Mom curtly responds.

She looks tired and weary. When she talks to us, she forces out a smile.

"What happened?" I ask her.

"I... I... I failed," she says in a stupefied tone.

"Failed?" Lucy says. "Not used to hearing such words. How is it possible?"

"I went to Mark Allen's compound, just like I saw in my visions," she explains. "I followed it to a tee. I even levitated through the window. When I got there, I heard the footsteps, like I predicated. I was certain that was him. But then..."

She pauses. Something is obviously troubling her.

"The footsteps, they ran in the other direction," she continues. "And instead of Mark Allen, I was confronted by someone else, someone I've never seen before. She attacked me without hesitation, as if she were hunting me. She wasn't holding back either. She was out to kill."

"What species was she?" Lucy asks.

"A human. A female human," Mom says. "She had on dark-green armor. It looked similar to Alliance gear but definitely wasn't standard issue. She was young. And beautiful. She also looked to be ethnically Asian. But she's a new face. I would have remembered her for sure."

"Did not acquire image? Could identify for you or figure out who sent her," Lucy says.

"No, I didn't," Mom says. "But I put a tracker on her and I doubt she'll find it. I'll figure soon enough who she is and who hired her. The main thing I want to know is why she was there and not Mark Allen like I had predicted."

Lucy and I look at each other nervously. We both know the little riff Mom had in her earlier assault at Eli Winde's place.

"This is result of mistake you made at Winde's," Lucy says. "Tripped on alarm sensor when shouldn't have. Winde's security activated and detected you. Probably had recording features. Now officials know you, The Collector, is back. Hired someone to kill. Puzzle pieces fit, explanation plausible. These unexpected events caused each other to happen, like dominoes."

Of course Lucy is the one to point it out.

"And Iris Lawton did not take precautions to recheck the changed timeline," she continues. "If did, could have seen the new consequences of earlier mistakes, could have known that Allen would not be there, but someone else."

My mother looks guilty, but not surprised. Perhaps she came to this conclusion already.

"I have to agree with you, Lucy," she says. "I have been too careless."

"Affirmative. However, not all lost. Can still head back to right path," Lucy says.

"Yes, I know," Mom says. "Before I continue on the plan, I need to take some time to look into the future. The timelines have changed, and I won't know what's going to happen unless I have patience and see what is different. Thus, that's the next step for now. It's time for me to regroup."

Lucy and I both nod our heads. My mom has always been a master planner, and I can tell this unexpected occurrence has rattled her. She needs our support to focus.

"Other than that, how are things going up in the Great North?" she asks.

"We have some unexpected visitors lurking nearby," I say.

"Ah, yes, I'm aware of them. I saw them in one of my visions. They're not Alliance, right?"

"No, they don't appear to be. They don't look official enough. I think they're part of some illegal operation. What should we do with them?"

"I don't know off the top of my head, but give me a few minutes. I'll consult my visions and give you a viable plan."

Mom disconnects from her communicator while Lucy and I look at each other a little dumbfounded. Mom does this quite a bit when she has to zone out for her visions. Right as rain, a few minutes later, she's back on her communicator.

"You have a few days, but eventually, those guys will breach through the teleportation pod you're worried about," Iris says. "You'll have to make preparations to take them out. Luckily, they are black market grunts, so they won't be missed. That explains why they're humans and pigs. Low members in the Fan Zui Bin totem pole. We won't have to worry about the Alliance following up on an investigation."

"Okay, so a simple telekinesis job?" I ask.

"Yes, but I also saw the brutes in my vision."

"The brutes? That's weird. Why would they be there?"

"It looked like they were assisting you in your attack."

"Really? I'm perfectly capable of taking out some thugs on my own."

"Well, my vision had the brutes in there, so it seems you need them there for some reason."

"Are you sure?"

It's one of the few times I openly question my mom. She looks a little concerned at first, but quickly shows a calmer face.

"Ivy," she says. "That's what I saw, and we need to follow these visions perfectly. You saw what happened with Mark Allen when we don't. You'll need the brutes with you. It's the only way the mission will be successful."

"You are certain?" I ask once more.

"Yes," she says.

"Well, if you say so, Mother."

"Good girl. I'm going to get off now so I can recuperate and get ready for the next phase. I love you both. See you soon."

She disconnects and the holoscreen closes. In the background, the live feed of the surface floats in the air. I look at it warily as our trespassers continue to make their way down.

Chapter 18 – Maya Lawton

Power

August 12, 3033 11:23 PM

So this is what Lionel Changer meant when he said Iris was special. I doubted him at first, but as I raised her, I started to understand what he was talking about. I just never imagined that she would be able to tell the future.

I don't fully comprehend what she can and can't do. Some days she knows what's coming. She sees what I'm making for dinner or what I have planned for the family, even when I don't tell her. She's not exactly a mind reader, as she can't hear my thoughts on the spot. She just knows things.

Iris tells me that sometimes these visions pop up in her head, and usually what she sees happens. Some days she'll be playing or doing the work I've assigned her and then they'll appear out of the blue. Sometimes she tells me what she sees, other times she doesn't. When she does tell me, though, it's almost always spot on to what's actually going to happen.

I was skeptical at first. When Iris told me she saw this or saw that, the only thing I could think of was that it was the product of a child's imagination. Yet, as predictions started coming true, I realized there was nothing imaginary about it. Iris's power is very, very real.

Not everything is solid, though. I find myself confused on how it works, like the scientific explanation about it. I've only heard about future telling, or precognition, from made up stories. I know there are so called psychics out there, fortune tellers, but I also know all of those creatures are con artists. I used to work in that crowd. Iris's powers are natural, and I don't understand how it came to be. There has to be an explanation. Perhaps that's why Lionel Changer wanted to pick and prod her.

She can't really control her powers either. She tries to but they just come at random moments. They also vary in subject matter. Sometimes she sees important things, other times her visions have little importance. I've been keeping a log of what she sees and when she sees it, hoping to find a pattern, but I haven't deduced anything.

I spend most of these nights worrying about her gifts. The children are already so different from the rest of the world, and now Iris has something that makes her stand out even more. Not only that, but it makes her a target. I've been hiding for about eight years now, but there isn't a day that I don't worry that Lionel Changer will take her from me. Changer doesn't seem like the type to let things go. His cronies could bust through this door at any minute and snatch Iris away. In fact, I fear that it's not a matter of if it will happen but when.

Of course, Changer isn't the only one who wants my babies. My life in Primm has been one of secrecy. My community is deserted, and the one or two people I do interact with have no idea of the half human creatures I've raised. No one must know. If word got out what my babies were, the Alliance would certainly kill them, or worse, take them in for experimentation. I fear what Lionel Changer would do to my Iris, but my fear of the Alliance is far greater.

I don't want my precious little ones to be hunted down like beasts. That's why I've told them time and time again that the world is a dangerous place. I don't want them wondering what's out there, for their desire to leave will expose them to the horrible truth: that society would kill them. I need to get them thinking like this now, while they're young and under my control. I do this because I love them and would do anything to protect them.

Not all of them enjoy being kept away from a sometimes intriguing and always foreign world. Many are at the age where they start to question everything, and the number one thing they wonder is why. Why can't I go outside unsupervised? Why can't I go into town? Why can't we meet anyone? I tell them the answer, the cold truth, but they don't want to hear it. I even tell them how they'll be discriminated against and killed because of their roots in genetic experimentation. They still don't listen. They only get angry with my explanations.

I feel for them, I truly do. I would hate to grow up and only wonder about the world outside instead of being a part of it. It's only going to get harder. Some of the kids are teenagers now, and like all teens, they're hard headed and think they know it all. How much longer can I contain them?

Sometimes I look at myself and worry if I am doing the right thing. I'm stripping away their chance to live a full life. But what choice do I have? This isn't exactly a normal situation, and the choices I've decided have been made to keep them alive. Yet, what's the point of living a life that can't be truly lived?

I suppose it's not only Iris that keeps me up at night. The children are all downstairs resting, but I'm unable to sleep. I have so many things on my mind. I fear that my children will rebel, and it'll only get them killed. I'm scared that this house will be raided by HORUS or the Alliance, and the kids will be massacred in front of my very eyes. I saddened when I look at myself. Am I a good mother? Are my actions justified? I'm trying the best I can with what little I have, but sometimes that's not enough.

And of course, I worry about Iris. Now I know she is special, but it's only a matter of time before her powers are discovered and they are used for evil. I'll do whatever I can to make sure that doesn't happen. It's the only thing I can do.

Chapter 19 – Ash Han

Berated

September 23, 3071 9:15 AM

I anxiously wait in the lobby of the Benjamin Palace Hotel, one of the finest establishments in Allied City. That's not an understatement either. The walls are painted gold and the furniture is lavish. It's versatile as well. The hotel has the newest chair shifters, sofas that can readjust shape based on the species it's accommodating. You know you're in the ritzy areas when the couches are so high tech.

And of course the place has a high-end bar, diamond star restaurants, recreational facilities for all types of species, spas, and a botanical garden. No wonder Ms. Van Faye wanted to stay here, it fits her style.

I, on the other hand, feel out of place. It's true I'm barely reaching twenty, but even as I grow into adulthood, I could never get used to establishments like this.

Ms. Van Faye has spared no expense to make sure I'm cultured enough to fit into her high priced world, but still, I find resorts like these off-putting. I lived in the slums until Ms. Van Faye took me in. I was raised in an orphanage. I've begged for food, fought for it, even killed for it at such a young age. I've always been a survivor, struggling for my equal share in the world.

Yet as I look around me, I realize this place isn't about survival. This is decadence, spending ones means to sin. This is the world I live in now, but it's also one I hate. As hard as Ms. Van Faye has tried, this lifestyle has never been for me. I belong back in the slums because that's the only place I know where I've felt like I've earned what I took.

I know, though, that I can never return. I'm bound to Ms. Van Faye. She is my master, and I am her assassin. It's what I've been trained to do, it's what I'm good at. Among killers is where I truly belong. It doesn't matter if the setting is the underbelly of Shogun or on the top of Fan Zui Bin, I'll kill where it's needed.

However, yesterday I failed. It's quite rare that it happens, but when it does, Ms. Van Faye will let me hear it. I dread the fact that she's decided to come to Allied City herself. As I wait in the lobby, my heart races. I have to brace myself when I see that massive body trot through the golden doorway of the hotel.

How am I going to explain myself? I can't say I wasn't expecting The Collector to be so powerful. I read Rox's reports and saw the streams. I knew what I was getting myself into. And to say I was overpowered would be a shot to my pride. I'm made of Alliance materials. I mean, literally, the military grade biotics inside me are from the best the Alliance has to offer. If an Alliance constructed weapon can't take on The Collector, who can?

The explanations race through my mind, but before I can think of any more, I see a giant, grayish-purple body coming through the doors. The jewels, the gaudy clothing, the styled-up trunk ornament, the fancy giant-sized shoes. Make no mistake, Two Van Faye has walked into the building.

A few bystanders pass by her, but not before they gawk with wide-eyed looks. I'm not sure if they're staring because of her, um, fashion choices or because they know who she is. I'm guessing it's a combination of both.

"Ms. Van Faye," I say tersely.

"Ash," she nods.

Van Faye has a small entourage of three gorillas behind her. I recognize none of them, so I don't think they're soldiers. All three of them have their hands full with her belongings, which makes me think they're simply hired help.

"How was your teleport in?" I ask. Trying to make small talk with the boss is always difficult.

"Fine," she says. "I'm a little lagged that it's morning here. Damn time zones. I don't think I can ever get used to that."

"Yes, they are difficult."

She doesn't respond. An awkward silence fills the air. She starts to stare darts into me, and I become nervous. *Oh God, say something.*

"Do you have my accommodations ready?" she asks in a grumpy tone.

"Oh, yes," I say nervously. "The penthouse suite, just as you asked. It has an elephant-sized pool, bed, and your other usual requests."

"Excellent. I'll have time to relax later. I want to discuss your status right away. Understood?"

Shit, I know what that means.

"Yes, ma'am," I respond.

"Good," she says. "These lackeys will drop off my luggage, and then we'll get down to business. Lead the way."

We make our journey to her room. This is one of those fancy hotels that don't have elevators. Instead, there's a large teleporter that ports you directly into your room.

I scan Van Faye's hotel keycard, and the teleporter activates. I walk through it, as does Van Faye behind me, and we're here.

Her room is as beautiful as advertised. It's painted the same gold color as the ground lobby, except it's softer on the eyes. The floor is a mix of a classic oak and newer synthetic material. Outside is a wonderful view of Allied City.

The furnishings are amazing. Pool, bed, tons of food, entertainment systems—hell, there's even a climate changer that allows her to adjust the view and feel of her room.

"This is the best you could get?" Van Faye complains.

"On short notice, yes," I say.

She observes a table nearby.

"This is much too small to fit my size," she notes. "Is this a human table?"

"It's adjustable," I respond. "Watch."

I activate a control and the size modification feature initiates. The table seamlessly expands out, adding a few more legs, and quadruples in length and width. In a matter of seconds, it's more than large enough to accommodate an elephant.

Ms. Van Faye hardly looks impressed.

"Is this supposed to amaze me?" she asks harshly.

"No," I say humbly. "I just thought it was a nice feature."

"Think again."

"I'm sorry, boss."

She rolls her eyes. I get nervous.

"All of the other things in this room are adjustable to fit any species," I say. "Simply use the controls and it will change from a human room to an elephant one catered for you."

"And how much more did this cost me?" she asks.

"When I explained who was staying here, they said it's free of charge."

"Well, I suppose I should be happy about that."

Ms. Van Faye takes a few moments to observe her surroundings. She's changed this past week. Before this Collector business, she would have been wallowing in this kind of luxury. However, now, she seems completely unconcerned with it.

"Anyways," she says. "I'm ready to settle down. Grunts, leave my things here."

The gorillas place her things neatly on the floor, stacking bag on top of bag. After they're done, they continue to linger around.

Ms. Van Faye gives them a dirty look.

"Don't expect a tip," she curses.

They look at each other, a little shocked and a little scared, and then quickly turn the other direction and leave. Ms. Van Faye then turns her attention back to me.

"You!" she starts yelling. "How on Earth did you let The Collector escape!?"

"I... I flat out was outmatched," I say. "The Collector was too fast, too powerful, and was more strategic. Nothing I saw in the tapes could prepare me for the real thing."

"Nothing but excuses!"

I've been a victim of Van Faye's verbal thrashings before, but this seems a little different. She has a paranoid look in her eyes. Gone is the confident, cunning criminal mastermind I was raised by. The Collector has put the Elephant Queen of Crime on full tilt.

"I've trained you to do only one thing in life—protect me—and you are failing!" she screams.

"But I am always protecting you," I uselessly protest.

"And you do so by letting The Collector get away? The creature is probably concocting another battle plan as we speak, and it'll come back stronger than before. Yesterday was your only chance!"

"There will be another one."

My response lights a fire in Van Faye. She quickly lunges toward me and wraps her trunk around my neck. She lifts me above and my feet dangle, barely touching the ground. Her grip becomes tighter, squeezing me until I start to choke.

I could literally rip her trunk off her face like a piece of rope, but I do not. She is my master. I cannot disobey her, so I take the punishment.

She then loosens her grip and drops me to the ground as I land on my knees. I gasp for precious breaths of air, but once I recover, I quickly hop back to my feet.

"The Collector has a vendetta against me," she says. "I betrayed this creature so Rox could give me the power I wield over Fan Zui Bin. After that, I thought it was gone from the face of the earth, but now it's back. Normally, I'm not scared of some punk coming for me after all these years, but The Collector is different. I can tell it's a killer, just like you. And with these types, it's never about business, it's always personal. Just look at what it's done to Eli Winde."

"The Collector also killed your rhino bodyguard, Sai?" I ask.

I know about Van Faye's beast. She and Sai had a much different relationship than I have with my boss. Mine is grown out of fear, Sai and Van Faye's relationship was out of respect. She was his boss, but she trusted the rhino and admired him for his brutality. He was her personal destructive machine, someone I could never live up to.

"Yes, the creature killed Sai, my true bodyguard, a true friend," she says, almost shedding a tear.

Van Faye starts to size me up, looking at me from head to toe. Her initial sadness brought on by Sai's memory fades. Instead, a look of disgust spreads through her face.

"Sai is something you'll never be," she says in a berating tone. "The Collector murdered Sai. I wish it had been you instead. This is what happens when I trust a lowly human with the job. Your kind has weak hearts. Fan Zui Bin is the only place in the world where the strong truly survive. It's because your species is at the bottom there."

The words pierce me like a dagger to the heart. The rage of a lost childhood boils inside. But I grit my teeth hard and do my best to hide the anger I feel. I've been Van Faye's property for a long time, and verbal putdowns like these are commonplace. Ms. Van Faye has called me every slur in the book throughout my life. Skinbag, naked ape, mother nature's abomination, two-legger—I've heard them all. She's raised me through insults and fear, not love and compassion.

I'd be lying if I said every time I heard it I didn't want to ram my yari right into Van Faye's head. I'm only human after all. She's the Elephant Queen of

Crime, though. She is the master, not only of me, but all of the citizens of Fan Zui Bin. I cannot win.

"I'm sorry I have failed you, Ms. Van Faye," I say. "It won't happen again."

"It better not," she says. "The Alliance's goals mean nothing to me. They could want a million creatures dead, and I could care less. Yet this one creature is someone I have a personal stake in. Killing The Collector would bring me a lot of restful nights. I've had many enemies in my life, yet I've always slept easy knowing they were simply pretenders, creatures with no real power. The Collector is different, always has been. I knew it after the first day I did business with it. It is not a pretender. It has the means to do what it wants. And if one of those things it wants to do is kill me, well then, you better get your act together, Ash Han. I didn't have the Alliance invest their biotic implants in you for nothing. I've had the best train you since you were a child, both from the Alliance and my personal thugs. This is what you were born to do, and if you can't fulfill your purpose, why should you exist, my dear?"

A chill goes through my spine. Van Faye isn't yelling like she was before. She says her callous words with a calm tone. She's serious.

"I could have picked any of my soldiers to go through the process, but I picked you because you were hungry and I knew you had the potential," Ms. Van Faye says. "That is why I say this: don't fail, because it won't be The Collector you'll be worried about. It'll be me. Understood, skinbag?"

Her speech sinks in and I start to think of my situation. I've always done well for Ms. Van Faye, and I've never failed before. But now that I have, I see I'm walking on a thin line. I can die at the hand of The Collector, or I can die at the hand of my boss. Either way, I lose.

"I understand," I say to Ms. Van Faye in a solemn tone. "The next time The Collector comes, I'll be ready."

Chapter 20 – Iris Lawton

Refocus

<u>September 23, 3071 10:01 AM</u>

"The world famous Benjamin Plaza Hotel," I say to myself. "You sure have fancy taste, Ms. Assassin."

After my little conference with Lucy and Ivy, I sequestered myself to a quiet area so I could focus on my visions. The timeline had changed so differently from what I originally saw that I needed to backtrack before I embarked on my next move.

I saw what had changed, the new futures that were created, and adapted. I scanned which course of action would lead to the best outcome, and this is the conclusion I arrived at. My vision told me in order to set things right, the first thing I need to do is to follow this bodyguard, who I discovered is named Ash Han. This will be the starting point to a series of events that will bring me to victory.

I have her in my sights right now. She's on the penthouse level of this fine establishment, talking to her boss. I knew she wasn't working independently. A tool like that is to be wielded by command.

My vision also told me the identity of her lord, and I can't say I'm surprised. Why, even as I see Ash Han chatting it up with her superior, all I can think about is that Two Van Faye was the most likely non-Alliance candidate who would seek me. We didn't exactly end things on a good note, and I'm sure she's spooked by my reemergence. Truthfully, she has every right to be scared. I never forget personal issues.

Two Van Faye appears to be her boisterous self. Yet I see a bit of paranoia in her body language. She's not as confident, or arrogant, as usual. And Ash Han appears to be tolerating her. Their body language suggests there is anything but a respectful relationship between the two. This doesn't seem to be a voluntary job. Then again, her boss is short tempered, gaudy, and reckless. I'd hate to work for the Elephant Queen of Crime, too.

Thanks to the tracker I latched on Han, I'm able to spy on Ash Han and Van Faye. The placement occurred when I used a gun during our showdown. She thought that blast into her armor was a lethal shot, but actually it was a delivery shot. The package was a small, microscopic tracking unit, invisible to almost any eye. She has had it on her the whole time since our fight and has no clue. Thus, I've been observing her every move, studying my opponent, waiting for the right moment to strike.

Thinking about our earlier battle, I found it odd that Ash Han attacked me at Mark Allen's loft. It wasn't a coincidence, it's was more like she knew I was going to be there. She was waiting for me and I was walking into a trap. However, the only way she could set something up is if her or Van Faye was working with the Alliance.

It's entirely possible. Everyone knows the Alliance has Van Faye in their back pocket after they practically inserted her as leader of Fan Zui Bin. I don't have any concrete evidence, though, not even a vision. I was only looking for futures involving me, not two separate parties. I'm confident, though, that these paths, Alliance and Van Faye, will intersect at one point. And when they do, I will be ready to foresee what will happen.

However, first thing's first. Now that I know there's someone out to kill me, I'll have to make sure that doesn't happen. Ash Han is no longer the major threat. She's simply a pawn. No, the real target is the queen, Two Van Faye.

It seems the two are getting comfortable. It's the calm after the storm. Their guard is down, they think they're safe. This is the time to attack, right in the safety of their home.

I didn't consult my visions earlier to draw my battle plan for this particular ambush. For specifics, I've decided to wait before the moment, to make sure the future I choose is as set as possible. So I will consult them now.

I also don't have time to look through the thousands of different scenarios, but for something like this, only a few will be necessary. I want to see what happens if I do an attack now. I close my eyes to see what the future holds.

The first one that pops up shows me crashing through the window, armed to the teeth. There's no covertness at all. I suppose what I see is the consequence of a more reckless battle plan.

I quickly throw my spears at Ash Han, but she uses that same trick she did before, spinning her yari like a propeller. All my projectiles are batted away. With that attack failing, I pull out my blades from wrists, but Ash Han is able to block every strike. It appears I grow frustrated, so I lunge at Han with one mighty blow.

Unfortunately, she dodges it completely and counters with a plunge of her blade into my stomach. I'm dead.

"Well, that one didn't work out," I say to myself. "Let's try another."

This time, I concentrate on a path where my attack is much stealthier. Instead of diving through the window like before, this vision shows me gracefully entering from a smaller window in the bathroom while Han and Van Faye are preoccupied in the main room. I stay hovered in the air, traveling through the penthouse. I stop right before I make it to Han and Van Faye's location.

I peer around the corner cautiously, making sure Van Faye or Han hasn't spotted me. They don't. I then lie on the floor and levitate myself only a few inches off the ground. My head tilts up, and I move forward, flying right above floor level like a superhero. They definitely won't see me coming now.

I'm only a few feet away from both of them, and I get my spears ready. I set them out, and wait for a moment to release them. After a few seconds, both Van Faye and Han are completely turned away from me. I have my shot. I'm going to take it.

One…

Two…

Without warning, Ash Han turns around and swings her yari at my head.

Slash!

It gets cut off clearly. Once more this vision has led me to my death. I'm flabbergasted that I've seen failure in such a spectacular fashion. So far, I'm zero and two.

"There has to be a way to kill these two," I say to myself in a frustrated tone.

I spend even more time going through all the possible futures. I won't quit until I find a way to kill them.

What if I attack from the front? No, that doesn't work. Perhaps if I do a ranged attack? This vision tells me I'll fail too. How about throwing a bomb through the window? Han simply bats it back to me and I become an exploded mess. Damn, she is good.

I look through countless more visions and I see nothing but failure. No matter how hard I try to find a future that will work out, I find nothing.

"This can't be. It only makes sense for me to attack them now," I say.

I start to think of the reasons this isn't working. Stealth is harder to work in during the day, as the cover of night is not on your side. And it's morning. Van Faye and Ash Han are both fully rested. Han looks stronger and quicker in my visions compared to when we first fought.

That's when I realize perhaps I was looking in the wrong place. It's not about going for an ambush in broad daylight. No, a night attack might yield a more successful outcome.

I switch it up, this time only looking at what would happen if I delayed my assault until later. I close my eyes and scan through the results. The first one I see results in a failure, but that's only because it was the same reckless plan I initially saw before. I must use the darkness as an ally, so stealth is the only way to go.

Even then, as I look into more and more visions, I see many possibilities that will lead to my end. And in grisly fashion. I'm talking about chopped off heads, legs getting pierced, hell, even one where I'm burned alive. Looking at yourself die so many times is quite depressing.

On the other hand, I do see some where I come out victorious, but getting there is difficult. It would require me to be on top of my game, completely flawless in my skills of battle, precision in every movement. I'm confident in my abilities, but not that confident.

Perhaps now is not the time for me to claim their lives. I'm disappointed. Why am I here, then? Why did my earlier visions tell me to follow Ash Han? What purpose does she bring?

For the hell of it, I dive into the views of other futures, ones not necessarily related to their deaths, but ones where I still ambush them. Ash Han and Van Faye are somehow related to my goal of obtaining the GTS, so it's a good idea to see all the possibilities out there.

I close my eyes and look. I see the attack against Ash Han and Van Faye. I see myself and Ash Han fighting it out like we did in all the other visions. I don't get it. What's different here?

And then I see it. The tangent, the change in the timeline, the alternate set of actions that is unlike the others. It's like watching a movie or play, where you get the next juicy piece of plot. Except this could be real, not fantasy.

As I watch the scene unfold, I become more and more satisfied with what I see. So this is what I'm supposed to do to get to the next step. I was so focused on personal vendettas, getting the kill, that I failed to realize the bigger picture. Now that I have concentrated on another path, the true one, I see what must be done in the following hours.

So it appears the battle still is on. I will have to be patient and intercept them at night. I've seen what I need to do in this vision, and waiting is the key. Now is too risky anyway.

Ash Han and I will go for a round two, only it won't be a death match. Instead, I'll get something else, something much more important. I've been foolish lately, focusing only on a one-track path. Time to refocus.

Chapter 21 – Falena Snow

Unplugged

September 23, 3071 1:00 PM

It's been a week since I fled my home and narrowly escaped my pursuer's clutches. That dive from the window could have seriously injured me, and I was lucky to land unscathed. I was even luckier that I was able to run fast and far away from him before he could continue his pursuit.

After I ran, I made my way away from the city. There's no doubt in my mind the intruder was there to silence me, so if I'm to stay alive, living off the grid is the only way.

That's a lot harder than it sounds, though. Everything I do is traceable. It's not difficult to track my purchases via insta-item. And since I believe the Alliance is at hand for sending this human, they'll certainly have the means to find me from my transaction trail.

Other than transactions, I have to be mindful if several other things. Obviously, any communication, by infospace or a communicator, is a definite no-no. That would lead them to me faster than a purchase would and endanger the creature I reached out to. No soul must know where I am. Co-workers, friends, family—I have to temporarily stay away from all of them. Hell, right now, I don't even know who among them I could trust.

Even trickier is keeping my transportation methods off the grid. When I fled my home, the best chance at evading my stalker was with a teleporter, but it was out of the question. Those things keep a log of every user that walks through the lighted gates for the exact purposes of tracking. Once I used one, the Alliance would know where I was and where I was going within a matter of seconds. Traveling far distances without a teleporter was near impossible, so I had to think of a more practical way to travel.

Hovercars were also a risk. I didn't own one, I couldn't steal one, and renting one would count as one of those liable transactions. The only safe, trail-free way to travel was on foot. It may not have gotten me hundreds of miles away from my pursuer, but it would keep me out of his sights.

Before I left, I did make a stop to some underground arms traders. They're not wolves I normally deal with, but I know of them thanks to some familial connections. I purchased a few explosives, a helmed weapon, and some food and supplies from raw credits. They're untraceable transactions.

I headed to the outskirts of town and into the woods. I had to leave the city of Orf and hide under the canopy of redwoods that bordered the small town.

I wasn't wandering aimlessly around, though. I knew of a place I could hide. There are some perks to being daughter of a former high-ranking military family. One of them was that we spent a lot of time going back to our roots, living in the woods and engaging in survival training. And because of that, I developed an instinctive desire to know everything about where I lived. That's how I discovered that hidden in the woods was an abandoned cabin for me to use. It was built long ago by humans, and though it's old and decrepit, it's still usable for a temporary living space. I hope my pursuer and the Alliance know nothing about it.

For the past few days, I've lived unplugged, using the things I've learned from my mother when I was a pup. It was tricky at first. My skills were rusty. Since my mother's disappearance, I've taken a few wilderness trips here and there to sharpen my survival skills, but they were far from frequent. It was more or less like a vacation for me. I'd go out with my gear—yes, that's right, gear—and live off nature for a few days. I caught my own food and stayed away from modern conveniences. Then, when I was done, I'd head home back to my nice, hooked-up home. This is different. This isn't a vacation, it's for real.

My mother taught me everything I needed to know. She taught me how to locate prey, stalk them, chase them, and finish them off both with helmed weapons and old-school methods. I'm talking about bare teeth. Many wolves these days think such activities are barbaric, but my mother told me our creator gifted us with such natural tools and it'd be disrespectful not to know how to use them. I was very young at the time, but I kept those lessons to heart.

Back then, I always thought these trips were simply for leisure, and I never thought I'd actually have to use the things I learned. It's been a while since my last trip. I had to once again familiarize myself with activities such as finding water, hunting meat, and keeping warm all without the use of technology.

I'm not sure how long I'll be on the run, and the food I bought can only last so long. I had to get meals the old way, the savage way. Fortunately for me, everything came pretty quickly. The things I learned from Mom never went away. For example, I've just finished a lunch of wild rabbit. It's not exactly a deer, but it's good enough to get by. I had to be patient, tracking my prey with its scent. Then when I found it, I stayed in the shadows, stalking it gracefully. I may be a tech nerd, but I'm quite agile when needed. The rabbit had its guard down, I started the chase. One snap of my jaws later and it was dead. I tried to be as clean about it as possible, killing it with one blow. I brought it back to the hallowed-out cabin and ate it, cooking it slightly with a compact burner I salvaged. I suppose I could have blasted it with my helmed weapon. But in a strange way, as unrestrained as it was, I'm glad I can still kill the old way. It's what makes me feel close to my kind.

I also used my nose to find a nearby stream. The water is clean, at least clean enough for me. It'll be suitable to drink and bathe in when needed. I may be going back to my roots, but it's nice to feel fresh once in a while.

Now that I'm done with my meal, all I have time for is to think about what to do next. In one week, my life has been turned upside down. I'm on the run from a human, possibly sent by the Alliance and possibly sent to kill me. I've survived so far, but this isn't a life. I can't do this for another month, another year. Living offline, unplugged might have been a viable option for wolves during the unintelligent era, but it's not for me.

More importantly, I can't simply sit around, waiting to die with what's stored in my brain. The reason I'm on the run in the first place is because I have information, data that could change the world. It could start a revolution or push the Alliance to the total destruction of its enemies.

Before I left, I hastily took my compcube with me in an effort to preserve the reports I stumbled upon. With so much time to kill here, I delved further into the Operation Alphas file. That's when I understood the full scope of it, beyond just how it affects the relationship between the Alliance and the Brotherhood of Wolves.

Implants have been around for some time, but their rise in prominence has been possible thanks to what the Alliance found at HORUS. The research harvested from its remains is what allowed the Alliance to develop their own designs and disperse it worldwide so the general masses could consume them.

Medical implants have always been public. Animals use them to expand their already expanded lifespans. Broken bones are fixed, common annoyances are gone. And the Alliance has been making a killing in profits thanks to them. No one really questions how they were created, and barely anyone knows of Lionel Changer. I certainly didn't before I stumbled upon these reports. The man faded from the public eye long before the downfall of HORUS.

There's always been an understanding that implants were only used to heal and nothing else. In fact, it's common knowledge that the Alliance put out their own sanctions barring any creature from dabbling into implant experimentation, much like they did against genetic experimentation. The Alliance was afraid shady groups would have implants applied for unlawful purposes.

That's when I was shocked to learn the purpose of Operation Alphas wasn't simply to turn wolves into fighting machines. No, the ultimate goal was to weaponize implants using the Alphas as a prototype. They wanted to create super soldiers from these implants, and the owner of the data I hacked, one General Rox, appears to be the leader.

The Alliance banned any implant modification because they wanted to be on the forefront of implant technology. Thus, they have one of their own working on ways to have implants developed outside the medical market. Yet, after reading some of the supporting documents, I'm not even sure who in the Alliance knows about this. I had to hack through some pretty high security clearances to get to this data. Other than a few superiors, it seems Rox and his group are the only ones who know about implant weaponization. Even high-ranking Alliance members are probably blind to what Rox is cooking up. Just shows you the layers of deception within the Alliance. Secrets are being withheld from the secret holders.

That explains why what I have is so confidential and it explains why I have someone coming after me. The world is in an era of peace right now. News of a top-secret, government super soldier army would no doubt unleash a wave of paranoia so severe that the Alliance would lose any trust the citizens had in them. In fact, it'd probably be the cause of extreme distrust within Alliance circles as well. And then on top of that, add in the drama with the Brotherhood of Wolves, and well, you have a recipe for disaster.

What I have in my paws is a pipebomb of truth. Is it worth it to expose that truth, knowing the repercussions that will come? Yes, it is. My mother was a pawn and used by creatures with power. Her life was thrown away and she was turned into a soulless beast. They'll never get away with this. The world will know.

Years of searching and hacking and it's come to this. This data is priceless. I have to make sure it's somewhere safe. My compcube isn't a reliable place to hold such sensitive material. That's why I transferred it somewhere that no one can get to, somewhere only I can access it. That place is within me, that place is my brain.

Implants go beyond just medical and military purposes. There are some everyday kinds of implants that have practical uses. Once such implant is the NDT, or the neural data transfer implant. It was developed as an offshoot for curing memory degenerative diseases. Think of it as a personal hard drive implanted in your memory. If you have a document or data that needs to be saved, you can store it directly into your brain via a wireless transfer for safekeeping. Then, when the time comes to access it, simply connect your compcube to your brain and voila, instant file transfer. It literally implants nanotech into your mind, setting up an information cloud in your head so you'll never have to worry about anyone stealing your stuff.

Naturally, advanced implants like these aren't available for the general public to use. They've figured other, less potentially destructive ways to combat memory degeneration. However, I know for a fact that most members in the Alliance have them installed, all animals, from humans to dogs to chimps and so on. It's a convenient way for the Alliance to keep track of the sensitive data they entrust with their employees and it also enables them a level of control. Once the individual is done with their service, they go through a painless data removal and uninstallation process so the Alliance can scrub out any security leaks that could arise.

So how did I get my hands on such innovative technology? Well, I said unsanctioned Alliance implants are illegal, but that doesn't mean they don't exist. There's a whole black market for the stuff. That doesn't mean you'll find implants as advanced as the ones they are using for this Implant Program, but you will find simpler stuff. An NDT qualifies as one of those simple things, and I went through with the procedure a few years ago. Granted, there was a lot of risk involved as you can never trust yourself in the hands of a black market implant surgeon, but it was a risk I was willing to take. I knew I would need it for my hacking activities, and I haven't regretted it since.

It's time to make sure this world-changing information stays safe. I put away my scraps and go to the compcube I was able to grab right before jumping out of my window. Just like my body, it's a miracle it's still intact after the fall.

I have to be quick about this. I've been offline this whole time, but to transfer the information to my NDT, I'll have to temporarily be back online. I run the risk of being found electronically, but that's one I'm going to have to take. Transferring the information to my brain is the only safe measure I feel comfortable with. Anything else is too damn risky.

Here goes. My holographic display pops up in front of me and I quickly navigate my way through the screens until I locate where my files are stored. I quickly run the decryption program to unlock them, and then connect to the drive on my NDT. As soon as I'm linked to it, I do a transfer. The upload begins. The seconds go by and I get nervous, worrying that something is going to go wrong. But luckily, I get the confirmation. The transfer is successful, General Rox's report and all his confidential information are securely stored within my brain. I quickly disconnect from the infospace and shut down my compcube. I hope that small window of time left no trail.

Now that I know the information is safe, there's only one thing I need to focus on: staying alive. Yet that's easier said than done. I don't know who I'm up against really. All I know is that he's a human and he scares the shit out of me.

I have a hard time picturing what he looks like. Everything happened so fast that it only seems like a blur.

I do remember a few things, though. He was massive. I've seen humans who are ripped from head to toe, but this guy was ridiculous, hulking. And the man was armed and armored. He wielded a heavy-duty blaster while tactical gear hugged his body. Yet that's all I could remember about him. The rest is simply a shadow.

I know for sure it was the Alliance that sent him. He looks like one of those government soldiers. It wasn't only because of his uniform, it was his demeanor. When he was after me, it was a mad scramble for me, but not for him. He approached me calmly, like a soulless drone coming in on its target. I didn't sense any urgency from him, even when I jumped out the window. He simply watched me from above.

It's because he has confidence. He knows eventually he'll catch up to me, his prey. And that confidence is what terrifies me. If I could identify some haste from him, then I could detect fear. But I sense none.

Now all I can do is hope to hide and survive. The world will know what the Alliance is up to. They control the masses, but they don't own them. When their crimes are exposed, we will demand justice. Not just my family, not just wolves, every creature on this planet of every species.

Yes, all I have to do is survive. In the distance I hear leaves rustling. Is it my pursuer? Do I dare look out? No, I will stay here, hidden. It's all I can do for now.

Chapter 22 – Two Van Faye

Paranoia

September 23, 3071 10:02 PM

"I just got off communication with Rox. He'll want you out doing security detail on Mark Allen soon," I say to Ash Han, who is sitting leisurely at the dining table of our penthouse.

"In Sector Six?" she replies.

"Yes, in Sector Six. You'll only be given clearance to the guest corridors, though, where he is currently being held in his off hours. Rox has made it clear he doesn't want you doing any snooping. Don't go looking for any Alliance secrets."

I take a quick glance around.

"But if, you know, if you find anything good, be sure to tell me," I say slyly.

"Yes, boss," she responds.

"By the way, Rox was very satisfied at how you were able to go toe to toe with The Collector. He said fighting to a draw during your first encounter with the creature was very impressive. That's the main reason he wants you out in Sector Six as soon as possible."

"Thank you, boss."

Her response is monotone. She lacks any emotion. She looks calm and relaxed. She casually sits there, cleaning her weapon, when I gave her the order. She's completely full of composure. And that really pisses me off.

"That's all you have to say!" I scream. She becomes alarmed with my outburst and quickly gets off her butt and stands straight.

"Um, no boss," she says in a flustered tone.

"Well then, what is it?"

"What is what?"

"What do you have to say?"

"Oh, um…"

She only mutters out noises.

"Just shut up, Han," I say. "You must think you're hot shit because you fought The Collector and lived to tell about it, but remember, you failed. Is The Collector dead?"

She's still speechless.

"It the creature dead?!" I shriek. "Is it, you piece of shit human?"

My words cut her like a blade. She winces through my tirade.

"No, it isn't," I say. "So don't act like the mission is over. You need to be on full alert. I've seen this thing kill. It's unstoppable, probably one of the most purely powerful beings I've ever seen. I don't know how you made it out of that first encounter, but trust me, that creature will have your head if you aren't careful. And after it's done with you, it'll be after me. I don't give a shit about what you want, but I want to live, so don't fuck this up!"

Am I afraid of The Collector? Hell yes. It didn't hit me until a few months after Sai died. I started experiencing flashbacks of its assault on the both of us. The creature smashed his head like a jelly sandwich. I've seen a lot of atrocities in my life, but they were always doled out by me! Never has anyone been so close to offing me as The Collector had been. I'm in the prime of my career, the ruler of the crime world. It is not my time to die. I refuse it! I will live. I won't lose my life thanks to this fuck-up human who doesn't take these threats seriously!

And look at her, cowered in fear after a simple scolding. What kind of warrior is this? Sai would never show such cowardice. He'd simply remain his stonewall self. He was a true fighter, not like this pathetic excuse I've raised to be my bodyguard.

"I'm sorry, Ms. Van Faye," she forces out. "You know I would never fail in my duties to protect your life."

"Yeah, whatever," I say dismissively. "Now, as I was saying before, you will be spending some time in Sector Six. Unfortunately, I can't come with you. That mutt Rox has guaranteed to send some guards to protect me in your absence. But shit, I trust them less than you! Alliance cronies are pathetic. You never can find good help these days."

"So when will I start these shifts?"

"Tomorrow, and for the next few days, or weeks, depending on their needs. Know that Rox is paying me straight creds for your services, so you better on top of your game. The last thing I need is for my relationship with the Alliance to go sour."

"Yes, Ms. Van Faye."

"You'll be on stakeout duty. You won't be some slack-jawed guard. Your role in this is always to be the hunter. You will wait for The Collector to come, like a fly to a web, and when it does, you will attack. That's your objective. Understood?"

"Yes, boss."

She says so half sad and half begrudging. Whatever, I don't have time to deal with her emotions. Is an owner concerned about the feelings of their pet? I think not.

"I can't wait until this Collector business is over," I say exasperatedly. "It's been putting me high on tilt ever since it's come up."

It's true. I haven't even gotten to go about my usual schedule. No massages, no business calls, not even a day out in the fabulous Allied City. Instead, I've been confined to this penthouse, bored out of my mind, scared half to death. Going in public could risk an assault by The Collector. In fact, everything is a risk. As long as The Collector is out there, I could be killed any second.

"I want that creature dead!" I burst out.

I pick up a nearby chair with my trunk and hurl it at a wall. Han looks at me in utter shock. I'm not usually prone to violent outbursts. I'm often much more composed than this. The Collector has truly gotten to my head.

That's when I hear something scratching at our window. I look over, but there's nothing there.

"Do you see anything at the window?" I ask Han.

She glances over.

"No," she responds.

I hear the scratching noise once more.

"What about that?" I ask. "Do you hear that?"

"What?" she says.

"Quiet. Just listen."

We both stand there, our focus on the window. I hear it again.

"That!" I exclaim. "Did you hear that?"

"I did," she says with a surprised expression. She quickly grabs her yari. "But there's no balcony out there, and it's a long way down."

We walk closer, slowly and carefully. Ash Han has her weapon in her hand and she follows closely behind me. I start getting jittery as apprehension encompasses my body. Is this it? Is this my end?

We arrive at the window and I look outside. Nothing is out there. Strange. But I spot a blur in the corner of my eye. It's from the reflection on the window, a small flash, like a glimmer. And it's making a whizzing sound.

Oh, shit.

Before I can even react, Ash Han does a complete about-face and swings her weapon across her body. She bats an object out of the air, and it flies directly into the wall. I look closely at it and see a needle-like spear stuck there.

I shift my attention back ahead, and that's when I see the creature standing motionlessly. It's been over ten years, but The Collector looks exactly the same. The armor and that soulless feeling are all too familiar.

I'm terrified inside, but I can't lose these mind games. I use all my willpower to collect myself.

"Long time, old business partner," I say haughtily. "I'm surprised you still remember me."

"Indeed," The Collector says through its synthesized voice. "I always remember those who betray me."

That's reassuring.

"Ah, yes, well, that was a long time ago," I say.

"It was," the creature responds. "But things don't change. You were scum then and you're still scum now."

The creature tilts its head so it faces Ash Han.

"And this must be the assassin you sent to ambush me," the creature says.

"Indeed, it was me," I say. "But not under my direction, of course. If it were up to me, I'd rather not get involved."

"Then who forced your hand?"

"You know who."

Our conversation pauses. We engage in a stare-down, sizing up each other. I decide to start it.

"Han, begin," I say.

Ash Han draws her gun and starts firing at The Collector. I quickly run for cover, going to the large table capable of partially hiding my enormous frame. I reach it, flip it over, and start ducking. I peer my head from the side to make sure I have a good view of all the action.

Han continues her assault on The Collector. She stands stationary, focusing on her aim as she fires her blaster. Spurts of light fly at the cloaked figure, but The Collector easily dodges them, juking from side to side as every shot misses. The creature has lightning-fast reflexes, as if she knows where each shot is going to be before it comes out.

The Collector makes one dramatic duck, and then it goes on the offensive. It retaliates with the needle-like spears it came with and fires one from its cloak straight at Ash Han. Han, who has her yari in her other hand, swipes at it and knocks it away harmlessly.

However, while my bodyguard was distracted by the initial shot, The Collector lets another one rip right after. It screams through the air toward Han's hand and makes contact with her blaster. The gun flies away and out of reach. Han helplessly looks at it and starts to think of another approach.

The tip of her yari begins to glow. I've seen her do this a thousand times. Actually, it's something I implemented for her. You see, when I had Sai, he had a marquee weapon, something to stamp his name on his victims. It was his electrified horn. Thus, when I trained Han as a child, I knew I wanted to give her a similar signature.

Enter her yari. I wanted to make my bodyguard's weapon go beyond a simple gun. It had to draw images of ancient warriors so her legend would grow. She's a human, thus, I equipped her with an ancient weapon used by humans of this land long ago. Of course, I modernized it. I gave it energy capabilities, both in blade and ammunition. Her yari can fire energy shots that vary in caliber. That is what she's prepping right now. She'll shoot a ball of plasma that could tear through walls.

Her weapon is primed, she's ready to fire. She points the tip of yari at The Collector and shoots a sphere right at the creature. It's large and bulldozes anything in the way.

The Collector only has a split second to react, so it reaches its palms to a nearby nightstand and uses the table to shield itself.

The shot makes contact and immediately dust explodes into the air. The nightstand is obliterated and shards of it turn into burning, powdered embers that light up the penthouse of the Benjamin Plaza Hotel. A cloud of illuminated debris forms, obscuring Han and me from what lies beyond. It's like someone fired an indoor firework. Through all of this, Han and I simply observe quietly. We're on pins and needles, hoping the attack connected.

The dust starts to settle and the room becomes clear. As the air is less obscured, we start to wonder if the attack hit.

Han and I are stunned to see that nothing is there. No charred remains, no butchered body, not even a corpse. Either The Collector got disintegrated completely and is now part of the ash that surrounds this room, or it disappeared into thin air. Given its track record, I wouldn't be that surprised if it were the latter.

That's when I see Han looking at the ceiling. The Collector latched onto it, back facing the top. Damn, it must have used its telekinesis to make a last-minute dodge.

In an instant, The Collector rockets itself from the ceiling and flies fist forward to Han. Han takes a swing with her yari, but The Collector rolls into a ball and ducks under it. The creature lands with a somersault forward and then spins its body. Using the momentum, it swings its leg and performs a sweeping roundhouse at Han's leg, knocking her clear off her feet. Han falls to the floor and hits her head hard with a loud thud. She's temporarily out for the count.

The Collector then gets back to its feet and turns around, right toward where I am hiding. Shit. I can't do anything. My body stiffens and I lose control of myself. I can't move, I'm too frozen in fear.

The Collector approaches me slowly, like it is an executioner sauntering to its victim. I think of how I can fight back. Perhaps I can strangle it with my trunk. Or maybe if I charge at it, I can crush the creature.

But I know it's useless. This feeling of fear is all too familiar. It's what I felt ten years ago during the battle at my own penthouse. The Collector had just killed Sai, and I was next. I thought I was a goner then, and I think it now. The mighty Elephant Queen of Crime dies like a coward thanks to this black-armored menace.

Then, a miracle happens. Han regains consciousness and gets back to her feet. The Collector turns around, attention once again shifted to its opponent. Looks like the fight isn't over.

Chapter 23 – Ash Han

Rematch

September 23, 3071 10:21 PM

Round two, here we go. The creature pulled a dirty move with that sweep. I fell hard on the side of my head, but I'm back on my feet and I'm ready to try again.

I have to if I'm to protect Ms. Van Faye. I see her crouching behind the oversized table we adjusted earlier, though the table is still much too small to cover her gargantuan frame. She actually looks afraid. She watches the action, wide-eyed, and her face shivers, petrified by the sight before her. When she first heard about The Collector, she was her usual cocky, flashy self. Yet as things become more real, and The Collector has become a closer threat, I've seen her change from a fearful boss to a cowardly shell of what she used to be.

I'm somewhat surprised. Or more accurately, I'm unimpressed. This is the elephant that I've dreaded most of my life? For as long as I've known her, since childhood to now, she's always been a creature that was my master, and a volatile and terrifying one at that. I only obey because I am afraid. Yet the paranoid mess I see in front of me doesn't look like that at all. It makes me wonder what I've been so petrified of and makes me second-guess everything I've believed serving under her. This is no ruthless leader, the Two Van Faye I see is a pawn.

Perhaps she has reason to be afraid. I know I am. Even at my young age, I already have years of experience doing things for Ms. Van Faye, things I will regret doing one day. I've decapitated legions of rival crime bosses. I've plowed through armies of lackeys, killed every kind of species, simply because I was told to do it. I've never faced a threat that I couldn't handle. Until now. The unnatural power, the technology, the pure fighting skill and reflexes—all of that has made The Collector my most dangerous target.

I don't make a move, not yet. Instead, I remain there panting for breath as I stand on defense and wait to see what The Collector is going to do. So far, I've been too aggressive with my game plan. I've attacked first, often recklessly, when I should be like The Collector. I can't see what's behind the mask, but I can tell the creature is patient. It knows how to wait for an opening, and that's why it's still alive.

I also need time to recover from the injury I sustained earlier. I hit my head hard on the ground, any other human would have received a concussion. But I'm different thanks to my implants. They've done a lot of things. They've made me stronger and quicker, but the greatest advantage is that I am much more durable than the average human. Since I was a girl, Ms. Van Faye has had them installed everywhere: on my bones, in my muscles, and in particular, on my skull.

It's like my brain isn't encased with bone, it's encased with metal. It's still light, but it can take the damage. A punch to the head that could kill someone only leaves me temporarily dazed. In fact, I'm pretty sure I should be dead, or at least in a coma, but I'm not.

The average Fan Zui Bin citizen can't get their hands on this either. I have it thanks to Two Van Faye's connections.

Despite that, I'm still a little dizzy, but I'm recovering at an accelerated rate. I look to my right and see my blaster is on the ground. It's too far out of reach for me to make a run for it. I still have my yari, and I can charge it up to fire the heavy-duty shot, but that might be too slow. In fact, I think any projectile is useless against The Collector. Everything I've thrown at it has failed. The only thing I can use is my yari and my fists. It's what has given me even a sliver of a chance.

My headache has disappeared. I'm ready to go. This whole time The Collector has just stood there. I can hear the creature breathing. Well, at least I know it's not a drone. It hasn't moved, not an arm or leg, hasn't even tilted its head. It's like a statue.

I don't know if it's trying to goad me into an attack. I stay defiant and refuse to budge.

Naturally, though, Ms. Van Faye isn't a huge fan of this strategy.

"What are you doing, you idiot?" she hollers. "Hurry up and attack your enemy."

I don't respond.

"Do it now, you moron!" she yells.

I want to turn around and fire a warning shot at my boss. She can be quite distracting.

And distracted me she has, for during those slight seconds when she was barking out her commands, The Collector at last moves. The creature lifts its arm and spreads out its palms. I've seen this many times now. She's using her telekinesis. I look and see it directing its efforts toward a chair. I have to act fast because once the creature starts to use this power, there's no turning back.

I make a mad dash to the creature. The creature notices my charge and releases its mental hold on the chair, focusing all its attention on me. I'm a foot away, so I whip a mighty slash at its head. The Collector quickly ducks under it and my swing hits nothing but air. But I readjust and promptly throw another swipe downward, aiming at the creature's head once more.

The creature sidesteps to the right, and my yari misses and smashes onto the floor. The Collector now kneels to my left. I try one last desperation slash, aiming for the creature's torso, but it simply jumps back. My yari fails connect once more.

That's when The Collector makes its move. She stretches out her arm and the blades hidden in its gauntlet extend. One cut from those and I'll be sliced to ribbons.

However, this fraction of a second delay is enough time for me to react. Before the creature can even make its move, I grab its arm and slam my back into its chest so its body hangs over mine. Then with all my strength, I throw the creature's arm forward, finishing a perfect judo throw. The Collector smashes into the floor, back on the ground, face up toward the ceiling.

With my yari still in hand, I lift it up and get ready to drive it through the creature's skull. Good game, but this one's over.

"Han, above you!" a voice screams. It's Van Faye, yelling from behind her table.

"What?" I instinctively say.

I turn my body and look above to see what the commotion is about. There I see a ceiling of those needle-like spears The Collector has been using as ammo. They hang above me, stationary, like a sky of icicles ready to fall. I'm completely floored. When did this happen?

I turn back around and face The Collector. I look into its mask as my shocked expression tells the creature the story. In response, it nods its head satisfyingly.

Then it snaps its fingers.

I immediately jump away from the creature, scrambling in a completely random direction. I take a quick glance at the spears and watch them crashing down. I then turn my head back forward and continue to flee.

I have no particular place I'm going, only away from the spears. I can hear them behind me, pattering on the ground like heavy rainfall. There's so many of them. But my legs keep churning, hoping an errant one doesn't hit me.

I forget grace in the moments of my haste. I miscalculate a step and stumble forward, headfirst. As I fall, I do a complete summersault. During the roll, I get a momentary look at the rain of needles. I can see one coming down on me, right at my head, so instead of halting my tumble, I carry its momentum. I roll and roll and roll, and with every tumble, more of The Collector's weapons miss.

At last, a good minute after it started, the attack stops. The Collector has run out of ammunition. I get to my feet and observe the damage. Before me lies a trail of these spears, stuck firmly into the ground, the result of every one of them missing. I've jumped, run, and rolled my way out of getting impaled. I am alive, and The Collector stands there ready for the next move.

I barely escaped with my life, and I got trapped into making the first move, again. I have to be more careful.

While I think it out, The Collector points its palms toward the trail of spears on the ground. The floor rumbles a little, but then, in unison, all of them pop out of the ground into the air. I get ready for another onslaught, but instead, the creature clenches its fist and all of the spears gather in a bunch. Then The Collector throws a small device at the grouping. A blinding light flashes and I close my eyes. When they reopen, the spears are gone. It looked like the same teleportation trick The Collector used on itself.

"We can't fight on a dirty battlefield," the creature says.

"Agreed," I respond. "Now, let's continue."

"Let's."

The Collector gets in a fighting stance, and I get in one too. It has its blades out, and I have my yari. No more guns, no more spears, just pure hand-to-hand combat like in the old times. Though I face possible death, I wouldn't have it any other way. The creature is truly a worthy foe.

This isn't about Van Faye. I know this because I feel no honor when I look at her sniveling behind her cover. And this isn't about the Alliance either. No, this is just about two combatants locked in a primitive struggle.

I wait for the creature to make the first move, and surprisingly, it does. It comes to me with a wild right hook that I see coming a mile away. I twist my yari and block off the first blow, but the instant I do that, The Collector tries to jab me in the face, pointed tip first. But I quickly slip past it and throw a kick of my own. Naturally, The Collector sidesteps that. It backs away, relenting from the initial attack, and we stand again in a stare-down. No hit has been landed.

The Collector decides to go on the offensive once more. It spins and throws a roundhouse kick with its left leg right at my face. But I block it and grab its foot. I then throw a low kick of my own, aiming for its other leg. But The Collector hops back, which causes me to release my hold on the creature.

Right when it recovers, it tries another slash. It probably thinks my guard is down. It's wrong. I block the attack once again with the bladed side of my yari. Then I do a full rotation, hoping to land a blow to the head with the handle side of my weapon. Instead of landing, The Collector catches it with its bare hand. I can't hide my shock. I look at the creature, and the creature looks at me for a second before letting go of my weapon. How does it always know my moves?

Still, I am satisfied with how the fight has turned out so far. We're old-school sword fighters striking and sticking each other's moves, going back and forth like a well-played game of chess. And we don't lack confidence. This is child's play to both of us.

If The Collector wants to win, it has to draw upon the advantages given to it. It does. The Collector turns to a chair nearby and crashes down a thunderous punch to it. Van Faye and I both watch the piece of furniture crumble into several small pieces. The creature then uses its telekinesis to levitate the debris in the air. Slowly, the shards and chunks start to float around the being, orbiting around it like a moon around a planet. The pieces start to rotate faster, picking up speed by the seconds. I watch helplessly as a few moments later the chunks fully encircle The Collector, creating a tornado of debris that's both distracting and dangerous.

The Collector then gets in its fighting stance. This is going to be interesting.

The creature approaches me slowly, and I'm forced to back away unless I want to get hit with an errant piece of broken chair. They rotate around The Collector so quickly that it's hard to keep track of everything, both her and the debris.

Then something flies at me. I think it's her fist, but I see her outstretched palm in the distance. It's a piece of debris. I make a slip to the right to avoid it, and it goes flying behind me. The Collector throws another and I dodge that one too.

Then the creature throws its own fist my way. I'm caught off guard at first, as I was expecting it to hurl the broken bits of chair instead of a punch. Yet I'm able to react at the last moment and duck under it. Right when that's done, another piece of debris shoots at me, and I move just in time, like the others.

The Collector continues her assault in this manner, launching debris here, throwing punches there, alternating between the two attacks as I do what I can to avoid them. And for the most part, I'm successful. Though, I must admit, the pure amount of things getting thrown my way and the variations of attack, going from debris to punches, has made this task quite difficult. Things are coming out so rapidly that sometimes I can't tell if it's the creature's fist or pieces of chair. All I can do is dodge.

I duck and weave, slide and bob, and through it all, nothing hits me. I'm like this when I've hit my stride. I only concentrate on the blows that are heading my way. The world slows down and I'm able to see things coming with precise vision. I feel the adrenaline rush, and I force my body to move faster, pushing it to the limit.

I don't get tired, I don't feel pain. I only focus on the task at hand.

After it's all said and done, the attack ceases. The Collector has no more debris to toss my way. It must have thrown hundreds of punches, and all of them missed. It sees things are at a draw, and we both stand in a mixture of amazement and silence. I breathe in heavily, panting for air, but I am proud of what I've accomplished.

"You've run out of ammo," I say with gratification. "Guess it's pretty tough hitting me, huh?"

"Perhaps it is," the creature responds. "Yet, then again, I'm not really throwing ammunition at you. Ammunition is useless after it's fired."

"What?"

"If you weren't so focused on my attacks, you would have taken a look at where they were going."

I look above and behind me, and to my utter bewilderment, the pieces of debris The Collector levitated past me remain in the air. They surround me like a swarm of bees. I was concentrating so hard on dodging its attacks that I didn't even pay attention to where they were going. And now I'm ensnared in a cloud of chair bits.

"You're trapped," The Collector says.

It closes its fists, and like a giant magnet, I attract them all. The pieces attach to me in unison, slamming into my body hard. I grunt and grimace through the pain until every piece is stuck to my body.

Still, that wasn't too bad. I was expecting it to be a deadly blow, but it was no more deadly than a few punches. Now it's time to counterattack.

Except… I can't move. I try to lift my arms, but they're glued to my sides. Same thing with my legs. I don't recall being in this position earlier, before the hail of debris rained on me.

"What did you do?" I ask the creature in a desperate tone.

"I found a way to bind you," the creature responds. "You see, I can't control something as complex as a living creature. Too many moving parts. And I can't lift you using your own armor. It's too intricate and I need to gain a level of familiarity with what I'm lifting. And you need to stay still. But I can control the stuff that surrounds you."

That's when I take a look around my body and realize the debris didn't just stick to me, they actually entombed me like a mummy. That's what The Collector did. It wasn't trying to attack me, it was trying to trap me. It has complete control over the chunks it threw, and now the creature controls it to wrap my body. I'm stuck, encased in a coffin of debris that hugs my body.

"Thus, you're now bound by something I can lift with my mind. Why, I can lift you right now," the creature says.

It's right. I can only watch helplessly as I feel my body being lifted. It rides the container of debris I'm wrapped with. I go where it goes. I struggle all I want, hoping to be released from this quandary, but it is useless.

"Release me!" I yell.

"No can do," it says. "I have some business with your boss and I'd like to conduct it in a civil manner. That won't happen if you keep buzzing around, so I'll have to put you on a time out."

"Time out?"

The Collector then lifts its other hand and points it at Van Faye's table. Ms. Van Faye quickly gets to her feet and runs the opposite direction. The table, as heavy as it is, starts to float in the air and starts to rumble. I see fissures being formed in it, cracks and splits. Then, with one mighty crunch, the table separates in half, forming two large slabs.

"What are you doing?" I ask.

"Like I said, I'm putting you on time out," it responds.

Those are the last words I hear. Immediately, she swings her arm and the two pieces of table go with it. They fly in my direction, and moments later, they crash into my helpless, floating body. I collide, stuck in a storm of debris and broken furniture. And in this storm, I see nothing but darkness.

Chapter 24 – Two Van Faye

Threats

September 23, 3071 10:34 PM

"Get up, Van Faye," The Collector says to me. "You look ridiculous."

With the large table I was using for protection gone, I've resorted to hiding behind a couch. It barely covers a third of my body. My head sticks out. My ass sticks out. Actually, almost everything sticks out. The Collector is right, I look ridiculous.

I glance over to Ash Han. She's alive, breathing, but knocked out indefinitely. Now is the time I need her services. What luck.

I quickly gather my composure and get up from my crouched position. I use my trunk to dust off parts of my body. It's a mind game with this creature. I may be terrified, but I can never give off that vibe, for if I do, I'll be dead.

"You've knocked out my bodyguard and trashed my penthouse," I say with forced arrogance. "You must want to talk to me really badly."

"No, I despise talking to creatures like you," The Collector retorts.

"That hurts my feelings. So what do you really want, then?"

"What I want is some information."

"Like what?"

The Collector inches closer to me. I instinctively back away, but once I realize what I'm doing, I stop and take a firm stand.

"I know you're aware of who I'm looking for," The Collector says. "And I know you know where he is, so tell me where the Alliance is keeping Mark Allen."

"Why would I tell you?" I say. "I only negotiate when there's a profit to be made. What do you offer? Credits? Business?"

"I've learned in the past that dealing with you can be a very... risky venture. Thus, the only thing I offer you is this."

The creature extends the blade in its gauntlet and points it at my head. It's finely sharpened, and only a few inches away. At a moment's notice, my head could be cut like ribbons.

"I offer you your life," The Collector says.

I start to panic. Never before has someone gotten so close to ending my life. The Elephant Queen of Crime has conquered all her enemies mercilessly, except this one.

"Please reconsider!" I desperately yell.

"There's nothing to think about," the creature says. "The information or death. It's your choice."

What a choice. I look at the ground despondently.

"It doesn't matter what I do," I say. "I don't tell you, you'll kill me. I tell you, the Alliance will know I ratted and I'll say good-bye to their support. Fan Zui Bin will be out of my grip. I might as well die then."

"I'm sure you'll find some way to skirt around the Alliance," it says. "It's a safer bet than going against me."

I think about her response.

"I suppose you're right," I say. "Lift your blade and I'll tell you what you want to know."

"Okay, but no tricks, Van Faye. Your bodyguard is knocked out. It's only me. You'd be unwise to even attempt one of your famous betrayals," the creature says.

"I begrudgingly agree."

The Collector puts the blade away in its gauntlet, and I sigh a breath of relief.

"Your mark is in an undisclosed Alliance research facility called Sector Six," I respond. "It's one of the many Alliance sanctioned buildings where Rox runs his Implant Program. When they heard you were back, they secured Allen to that building alone. That is where you will find him."

"Excellent," the creature says. "That's all I wanted to hear."

The Collector turns its attention away from me and messes with some buttons on its armor.

"Do you need me to draw you a map?" I say sarcastically. "Sector Six isn't exactly easy to find, even if it is near Allied City. It's not like there's a big sign telling you where it is."

"Don't worry, I know where it is," it says.

"How?"

"I have my methods."

I look at the creature curiously.

"What do you want with Allen anyway?" I ask. "He's just Rox's implant lackey."

"You underestimate him," the creature responds. "He holds quite a bit of data in his head."

"And what in particular are you interested in?"

The Collector's head turns to mine.

"Nice try, Van Faye," it says. "But you won't be getting out any information from me. I know how dangerous knowledge can be in your hands."

"Very well. I hope that helps. And I hope I won't have to worry about retribution anymore," I say.

"You won't. It won't be by my hand that you'll face your end. My word is always solid. Even when we did business, I wasn't the untrustworthy one. You were."

"Those words wound me."

"I'm sure you'll get over it. Until then."

The Collector stops fiddling with its controls. Like the many times I've seen before, a flash appears, and the creature disappears in a ball of light. It's only Ash Han and me left.

The penthouse is damaged. The chairs and tables are a mess, and the walls and floors are filled with cracks. I can't imagine how much this is going to cost me.

And then I hear a cough. Guess who starts to come back to consciousness? Ash Han. My life has been threatened, a blade was put to my head, and now, after all that, my idiot human decides to wake up. How convenient.

"Get to your feet, you waste of carbon," I say. "The Collector is gone."

Han stands up and looks like hell. She massages her head and struggles to maintain her balance. Her legs are wobbly, her armor scraped, and she's constantly shaking.

Fortunately, though, she's not seriously injured. And she's recovering rather quickly. Not like I give a shit about her, but I still need my bodyguard to be physically capable of carrying out her job.

"Are you coherent enough to talk?" I say demandingly.

"Uh, yes, Ms. Van Faye," she says slowly.

"Good. A lot has happened in the few minutes you were out, and I'll require your services. Nothing is broken I assume?"

"No. Everything just hurts like hell."

"Good. I'll have a bioscan run on you to make sure. Anyway, The Collector knows Mark Allen's location. You'll need to head over to Sector Six right away."

Han looks confused by my revelation.

"How'd the creature find out?" she asks.

"I told the creature," I say. "I had to. My life was in danger. It wouldn't have been if you did your job correctly."

Han looks at the ground in shame.

"Sorry, Ms. Van Faye," she says.

"Don't grovel to me," I say. "It's unfitting for a warrior. Now, we'll need to tell General Rox and give him a heads-up, but any mention that I was responsible for leaking the information and I will kill you. Do you understand?"

I say the words with the harshest tone I can muster.

"Yes, I do," she responds.

"Good. Now get me my communicator," I say. "I'll need to link up with the dog."

She grabs my communicator and puts it on my head. I connect out to General Rox and in seconds, he's on a holoscreen in front of me.

"Rox, we have a development," I say.

"What is it, Van Faye?" Rox asks.

"The Collector attacked me in my penthouse."

Instantaneously, a look of surprise shoots across his face.

"What?" he exclaims. "Why?"

"The creature probably figured out who Han was and connected the dots," I say.

"You appear unscathed, though. What happened?"

"Han successfully defended me and the creature retreated."

"Interesting."

"Not all is good news, though. During the battle, the creature mentioned something about Sector Six and Mark Allen."

Rox appears even more surprised than before.

"What did it say exactly?" Rox asks.

"I'm not sure," I respond. "It was talking to a third party on its communicator. I simply heard those words."

"I see. And you said Han was able to fend off The Collector?"

I nod my head.

"Well, we'll need her over here posthaste!" Rox exclaims. "Your bodyguard may be the only hope we have of protecting Mark Allen. If the creature is coming straight here for him, we'll need to be prepared. Understood?"

"Yes," I respond.

"Don't get any ideas, though, Van Faye. As I stated before, your bodyguard will only be given access to the secure wing. You won't be getting your grubby trunk on any of my secrets. Got that?"

"Of course."

"Good. I will send over the details, but I'll be expecting Han to be here as soon as possible. Thank you for the update, Van Faye. This is Rox, out."

The holoscreen closes, and I turn my attention back to Ash Han.

"And that's how you deflect blame and lie to the Alliance," I say. "Let's make sure the Alliance doesn't suspect I confessed."

"Yes, Ms. Van Faye. So I'm heading to Sector Six?" Han asks.

"It seems so. Gather your gear. You better not mess up this time, Han. You've already failed twice. The Alliance may tell you your mission is to protect Mark Allen, but remember what I really want you to do. You need to kill The Collector. I want the creature's head. Don't come back empty handed."

Chapter 25 – Falena Snow

Spotted

<u>September 27, 3071 5:01 AM</u>
My God, it's early. The sun isn't even out yet and the forest is eerily quiet. Perhaps it's my imagination. I've been rather tense. It's hard to stay focused when you've been up for hours. With an assassin chasing me, I've barely been able to sleep for the past few days. Then again, I don't think anyone in my situation could.

A few days ago, reality started to sink in. I realized I was against the odds. I'm a simple hacker. My enemy is probably a highly trained Alliance soldier. Once he makes contact, I don't think I have much of a chance to survive.

Sure, I have some minor combat experience thanks to my family lineage, but seriously, I'm a rank amateur. There's no way I can physically outmatch this enemy. Yet I'm not one to give up. I knew my brawn couldn't resolve anything, but my brains could. I had to think strategically.

I had the bombs from the arms dealer. I had a helmed weapon. And my cabin was my shelter. Thus, I proposed to fortify it. If my stalker wanted to come get me, he'd have to endure a bunch of traps, ones that I will lay before him. That's what I plan to do this morning.

I'm right outside my cabin with a tote full of bombs tied to my leg. I have my helmed weapon and I'm ready to go. The goal is to set a bunch of them on the ground, like land mines, to protect the cabin. I'll transform the perimeter into a warzone. The bombs are wolf manufactured, designed to be activated orally. I won't have to worry about needing hands to arm them, which is good. The last thing I want is to accidently blow off my face.

I stick my head into the bag and get a bomb, wrapping my jaws around its gripped handle. These bombs are remotely activated through the interface on my helmed weapon. All I have to do is place them where I want and then give the verbal command to arm it. The bomb will beep, and I can go on to the next one. They're already set to proximity mode, but the bomb also comes with a plethora of other features. You can do timed mode, remote mode, and a host of other things. You can even monitor all the bombs' statuses right from the helmed weapon. A holoscreen pops up and shows you where they are located and gives the user access to set them. Everything is controlled by my weapon.

I'm not looking for anything fancy, though. I simply want to have them go off like mines. If my pursuer is foolish enough to come by the cabin, a firestorm of explosions will be here to greet him.

The bomb is still in my mouth, so I find a nice location to set it down. I then go on to the next one. I decide to set them first, sowing them like seeds. My plan is to cover the entirety of the perimeter, from the front to the back to both sides. I'll also be wearing my helmed weapon for the remainder of the week. It's always good to be prepared for anything.

I've installed some on the nearby trees. My hope is that if the enemy is nearby, it'll trigger and cause the tree to collapse on my foe. Or, at the very least, it'll give me enough warning for me to be ready to attack.

I have about twenty bombs in my tote. It may seem like a lot, but the bombs are relatively small. I'd say they're no bigger than the size of a lemon. And they're amazingly light. Don't be deceived by their size, though. I've seen them in action, and they pack quite the powerful punch.

I finish dropping them in the front and continue around the house. I take my time with each one. I use my paws to dig a small hole in the ground so the bombs remain. I carefully place it within the earth and then cover. It's a slow process, and by the time I'm done, an hour and a half has already passed.

Still, my bag is empty, and I'm quite pleased.

"Not a single one wasted," I say.

I prepare to go back inside the cabin and get the rest of my preparations ready, when I hear a rattle in the distance.

"What was that?" I say with a suspicious tone.

It really could be anything. A rabbit, a mouse, hell, even the wind. Strange noises are common. This is a forest after all.

Yet the rattle continues, and paranoia gets the best of me. It sounds like it's only about a hundred feet away, close enough for me to investigate. Before I leave, I make sure my helmed weapon is armed, just in case.

I slowly make my way through my minefield. I don't have to worry about accidental trips, as I haven't armed anything yet. And the sensors are coded to my genetic structure, so it knows if it's me it's attacking. It's another nice little feature that acts as a safety.

The rattling is still going, and my nerves start to build up. I trek more cautiously into the woods, trying to locate the source. I don't see anything, so maybe I'm right, maybe it is a small animal. Lord, I hope that is the truth.

That's when the rattling gets louder. I look around and see it coming from straight ahead. Underneath two small trees, a leafy bush violently shakes. It's not the wind that's causing it to move. There are several bushes around, and none of them vibrate as harshly as it. And it's rather large, so anything could be hiding behind all that green.

My helmed weapon is now set to fire mode. I'm armed and ready.

Before I can say "fire," someone steps out. It's a human, a man, the same man from before. This time I'm close enough to get a good view of him. He's decked out in Alliance armor, covered head to toe. He even wears a mask, and the only things exposed are his strong, focused eyes.

The man is as I remembered him. He's built like a brick and huge. Muscles sculpt his armor and a cadre of weapons hang from his oversized frame. He must stand close to seven feet tall, which towers above the average human. He towers over me as well.

I'm too scared to do anything. I want to shoot him, but I can't muster the words to do it. Instead, I turn around and run to my cabin. I don't look back, I don't even think about my pursuer. The only thing I think about is getting back to safety.

The automatic door opens and I bolt through it. It then shuts, and I command it to lock. The gears turn and the entrance is secure. I quickly turn on the holoscreen and activate the mines. The statuses light up and the bombs are ready to detonate. If my stalker even thinks of coming here, he'll have another thing coming. I grab some spare grenades and place them in my helmed weapon's launcher. I also charge up the plasma shots. I'm ready to get this started.

I wait for him to come. And wait. And wait. After a solid ten minutes, he still hasn't approached. I don't see him in my surveillance streams, nor do I sense any heat signatures coming through. He's found me, in the woods, by myself. If it were ever his chance to attack, now would be the time, but he doesn't. He doesn't even come near me.

Why?

I peer outside a window and put on my specs to get a better look. I zoom in on the bush from where he emerged, and to my shock, he's still there. The guy is just standing there like a statue, face pointed at me, but the eyes convey nothing. I look closer to see if I'm missing something, but I don't find anything.

I'm puzzled. What is he doing? Is this some kind of ploy?

As I continue to guess what's going on, he finally does something. He takes out an object from his pocket. It appears to be a large hunting knife. He holds it in the air and inspects it for a few seconds. I'm still confused by these actions.

He then lowers it and points it straight ahead, right at me. Does he know I'm looking at him? Is he trying to send a message?

It becomes all too clear. He raises the knife again, up to his shoulders. Slowly, he mimics a throat-cutting motion while nodding his head reassuringly. He doesn't say anything, but his eyes tell me everything. And I have received his threat in full force. Dread takes over.

After that is done, he squats down and starts to unload his gear. He unbuckles the weapons that are strapped to him and takes out some sustenance from his sack. He's setting up camp, not going for a direct attack. Instead, he's on a stakeout, waiting for me, his prey, patiently, like a hawk.

I just realized what I've done. I'm trapped, surrounded by bombs I've set, stuck in a cabin I can no longer flee from. He knows where I am, and he's going to wait it out.

Now the game starts. I must take this time to adjust my strategy, for when it's time to play, I need to win. My life depends on it.

Chapter 26 – Ash Han

Orphan

September 27, 3071 9:13 AM

After that deadly, arduous, yet exhilarating fight a few days ago, things certainly have died down. We haven't heard anything about The Collector, nor do we have a clue what the creature is up to. Instead, the main focus has been safeguarding Mark Allen until The Collector inevitably shows up to confront him. Then we'll be ready.

The morning after our encounter with The Collector, I was shipped off to Sector Six for security duties. Rox didn't want a minute wasted. A hovercar was sent to pick me up, and to my surprise, the dog was inside. We didn't exchange pleasantries, though. He simply briefed me on what I'd be doing and then remained silent for the rest of the ride. It was very businesslike and something I would expect from the Alliance.

The hovercar itself was completely shielded from the outside, so I had no idea where we were going or where Sector Six was located. Once it had stopped and I got outside, we were already in the hangar of the building.

From there, General Rox left and his cronies showed me to my temporary living quarters. The escorts were just as stern as Rox. They had that stuck-

up Alliance way about them and most definitely were
unhappy with my presence. I suppose I would be upset
too if there was some gangster's lackey doing the job
that I was supposed to do. Their attitude indicated this,
as they barely wanted to show me around. But being an
outsider is nothing new to me. I've lived like one all
my life.

After I set aside my gear, the grunts showed me
around the rest of the place. I was only given a small
tour, as my access was and will be limited during my
mission. Rox was very clear to Ms. Van Faye that any
suspicious behavior will lead to an end to their
agreement, so I won't be doing any snooping. I don't
care to anyway. Ms. Van Faye may want to know their
dirty secrets, but I couldn't care less.

The whole facility is located underground to
maintain secrecy. Above, there's a cloaking field and
several armed drones incase a passerby, or spy, wanders
around. Sector Six is part of the larger group of
"sectors" that are scattered around the world. Other
than the research prisons, most Alliance R&D is done
here. The place is equipped with labs, barracks,
armories, and cafeterias to keep their staff happy. I'll
only be given access to the barracks and cafeteria. Staff
are not required to stay on premises, but the Alliance
keeps very close tabs on anyone who lives offsite, like
Mark Allen.

Speaking of which, I actually met him. I had to
interview him if I was going to protect him. I know he
was one of the head guys running the Implant Program,
but we never crossed paths when I was getting my
implants installed.

Finally, I have another human to talk to. He's kind
of a wiry guy. I don't sense much confidence in him,

despite all he's accomplished. He speaks in low tones and mumbled phrases. I suppose I can be intimidating with my armor and gear. He probably also knows I work for Ms. Van Faye. He's a civilian. Still, it goes beyond that. He's been a prisoner most of his life, and even when given freedom, he's still working for the Alliance. All he has been doing is serving someone his entire existence. A lifestyle like that often comes with a certain fear. I can relate. It's the same feeling I have working for Ms. Van Faye. How odd is it that the two humans are slaves to their master?

It makes me wonder why this man is such a high priority target for The Collector. I keep hearing talks about how he holds sensitive information deep within the crevices of his brain. Makes sense that he has it. He is in charge of one of Rox's biggest projects, and I imagine there's a whole boatload of confidential info to get. I just find it odd that this man is the person who is the gatekeeper.

During our meeting, I went over his schedule. When it's day, he spends time on his work. He gets started anytime between five in the morning until seven, and ends his day late in the night. He eats sparingly during his work hours, and afterward, he hits the hay to start all over again. The research facility is heavily guarded, so I'm more worried about The Collector attacking when he is most vulnerable, in the barracks, where security is not as strict. Thus, my duties are to guard his living quarters when he's in them and sweep the perimeter of the research area when he's working in the lab.

Logistically speaking, guarding the living quarters shouldn't be too difficult. They're in an isolated part of Sector Six, and there is only one hall leading to it.

Thus, once Mark Allen is inside, I can guard the connecting hall without worrying about a possible rear attack. Also, we have motion sensors that can detect foreign entities and will alert me and the enclave of other soldiers when an intruder arrives.

The hallway itself is rather narrow, so it'll be a good place for me to have the advantage if The Collector decides to strike Sector Six directly. With the creature's powers, an open space could mean a lot of trouble as its telekinesis has more room to travel. We've also cleared the space of any possible projectiles The Collector may use. That way, I can make sure the fight is as even as possible. Every precaution has been taken.

Now all I can do is wait. I know The Collector will come. It's just a matter of time. Mark Allen is already off in the lab, so as of this moment, I am on watch outside the restricted area. It's pretty boring work. I've been standing here like a damn statue, bored out of my mind. I've been on stakeout missions before for Ms. Van Faye, but at least those had a hint of excitement.

Accompanying me are a few Alliance guards. They aren't as dickish as the ones that have been escorting me around. In fact, they're almost like teammates. They vary in species but are extremely professional. I was even given a communicator so I could coordinate my position with them.

It's nice working with a group that has professionalism. It's not something I'm used to and I need it now more than even. Everyone is tense over The Collector. I'm nervous, the Alliance is anxious, and most of all, Ms. Van Faye is on edge. Having this kind of support helps make things run smoother.

I never had such support growing up in the hardened city of Shogun. I've always done everything on my own. Before I was introduced to the world of Two Van Faye, I was an orphan. I never knew who my mother or father was. Ms. Van Faye eventually told me that my mom was probably a drug user and my dad one of her one-night stands. I was dumped off to the orphanage from day one. Why I wasn't aborted is beyond me.

It's not like I have any desire to meet them anyway. They're nothing more than a bunch of strangers. I call no one my guardian.

Life at the orphanage was hard. From the onset, I was an outcast because I was a human. Shogun, no wait, all of Fan Zui Bin has a complicated history with the human species. The original crime bosses that ruled the territory were human. And the general population was comprised of other species. Humans were the only ones with the capital to build a place like the FZB. The bosses built their empire and preyed upon the desperate creatures that moved in. They governed the land like tyrants, only caring for themselves, and ignored the lower class. Considering the history the other species had with humans, this only left a bad taste in their mouths.

Eventually, though, the animals got their way. They overthrew the upper-class humans and ruled for themselves. Any human left in Fan Zui Bin fled and only the few, unfortunate, lower class humans who had no credits to leave stayed behind. My kind became the minority. We felt the wrath of the new power.

Thus, as it is today, humans are discriminated against. Everyone knows this, even the cubs. When I was in that orphanage I was treated like any other human, I was garbage. None of the other young ones wanted to play with me. Water was limited at the orphanage, and I couldn't bathe every day. I didn't have fur to conceal the grime, so the others would call me the "dirty girl."

I'd often get thrashed by the others. I recalled one time I had to fend off a lion cub, a tiger cub, and a pup at one time. I didn't win and was in the medical wing for one whole week. I would get slashed, bitten, and bulldozed over by my non-human colleagues.

The headmistresses didn't seem to care for me either. They were all also non-humans and would often play the blame the victim game. To them, I was unwanted, the symbol of repression that ruled over the world for so many centuries. They took their prejudice out on me. I was a child, I didn't understand why they were so mean. I thought they were supposed to be my guardians, but they were as bad as my bullies. I cried and wondered where my parents were and where I belonged. I never could find an answer.

Eventually, I got tired of it all. A child can only take so much. I developed a cold and distant attitude toward society, one that I harbor today. I ceased my attempts at fitting in. I didn't care for the other young ones, and I stopped yearning for the affection of the headmistresses.

I was never combative about it. I was simply apathetic. To me, they were nothing, but I wouldn't fuel their satisfaction by giving in to their taunts and threats. I remained defiant, standing up for what I believed. If a cub tried to bully me, I'd fight back, but I would never be the bully. If one of the headmistresses did something I thought was unjust, I would speak my mind. I was only no older than five, but I was mature enough to understand what it meant to hold your ground.

Looking back, I can't help but admire the person I was as a child. I was a lot stronger back then, a lot stronger than I am now. I answered to no one. I was my own person. The cruel realities of life had yet to affect me. In a way, that was the only time I was truly free. All of that changed when the Elephant Queen of Crime entered my life.

I had heard the hubbub all week from my peers and headmistresses. Someone of great importance was supposed to stop by, and we were to act our best. None of the young ones knew who she was, nor did we know of her reputation. But when the headmistresses got in a huge fuss about something, you damn well knew something was going down. We all dressed our best, but inside I didn't care. The others may have wanted to put on a show, but I wasn't going to.

The day came. All of the young ones lined up and the headmistresses greeted our guest with great enthusiasm. All the young ones murmured with excitement, and I have to say that even I was impressed when I got my first glimpse of Ms. Van Faye. Even back then, she had this swagger about her. She was larger than the rest of us, towering over with tremendous might. She had such extravagant taste in fashion. She shimmered because of all the fine jewelry that adorned her large frame. She wore shiny silks that looked expensive and had beautiful patterns woven into them. And she was surrounded by several guards. If her clothing and jewels didn't send the message of her importance, the large entourage certainly did.

We couldn't help but be eager to please. Many of the others immediately started to suck up. They complimented her while the headmistresses showered her with praise. We all knew she was here to adopt one of us, and many of the others were dying to leave the ranks of poverty. However, through all the compliments and applause, she looked unimpressed by everything.

I didn't give in. I was the only one who didn't put on a show for this elephant. Instead, I remained aloof and indifferent, much like I did for most of my childhood. I tried to hide in the shadows and be as dull and apathetic as possible. Ironically, that's what drew her to me.

Years later, she would tell me she chose me because she could see past the act. She said I had fire in my eyes, a desire to fight that I don't unleash enough. She noticed it had built inside me, and I was yearning to go a place where I could take out my frustrations on the world. She knew I had a warrior's heart, even though I didn't want to admit it. And despite her arrogance and obnoxiousness, she was surprisingly right. Who knew Ms. Van Faye could be so insightful?

Within a few days, I was gone from the orphanage and sent to live with Ms. Van Faye. It was then she told me why I was being adopted. Her bodyguard, Sai, recently had been killed. She needed a replacement, and that replacement would be me. I was only eight years old at the time.

Behind all the confidence and talk, Ms. Van Faye was distrustful of most creatures. She didn't want her life in the hands or paws of an animal that worked for her. Her reasoning is that grudges are built when you are the boss of someone, and in her line of work, it's so easy for convenient mistakes to happen. Thus, she needed someone new, someone she could build from

234

the ground up. She didn't care if it was a child putting their life on the line, she simply needed someone she could trust.

In the orphanage, I had a shadow of a childhood. Living under Ms. Van Faye, I had none. Right from the start, she trained me. It wasn't the fun, rewarding type either. It was the "kick them while they're down" kind of training.

I first learned the basics of hand-to-hand combat, cognitive development, and firearms. My schedule would revolve around weekly routine, based on the type of training I would go through during the day.

Hand-to-hand combat training meant mastering the basic forms followed by sparring sessions. These sessions weren't against enemies my age or my size. It would always be a variety. I had to master fighting with a tiger, a lion, even a rhino. Naturally, I'd get my ass whipped. These opponents were mostly Van Faye's thugs, and they had little remorse for a child. Their goal was to beat me, plain and simple. I got slashed, bucked, and bumped by all of them. It was more or less learning by exposure. Slowly but surely, I was able to defeat my foes, adjusting to their various body types and styles.

It sounds incredible, a little girl out muscling beasts. But I never outmuscled them. I adapted. I learned how to use my skills to strike when needed. It wasn't about being able to lift a tiger above my head, I could never do that as a child. Instead, I learned where their weaknesses were and hit them where it hurt. I'd either end fights in a few blows or face the consequences of missing. But I improved, and soon, they were the ones who feared me.

Ms. Van Faye was impressed with how quickly I was learning, though she didn't show it. She knew she made the right choice for Sai's replacement. She picked the girl with the spirit of fire.

Yet she was always so cold. Ms. Van Faye was nothing like a mother. She often put me down and verbally abused me. Whenever something upset her, whether it be business or under the influence of drugs, I would be her whipping girl. I was given this role for her amusement. She loved to belittle me. She excuses it as building character. A soldier can't be tough if she's so easy to break. To a certain point, I agree, yet how can you explain that to a child? I never received the love and care I should have. I was denied it.

Eventually, I trained with weapons and used virtual simulations to create obstacle courses that sharpened my agility and speed. I became an expert marksman. By the age of fifteen, I knew how to operate everything, from simple blasters to advanced weaponry like tunnelers and force guns. But my greatest weapon has always been the custom-made yari Van Faye supplied me. It's like an extension of my body. I use it to anticipate my opponents' attacks, and it's much cleaner than using a gun. Firearms can be unreliable. They run out of battery and their circuits can malfunction. The yari cannot. The energy infusion was the icing on the cake. It was just what I needed for those long-range occasions.

I also did exercises to hone my mental skills. Though I was never educated formally, the training I was put through made my mind sharp. It helped enhance my observational abilities. And Van Faye made sure I was schooled by the brightest her contacts could bring. She didn't want her bodyguard to be a dummy.

It was like this non-stop for years up until now. You'd be surprised how much a young person can master given the right amount of time and dedication. Plus, I was young, and my developing mind absorbed everything I was given. I'm only eighteen, but I feel like I've been a warrior for decades. All this practice is what has allowed me to be the proficient killer and guard I am today.

Of course, there's only so much the human body can do on its own. We are the physically weaker of the animal kingdom, and our intelligence isn't really an edge given our new competitors. Van Faye knew I had the attitude and mindset to become a feared killer, but she was always disappointed with the limits of my human body. She wanted me to be able to kill on an even playing field.

Sometime around the age of ten, I went through a secret Alliance operation known as the Implant Program. Long ago, there was a man who wanted to gift humans the same abilities other animals had. This program was the result of the Alliance harvesting this man's data. They were able to create implants, physical enhancements, to bestow upon their own soldiers.

Van Faye was given the gift to have one of her own go through the procedure. Naturally, she wanted the person safeguarding her life to get these upgrades. She always believed nothing was ever good enough. If I was to be the best, I had to go through with it.

I don't really remember the first time I got my implants. I was drugged up, so everything was hazy. But I do remember the pain. It was like someone took a knife, cut open so many parts of my body, and jammed a device inside. They were still in the process of perfecting things so they weren't concerned about being delicate with their patients. It's a pain that haunts me today. They've covered up the scars, but the mental ones are still there.

It was worth it, though. After my first set of implants, things changed. I had gotten the works— muscle, mental, and bone implants. They increased my strength, mental ability, and durability. It was like I gained super powers. Overnight, I went from struggling to lift a few hundred pounds to being able to lift a few tons. My speed increased. I could run faster, jump higher, move quicker. And my mental sharpness was unbelievable. I remembered things that I never knew I remembered before. I could see things coming at me in slow motion. Punches, bullets, everything—I saw it all.

Best of all, I was practically a rock. A few sparring sessions post implant procedure proved this. The opponents Van Faye threw at me were nothing. Their clawing and rushes were harmless. Blows that would cause me to bruise for days no longer did so. I was invincible.

Since then, I've gotten some more work done. A few years had passed, and Van Faye started to send me on missions. I was her assassin in addition to her bodyguard. I still preferred stealth, even with my gifts. The job is much cleaner that way.

When I needed to, though, I would plow through enemies. Sometimes I could take ten on at a time, killing each with swift blows and unrelenting power. My abilities gave me a boost in confidence. I was easily recognized as Ms. Van Faye's top enforcer. I no longer feared anything or anyone. The only exception was her.

I suppose a childhood of fear will do that to you. Ms. Van Faye was absolute terror to me, a child abuser that tormented me. Back then, I couldn't fight back against her. It would mean death. And even now, with all that I've learned and the gifts I've been given, I still can't fight back. She cripples my psyche. When I look at her, all I can think about is that she's my master and rebellion is futile.

The sad thing is, she still verbally puts me down. I can't go a day without being reminded of my lowly human status in Shogun. She pines for Sai and throws it in my face that I will never live up to his legacy. She wields her power mightily so I can see what she's capable of. Don't be fooled by her boisterous manner, Ms. Van Faye is as cruel as they come. I've been ordered to do things, horrible things, all in the name of business. I've killed pups and cubs, mothers and fathers who owe my boss. I've taken out mob dynasties and have been ordered to eradicate anyone, including the innocent. It breaks my heart and fills me with shame some of the things I've done. But if I let Ms. Van Faye down, I'd be dead.

It's all been for her, always for her. Her behavior lately has been questionable. It makes me wonder what happened to the confident boss I knew, the one that I've been so afraid of all these years. Why am I doing this?

I suppose a part of me does yearn for her approval. She's the only guardian I've ever known. Yet I see the irony. Most of my childhood, I needed no one's approval. Now, as I reach adulthood, I desperately want it.

That is why I do the things I do. That is why I'm here, in Sector Six, anticipating a foe that outclasses me. I don't care. I have to get this job done. I've never failed before, and I'm not going to start yet.

Do I wonder why fulfilling these tasks are important? All the time. Questioning is stupid. At this point, it's in my nature to kill. It's what I do best, and this time I will get the job done. One way or another, one of us will be dead.

Chapter 27 – Ivy Lawton

North

<u>September 27, 3071 10:13 AM</u>
Lucy and I are currently in the security wing of the lab, looking at the holoscreens intensely. We've been monitoring the crime syndicate construction crew over the past week and they continue to push into our territory.

Soon they will make contact, and that's when we have to end it. We can't hesitate. If they're able to find our location, and even worse, find out we exist, it could mean the end of us. The Alliance believes hybrids ended when HORUS did. They even think Mom and Lucy were incinerated by the bomb blast that covered their tracks.

We need to prevent leaks at all cost. It's not only the risk of discovery we're worried about, it's the collapse of our plans. Everything we've worked hard for will be gone. The dream that mother had, the dream where our species is free living among society, will be decimated. Every step matters along the way, and the same goes for eliminating every threat. It doesn't matter how small they are. Anyone and everyone is considered dangerous. There was a time when my mother didn't believe this, but a lifetime of unrelenting persecution has told her the truth. Destruction, hatred, and prejudice are simply the ways of the intelligent animal.

Lucy and I are discussing how we're going to handle our unwanted visitors. Luckily, Mom has given us the blueprints to our attack. Having a precog on our side certainly has its advantages. Now all we need to do is execute. We have our compcubes out and begin discussing defense strategies.

"According to Iris Lawton, construction crew makes contact to teleportation pod DZ at midnight," Lucy says.

"Yes," I say. "They've been digging for quite a while so it was inevitable. Mother's vision confirms this."

Lucy uses her compcube and a holoscreen pops up. On it is a graphical representation of our teleportation network as well as live maps of the intruders' tunnel system.

"Crime syndicate crew has dug almost one thousand feet underground," Lucy says. "Unsure what original intent is. Most likely digging to hold illegal contraband in tunnel network."

"It's too bad they've gone so low," I say. "If they had stayed at around five hundred feet and no deeper, we could have remained undetected."

"Agreed, but even at above height, still need to eradicate hostiles. Can't take risks."

I look at the monitor and see they're no more than a hundred feet away. Nearby is one of our outermost teleportation pods.

"There's no doubt they'll be hitting pod DZ," I say. "Mother told us that we must wait to attack, though. We can't initiate while they're still digging."

242

"Correct," Lucy says. "Dangerous to engage while crew is excavating. Tunnel unstable. Space is narrow. Fight will cause disturbance, tunnel might collapse on you and brutes. Engaging in pod much safer option. It is fortified. Also fighting in teleportation pod allows more space for you and brutes. Rate of success higher with such advantages."

I flash Lucy a smirk.

"Hey, if Mom has seen our victory, then I have nothing to worry about, right?" I joke.

"Does not work like that," she responds. "Future can alter if actions executed incorrectly."

"I know, I know. I'm just messing around."

"Do not see need for humorous dialogue at current moment."

My smirk turns into a look of ambivalence.

"You never do," I say. "Anyways, back to the plan. So the brutes and I will be waiting for the construction crew to make contact. According to mother, they'll hit the outer shell of pod DZ while they are excavating. There will be a few minutes of discussion and curiosity on their part, but these are hardened criminals. They're not going to overanalyze anything because their M.O. has always been shoot first, ask later. Same thing here. They won't waste time talking, they'll just blast through the outer shell and spill into the pod. That's when we attack."

"Correct," Lucy says. "Intruders may engage in conversation. Will not affect outcome. You may talk to criminals if needed."

"I'll try to keep it short. The less I know about them, the better. I just want to get it over with."

Lucy pops up another holoscreen. This one contains dossiers of my intended targets.

"Will need to know something about opponent," she says. "Using live feeds, have figured out identity of intruders."

Lucy pulls up mugshots of each of the individuals and displays them.

"All are former criminals," she explains. "Obtained images from Alliance crime database. Each are low-level grunts. Part of the Penghou Triad Group, operating out of southern areas of Fan Zui Bin. Known drug smugglers. Small group but expanding."

"So I guess we were right about why they're up in the Great North," I say.

"Correct. Total of eleven individuals on dig in team. Six pigs and five humans. As they approach, all work is done underground. Thus, when Ivy attacks, whole group will be eliminated. Will not have to worry about witnesses."

I take a look at the mug shots. The pigs are of different backgrounds. Some appear to be Australian pigs, some are spotted, all fat. The humans are also of different backgrounds. Some are African, some Asian, others Caucasian. Human or pig, they all look similar in personality, nothing but a bunch of brutish thugs. They appear hardened, each with their own signature tough guy expression. They'll probably be armed with some heavy-duty stuff, but it's nothing I can't handle. I'll mop them up with my telekinesis. I learned from the best.

"I'll handle them, no problem," I say.

"Will be easier, too, with backup," Lucy says.

She's talking about the brutes.

"I don't see why they need to come," I say. "I'm perfectly capable of handling this by myself. Their presence could endanger both them and me."

"Iris Lawton stated how critical they are there. Plan won't work without them," she responds. "Need to go over again why Lawton's visions must be executed exactly as seen?"

"No, we've done that plenty."

There's a bit of sarcasm and spite in my voice. I love my mom, more than anything, but sometimes I question the faith she has in her visions. She follows them religiously. I know she can see the future, but I don't agree with the path she chooses at times, especially when it concerns the brutes.

I know I shouldn't have grown attached to them. They're mistakes, prototypes, failed products of a process we hadn't perfected. They're not intelligent like Lucy or Mom or me. They're beasts, animals. They are the furthest representation of what we had all envisioned as the future of our species.

Yet I can't help but feel sympathy. They never asked to be born, we did that for them. How could we simply abandon something we created? The brutes may be monsters, mindless muscle masses of raw power, but they have gentle hearts. I can tell. Every day, I go to their holding pod and feed them. I watch them look at me with eager eyes, like I'm their mother. Well, I guess I am their mother. I give them food, clean them, take care of them. I suppose I treat them like my pets, but I'd be offended if someone told me so. That's an insult to the brutes. They aren't animals to be domesticated, they are simply creatures that need care. It doesn't matter if they're smart or not, they deserve to be treated like any other hybrid.

Sometimes Mom and Lucy have such cold attitudes. I don't understand, why they aren't like me. Why do they lack such compassion to the brutes? They had as much of a hand as I did in creating them. But Mom and Lucy can't get past their raw, animalistic nature. They see nothing but hulking hybrids, monsters that cannot be tamed. Their lack of intelligence screams liability.

That's why I'm so suspicious about this order. I see no tactical advantage of bringing the brutes along on this wipeout mission. Mom is usually extremely careful with tactics, and this seems like an obvious mistake. It makes me think her command has nothing to do with her visions, that it's simply a personal thing. What easier way to get rid of a problem than to send it away? Maybe she's hoping, rather she knows, the brutes will get caught in the crossfire. She was awful vague about why they needed to be there. Perhaps it's because she saw nothing.

No, my mother wouldn't do that. She has a thing against the brutes, but she knows how much I care for them. My mom loves me too much to break my heart like that.

"Remember instructions Iris Lawton told you?" Lucy says as she interrupts my thoughts. "Have gone over movements? How to defeat intruders?"

"Yes, and I'll go over it some more as the time approaches," I say.

"Good. Must follow instructions exactly. Also remember where to command brutes?"

"I remember. Don't worry so much, Lucy. I'll get the job done. I'll do exactly what Mom told me. We won't veer into another path."

"Have faith in you."

Lucy actually says it softly and flashes a small smile. I'm glad to know despite her callousness at times, she's still the mentor I grew up idolizing.

I must admit, our relationship has taken its share of hits since we started this splicing endeavor. She's pushed both of us hard, working long hours to perfect our process. When the brutes came along, I saw progress, but she saw failure. Perhaps that's another reason her tolerance for them is so small. While I have grown fond of them, to Lucy, they are the physical representation of when she failed.

I know Lucy strives for perfection, but that quest often shuts down the already complicated emotions she has. Yet when I see these flashes of compassion, it reminds me that she's come a long way over the past decade.

Lucy turns off the holoscreen. We have our plan ready and there's nothing else to discuss. I have some time to kill.

"I'm going to check on the brutes," I say. "I want to make sure they're ready for midnight."

"Excellent idea," Lucy says.

"I'll be back soon."

I exit the lab and make my way to the brutes' quarters. I enter the lab's teleportation pod and program the porter to my destination. The porter rings, a light flashes, and a second later, here I am. Once I exit, I traverse through a narrow corridor and at the end, a door opens.

The room is lighted, but as I look around, all my little fellows are sleeping. Not a single one of them is awake. They're normally up at this time, but I suppose it's been a long week.

When Mother told me the brutes would be involved in the attack on our intruders, I knew that meant their lives could be in danger. Thus, we've been training the past week to make sure they're offensively capable of taking out their enemies. They spent a lot of time in the training pod, a place they're normally not accustomed to.

The brutes aren't intelligent enough to operate weapons, so when we trained, it was all about sharpening their abilities to kill. We tried going through some exercises, some simulations where they were instructed to take out their rage on some test dummies.

That was asking a lot of them. They've never faced a hostile situation before. My brutes are kind creatures incapable of committing destruction on their own. When I commanded them to tear the dummies apart, they simply looked at me, dumbfounded, confused by my directions. They didn't know how to attack. It was too new of an idea.

That didn't faze me. I knew they had a killer instinct hidden inside them. It's the same one all animals possess when they are put to the edge. I had the training dummies switch to drone mode, ready to attack. Instead of waiting for the brutes to strike, they struck first. They fired warning shots that stung and irritated the brutes. At first, the brutes were a little scared, but each hit, each fire of these stingers made them more agitated.

Then, after a few minutes, the brutes could take no more. They lashed out on the dummies with fury, tearing them apart. One brute literally ripped the circuits of one of the dummies out and slammed them against the wall. I've never seen them like that before, and it scared me a little. I saw an animalistic power that was uncontrollable. I realized why my mother feared them. They were indeed the beasts she claimed they were.

But once the simulation was over and I deactivated the dummies, they were calm again. The rage they emanated was a flash, a quick burst of anger that subsided once there was no trigger. They returned to the gentle state I've been accustomed to.

Days after that, I did the same thing over and over. I wanted them to get used to stimuli that would trigger their berserker status, to get used to this routine. They needed to sense aggression so when we attack at midnight, they don't get blindsided. The last thing I want is for my precious brutes to be slaughtered before the fight even starts.

I can't tell what they're thinking about during all this or if they even have a clue about what lies ahead. They must know something is coming up with all the weird stuff I've been making them do, but their interaction with me doesn't hint at any of it. They look at me with the same happy, eager eyes. I'm not sure if I can look at them the same, considering the brutality they've displayed in the past week. I wonder how much more my opinion will change when I have to watch one of them tear off a poor sap's head in the heat of battle.

Yet still, they sleep so innocently, my little guys. They need a good rest for tonight. I came here to check on them, but I shall leave them alone until the time comes.

I turn around and start to leave when I hear one of them grumbling. It's Croc, the reptilian hybrid. He tosses and turns in his sleep, and I can only guess it's a nightmare.

I walk over to his cot. His blanket has been thrown on the ground, so I pick it up and drape it back over him. He's unruly, but he's still asleep, though it's a desperate struggle.

"Poor guy," I say. "There there, it's okay."

I calmly caress his face. He, like all the other brutes, is comprised from splicing humans with animals. Yet even though he's technically one of us, he looks malformed and distorted. The only thing I feel when I see his face is sympathy.

Am I worried about tonight? Of course. But my mom knows best. After my experiences with the brutes, I understand how difficult it is to be a mother. That is why I will follow my own through thick and thin.

"Rest well," I say to Croc. I then get back to my feet and exit the room.

Chapter 28 – Falena Snow

Defender

<u>September 27, 3071 4:11 PM</u>
He's been sitting there this whole time. I've been in my cabin this whole time. I've been staking him out, and he's been staking me. Neither of us has made a move, and I wonder if that's a good thing or a bad thing.

It's a curious tactic for him. He has the upper hand. I'm trapped in this cabin, surrounded by a field of bombs. I suppose I could make a diversion and set them off, thus creating a cloud of cover for my escape. But I doubt I'll get very far considering his relentlessness and tracking skills. Plus, other than a few grenades and my helmed cannon, I'd be out of weapons with nowhere to buy supplies. I have enough food and water for at least a week, so the best strategy is for me to hunker down.

I'm uneasy, though. Why is he taking his time? Surely he's plotting something. A trained soldier like that doesn't wait for rest. It's like a game of chess. He's figuring out his next moves as I figure out mine. And then battle commences.

I've been watching him with the surveillance feed I had set up. I can't zoom in completely, but I have a good idea of what he's been up to. He has a heater and has just been sitting there in front of it. He eats and checks on his gear once in a while. There's no strong tell that he's preparing anything large, no battle preparations that have been notable. I don't know if he's toying with me or if it's all part of some kind of elaborate plan.

The time is now a little past four, and he's been stationary for a little under twelve hours. What is he doing?

The anticipation is killing me. I just want to get this over with already. If it's time to die, it's time to die, but prolonging it is cruel.

And then I get my wish. He stands up and stretches a little bit. His mask and lightweight armor are still on, but he kneels down and ruffles through his gear. After a few seconds of searching, he pulls out a pistol. Then he turns around and walks right in my direction. Oh shit, it's on.

His stride is slow and calm. He doesn't look alert or cautioned. Instead, he simply marches forward in a straight line like a robot. I've never seen anyone so relaxed while facing certain danger. His confidence frightens me.

Even more alarming is his weapon of choice, a mere energy pistol. When I saw him during our first encounter, he had a host of weapons on him. There were shotguns, hand cannons, even what appeared to be a laser rocket. Yet he's coming at me so naked. I don't even see any explosives or tactical devices. No stun bombs, drones, or surveillance equipment. It's just him, his armor, and a small gun.

I don't have time to analyze it anymore. I need to get into my own battle station. The bombs I have set up should decimate him, but just in case, I have some spare grenades locked and loaded in my helmed cannon. The helmet itself is a new model that can directly read my brain patterns. Thus, I don't need to verbally command a shot, I can simply think it, and my weapon will go out blasting.

My surveillance equipment shows what's going on outside. The man edges the minefield, but then he stops. He knows something is up. I'm not that surprised. The soldier kneels down and surveys the land. He rubs his chin and thinks of what to do next. Looks like I've stalled him.

I'm wrong. He simply stands back up and continues to walk forward. My jaw drops. Surely he knows about the danger ahead of him.

It's more like he doesn't care. The second he goes into the danger zone, the bombs start going off. The booms echo throughout the entire forest. I can hear it both from inside the cabin and through the feeds. Clouds of dirt and dust fly into the air, obscuring my surveillance video. The few windows I have are hit with a blanket of grime, and that was just the first wave of bombs.

As the dirt clears, I quickly look back at my feeds to see what's left of him. And to my shock, horror, and disappointment, *everything* is left of him, everything. He's grimy and dusty, but other than that, he's unscathed. No blown limbs or cries for pain. He didn't even get knocked off his feet.

"Who the hell is this guy?" I say to myself. "Or what is this guy?"

I don't have much time to think about that because he hits the next wave of bombs. They light up the sky just as they did before. This time, the tree bombs go off too, blasting wood fragments left and right. Their base is weakened, and they rock back and forth, creaking before they collapse on their weight. The bombs boom loudly, and the thud of the falling trees creates even more commotion.

When they're done exploding, I see the same thing I did before. The man is left standing. He continues his slow stride through the front. The landscape is now decimated. All the grass is gone or on fire. The trees that were there have been leveled. Nothing is left; my cache of traps has been depleted. In a matter of seconds, this man has traversed through the mines that I so intricately set as if they were nothing. And now he's only a few feet from my door. It's locked and secured, made out of synthetic steel, but I have a feeling it won't hold him back.

I start to panic. My defenses have been obliterated, and I only have my helmed weapon and a few bombs to defend myself. The stranger is right at the front door. This guy is a trained soldier, I am not. There's no way I'm coming out of this alive.

A knock echoes from the front door. It's him. I don't move. I hear another one, and again I stand still, frozen with fear. The next one comes and it's much harder, much louder. Another hits, so hard I think I see a dent forming. When the next one comes, I don't even think it, I see it with my very eyes. The synthetic steal starts to become malformed, bending as another pound comes from the soldier. The man is seriously damaging my door, using his fists like a battering ram. The synthetic metal isn't lightweight stuff, it's supposed to withstand gunfire. As I see the damage being done to it with bare hands, I get more and more afraid.

Then it stops for a second. I shake uncontrollably, waiting for him to make his next move. I don't even know if I can fire my gun straight with all this fear.

"Hello?" I say cowardly. "Who is there?"

I'm greeted with a deafening crash. Right in front of my eyes, the door has fallen to the ground. The clang vibrates the entire cabin. As I look up behind the dust clouds, I see a silhouette of the man. He's knocked the door right off the hinges.

I don't think. I just start shooting. Shots barrel out of my helmed weapon, pummeling my pursuer with a hail of ammo. They hit him like a storm of ice smacking into the ground, rattling out of my gun at rapid fire. He makes no attempt to dodge anything. There's simply too much.

The gunfire pushes him back, and I see his limbs flail about as I continue my assault. I force him to step backward all the way to the door he knocked down earlier. There's so many energy bullets that the room becomes obscured with smoke and debris. It masks what I can see, and my pursuer becomes lost in the dust cloud.

I stop my assault. I wonder if there's anything left of him.

Of course I'm wrong. I see him rising from the dust as it clears. The black armor that hugs his body has no tears, no dents, nothing. It barely looks worn down. My assault has done nothing.

He continues his slow pace and walks through the grime that my gunfire has created. I slip backward until I'm pinned to the wall. Shit. I have nowhere to go.

I mentally command my helmed weapon to increase in caliber. I have to hit him with something harder. But if these don't do the job, then I have to consider another plan.

He's only a few feet from me, arms outstretched, ready to lunge.

That's when I fire.

A huge ball of energy spirals out of my helmed weapon and hits him directly in the stomach. He goes flying across the room, back toward the entrance, and lands with an enormous thud. His pistol separates from him, and dirt flies into the air when he collides onto the floor.

He quickly gets back to his feet, but miraculously, I've damaged him a little. There are some scratches and a small tear on the abdomen area of his armor. I have a lot of ammunition, so if I can keep this up, maybe I can wear him down. He no longer has his weapon. Not like that really mattered anyway, but that's still a plus for me.

I get another shot ready. He sees this and quickly picks up the metal door and props it up for cover. I'm a bit amazed by the feat of strength. The door itself is almost three hundred pounds, and he grabbed it like it was a piece of paper. Still, I focus on the task at hand. I'm not fazed by his makeshift shield.

The ball of energy propels out of my weapon and into the door. Astonishingly, he's able to brace himself for impact and the door barely moves. I grow a bit frustrated and blast another one. Once again, he's able to handle the impact.

The man counters by sticking his arm out from his covering. At first, I think he has a weapon, but as I take a closer glance, he has nothing. What is he going to do, punch me from across the room?

I speak too soon. I've been surprised many times during this battle, and it appears my opponent has another trick up his sleeve. Right before my eyes, his arm transforms. The armor that covers it peels back like an amorphous sludge, receding back into his flesh.

Once his arm is exposed, small parts arise from his skin, assembling together in microseconds. They meld and combine into some kind of object, and a few seconds later, when it's all done, a large cannon is mounted around his entire forearm. I guess I was wrong about disarming him.

Within a flash, a shot comes firing my way. It's even bigger than the heavy-duty ammo I was using earlier. I hastily jump, landing on my feet, but not before a small, smoking crater has been made on the cabin floor. Another one comes, and I duck under it as it flies past my head and smashes the wall behind me. It's kind of strange that he's missing from pointblank range, but I could care less. All I want to do is survive.

He comes out of his concealment and throws another round of ammo. I dodge once more, but I don't know how much longer I can keep this up. All this jumping around has made me tired. Eventually, I'm going to foul up.

I try one last desperation move. I have a high-duty explosive bomb in my helmed weapon. It's the strongest, most powerful thing I'm packing, enough to take out a building. I look straight at the man and pray for the best.

A small orb whizzes at him. He sees it and simply swats it away like a fly. Damn.

The bomb flies in the other direction and smashes into adjacent wall. Right at collision, it goes off. A giant flash blinds me and it's followed by an ear-deafening boom. Immediately, the force of the bomb sends both of us flying against the other wall. My legs flail into the air and my back slams into it, as does the man's. I land on my tail with a thud. I see nothing but dust.

Yet through the thickness of the debris, I see hope. A dim light shines, seeping into the cabin that has been wrecked by battle. It's sunlight and fresh air. The explosion has created an opening, a path to freedom. I thought I was trapped in this cabin, but now I see a way out.

I don't waste any time. My body may be bruised and battered, my legs may be sore as hell, but adrenaline courses through my veins. I hop to my feet and make a mad dash to freedom.

I can make it. I can make it!

I'm almost there when suddenly I feel a sharp pain coming from my tail. It stops me dead in my tracks, and I stumble, falling to the floor belly first. I get back up and churn my legs hard, but I end up only scraping at the floor. I don't move.

That's when I look behind me and see him holding on to my tail. I struggle all I want, but I can't get free.

The man then lifts me by the tail with one arm. My hind legs get raised off the ground, followed by my front legs. I dangle in the air like a sack of oranges, all of my weight being pulled by my tail. The pain is excruciating

I tilt my head to try to get a good look at the man, but his face is covered by a mask. Still, I stare right at him.

"So are you going to kill me?" I ask.

To my surprise, he shakes his head no.

"Then what do you want?" I ask.

His response is a punch to my abdomen. The blow knocks the wind out of me and I howl in pain. I heavily gasp for breaths of air.

The man tilts his head at me curiously, and I glance back. Then I am hit twice more. They feel like sledgehammers pounding into my body. I become weak as consciousness fades in and out.

I take one more look at him, and he looks at me. The last thing I see is his giant fist ramming into my eyes.

Chapter 29 – Mark Allen

Sector

September 27, 3071 11:17 PM

What a long workday. I've been up since this morning, at it non-stop. I'm should be used to this schedule already, but the hours can drain you. At least I get to have a nice, relaxing night in Sector Six's barracks. I haven't eaten all day, but I'm not that hungry. I'll probably just get a snack and head to sleep, ready to do it all over again tomorrow.

I've been busy the past few weeks, working on some modifications to the leg booster implants I created. Their compartmentalized implants are stored within the calf. When in use, they assemble and form rocket boosters that allow the user to fly. The current model is designed for top speeds and maximum air mobility. It was one of the first things I had installed on the Alphas, which seems so long ago. They used flight and were quite formidable because of it. It's a necessity for soldiers if they wish to maintain their versatility. I've been installing them into the subjects of the Implant Program for years and it's one of the more popular upgrades among the soldiers.

However, lately, there have been issues for some of our users. When I first created the prototypes, I had no problem applying them to lighter species such as cats, humans, and dogs. Booster implants were easy for them. The real challenge came from our larger users, mainly rhinos and elephants.

There haven't been many rhinos or elephants in the Implant Program, so I never created the boosters with their anatomy in mind. However, as the years passed and more and more subjects were coming in, the species set was getting increasingly varied. I modified my implants for the different physiologies I was working on, but some implants couldn't be applied so easily to certain types. Thus, the booster implants that I crafted for these larger species were hastily slapped together.

The rhinos and elephants can fly, but it's clunky and unreliable. Most are unwilling to use them, so it's essentially a wasted space in their body. That's why I've been tweaking it a bit so they can dependably fly through the air with the grace of a human or dog. It's my next minor project, and I'm just about finished with it. Then, flying elephants will essentially be flying tanks, thanks to their armor and firepower.

This is just one of the many projects my team and I have been working on. New ideas get formed and new creations are made. We've been picking up speed, constantly improving the implants we already have while focusing on the military aspects as Rox has instructed us to do. We're also not only limited to implants either. There are a slew of other projects that we've been working on. In fact, it's hard to keep track. Luckily, I have the memory implant in my head for easy access to information. I'd be lost without it.

That's also the reason I'm in this mess, though, isn't it? The Collector wants this data and has already killed two Alliance officials just to get to me.

It's after the GTS project. I'm actually a bit curious as to why the creature wants to know about that in particular. The project itself only made it to the blueprinting stage. We never got a working prototype because the head Alliance officials shut it down. They deemed it too dangerous. Projects like those get stopped all the time and become nothing more than a fading memory, a blip that's the afterbirth of rampant, reckless brainstorming. Hell, I never even analyzed its feasibility.

Then again, I can see why The Collector would want it. Though everything is theoretical, if a creature could get a working prototype, they'd have a very big card in their hand. The world could be taken at ransom. Yet, still, it's quite a longshot that they could create the device. They'd have a better chance at winning the lottery.

Perhaps The Collector is after something else. Rox's information could be wrong. Either way, he's taking every precaution to make sure the data in my head is protected. I've been under the watch of guards non-stop. When I'm in the lab, there's a guard. When I'm taking a break, there's a guard. Even when I'm using the bathroom, there's a guard. I feel like celebrity or world leader with all the attention I'm getting. Unwanted attention, but attention nonetheless.

It makes me nervous. Why do I need so many guards for one creature? I've seen what The Collector can do, and while it is impressive, all of this protection is overkill.

The only reason there's so many involved is because my life is in danger. I've come close to death before, back at HORUS. I don't want to come so close ever again.

I asked General Rox if it's the information the creature wants, why keep it inside my head? Why not extract it somewhere else, away from me? Rox stated flat out, it doesn't matter where the data is. One way or another, my life would be at risk. If I didn't have the data, The Collector would force me to reveal where it is. Eli Winde didn't have the information it was looking for, and he ended up dead anyway. The same would happen to me.

Thus, the logical thing to do is to keep it centralized in a place where General Rox has control. Sector Six is that place, and until this matter is resolved, I am a prisoner here. This schedule reminds me of my time at Arkady. I'd work and afterwards, I was sent to a prison pod to rest. The only difference here is I have the barracks to stay in. My freedom has been stripped. I can't go back to my loft because of the risk involved. Rox has told me it's already been breached, that The Collector has already infiltrated it. Unfortunately, the only place I am safe is within the armed walls of Sector Six.

With a cadre of soldiers escorting me, I've made it from the lab into the barracks. Once I enter, the guards leave. It's just me in this room. I suppose I'm fortunate that I'm granted a small level of privacy during these times.

The barracks themselves have two entry points, one in the west, which I call the front, and another on the east side, which I call the back. There are guards stationed at both ends. The front end is fortified by a team comprised of various species—tigers, lions, crocs, and others that were handpicked by Rox to keep me safe. I believe only a few have implants. Perhaps Rox is using this as an interview of sorts, to see which guard is suitable for an upgrade.

The back end is secured by ten human soldiers, a more elite team than the front. All of them have implants installed in one form or another. Though they are Alliance bred, they are led by Ash Han, Two Van Faye's personal bodyguard. I met her earlier. She is surprisingly nice and shockingly attractive. It makes me wonder how such a beauty could get tangled in the seedy crime world of Fan Zui Bin.

I'm also aware of the work that's been done on her. Two Van Faye has installed a boatload of my own designs within her bodyguard's body. Ash Han should be extremely durable and well equipped to engage in the art of killing.

Overall, the barracks are probably the most safeguarded area in Sector Six thanks to all of Rox's precautions. The location and setup of the lot makes it ideal for defense. I feel slightly safer here than I do in other areas of Sector Six.

I head over to the kitchen area and fix myself something to eat. I'm not really a chef, and there's not much to work with, so some noodles will be that for me. I pop it in the insta-cooker, and a second later I have some hot soup. The broth is boiling and the noodles are salty. There's a hint of ginger in it too. It's actually the perfect meal after a long day of work in the lab.

As I eat my noodles, I take a look around. It's nothing like my loft, which is nice and cozy. The barracks in Sector Six have more of a warehouse feel. There are no windows or natural sunlight because everything is contained underground. It's not freezing, but the temperature is moderately cool. I normally like my place to be a little warmer, as my skin is sensitive to colder weather, but the Alliance could care less.

Everything is also out and open. There are no walls separating the different rooms. The beds are next to the dining area. They're all doubles, and they're all bunks. They range in size to fit various species, but there are a large number of human beds. This room has the capacity to hold at least fifty scientists or soldiers, but it's been cleared out just for me.

The bathroom and showers is the only area that has walls for privacy. There's a small, holographic projector that's capable of playing streams, games, and movies, but that's about it for entertainment. Nothing is on right now. The only noise is the sound of me slurping my noodles.

I must say I miss my loft. Being in this large, warehouse-like building is quite lonely. The guards outside don't talk to me or interact with me, they're simply there to protect me. I suppose they have to remain focused, but still, their attitude is unfriendly. They might as well have drones guarding me.

Their behavior also does little to calm my nerves. In fact, it exasperates me. I feel like these soldiers are expecting something big and that my life can be in danger at any moment. It's not a good feeling. Being here by myself only makes things worse. I wish things weren't so quiet.

Suddenly, I hear a thud coming from the front hallway. I become startled by it and get to my feet. The first thud is followed by another one, in which I can hear a faint yelp.

Three more thumps are heard ahead. I hear a howl, a shriek, and a roar echo through the walls. A door separates the hallway from the barracks, so all I can do is imagine what's going on from the other side. A desperate struggle is going on, and there's only one culprit I can think of: The Collector.

The creature has telekinesis, so I imagine the thuds are soldiers getting thrown into the walls or maybe debris colliding into them. The chaos I hear is the soundtrack for my imagination. I hear some crunching, and it sounds exactly like the creature tearing apart the hallway. I've seen it do it before. The foundations and the walls were ripped open with the creature's mind.

A crash is heard, followed by a bark. I know The Collector enjoys using debris as weapons, so I can picture it slamming into one of the dogs that was guarding me. I hear a roar, which must belong to a tiger or a lion, but it's quickly silenced. I'm pretty sure that guard is dead now.

Finally, the guns go off. I hear the ammo firing, hitting walls and hopefully hitting The Collector. I even hear a large explosion. But as the seconds pass, the gunfire becomes less and less. I thought I heard five shots going off simultaneously, then four, then three, until there's only one. And then that one ceases. No noise comes through the other side of the door. Things are silent once again.

My imagination goes wild with what has occurred on the other side. I see the images in my head. Walls obliterated, bodies strewn, blood everywhere, and The Collector standing above it all.

I'm too scared to approach the door. I sit at the table, shaking and sweating, fearful of what's coming up. My anxiety reaches new heights.

"Are you there!?" I scream.

I'm answered with a giant explosion. Debris flies my way and I swiftly fall from the table and on my ass.

Things become hazy and I quickly scramble to my feet, but the dust blocks my view. I wave my arms, trying to clear the air of grime. As it settles, I see two objects in the distance. One is the door. It blew completely off and lies on the ground.

The other is something I don't recognize. It's darkened and mangled, almost unrecognizable. But I take a closer look and realize what it is. It's a body, a dog, one of my guards. He's not moving and looks battle torn. I think he's dead.

A third object comes to me, this time floating in the air. The cloud of dust has completely settled and from it I see what approaches. It's a creature, bipedal, donning a large black cloak. I recognize everything— the armor, the power, the aura of death. The Collector has just entered the barracks.

I stand there frozen. Is this my time to die? Do I dare fight back?

I don't have to. Right on cue comes the guards from the rear hallway. All ten of them line up in a row, their high-caliber energy cannons pointed at The Collector. They're ready to go. The creature, however, pays no attention to them.

From behind the guards emerges Van Faye's bodyguard, Ash Han. Unlike the other men, who look petrified, she looks at The Collector with little fear in her eyes.

"Mark Allen," she says to me. "Find some cover. We'll take care of this."

I quickly dash to a nearby table and hide under it. The Collector barely notices. Her focus is aimed directly at Ash Han.

The battle for my soul is about to begin.

Chapter 30 – Ash Han

Elimination

September 27, 3071 11:22 PM

With ten humans to my left and right, we stand afraid, anxious, and ready to take down our opponent. I'm eye to eye with The Collector for the third time. Hopefully, this one is a charm.

The Collector hovers in the air, looking down on all of us. We have our weapons pointed at the creature. Some soldiers are literally shaking. I've briefed this team on what to expect. I described the telekinesis and the instantaneous reflexes. I told them about the creature's natural intuition to know the attacks coming its way. When I gave them the information, I saw each soldier encased with anxiety and nervousness. I shouldn't have said anything. They're not focused anymore. All they can think about is how they'll get crushed and impaled by The Collector.

Neither side makes a move. I want to tell our men to start their assault, that no time is to be wasted, but I know I can't command anything right now. Even I, with my yari in my hand, ready to strike, refrain from making any sudden movements. None of us are willing to attack first.

Well, almost none of us. An errant shot comes out from one of our teammates and flies past The Collector. The creature instinctively dodges it and, while in the air, controls a nearby chair and lobs it toward the shooter. The whole team starts to scatter in different directions, looking for cover. We were supposed to stay together, as one unit, but now, with a single careless mistake, we're broken. How is it that I, the supposed criminal, am the only one who's composed?

It's somewhat of a blessing in disguise. We're spread apart in such a fashion that The Collector is surrounded by us. Half of the soldiers are to the left of the creature and the other half are to the right of it. I stand in front.

I see a guard to my left holding something in its hand. The soldier grips it firmly and concentrates on the creature. The object is a grenade.

"No explosives!" I yell.

I've seen it telekinetically catch grenades, and I don't want the creature using our own weapons against us. Yet, of course, they ignore me. They don't listen to my commands because of my status as a crime lord's assassin. Still, I'm the only one who has seen The Collector in action. Idiots.

The grenade flies from his hand toward The Collector, but it doesn't travel far enough and lands at the creature's feet. Once I see what kind of grenade it is, I understand why. A thick smoke flows out of the bomb. It's not a simple screen, it's a mellyst cloud. It's so dense that you need special goggles to see through it, ones they all have but ones I don't. They really screwed me out of equipment. Freaking Alliance assholes.

I know it's useless, though. A valiant attempt, but don't these yahoos know who they are dealing with? I feel a strong gust of wind brushing my cheeks and see the cloud swirling. The force picks up and soon, the smoke from the bomb starts to form a concentrated whirlwind. Any bits of the cloud get vacuumed in, and soon enough, it's completely caught in a tornado. The cyclone of force the cloud is in causes it to dissipate in the air, removing any cover it provided. Within seconds, the room is clear and the soldiers' plans to hide have been thrown out the window. I warned them that such tactics won't work against The Collector.

And other tactics would definitely backfire!

"These assholes won't listen to me," I say to myself.

I'm furious. Not at the failed mellyst cloud, but because one of the soldiers to my right has a high-impact incendiary grenade in his hand. I told them nothing heavy duty! Didn't they see how easily The Collector disposed of the cloud? This is just asking for trouble.

"Stop, you idiot!" I scream.

Too late. He cocks his arm back and launches the grenade forward. His aim is off, but the homing sensor locks onto The Collector and hurls toward the floating creature. I'm a bit surprised at how fast it travels. Perhaps The Collector isn't fast enough to telekinetically stop it.

I'm wrong. I'm always wrong. It looks like it's going to hit, but right before it does, it stops in mid-air and in front of The Collector. The creature has its palms outstretched, holding it in place, stationary. The creature is predictable but skilled.

The Collector tilts its head in the direction of the soldier who threw the grenade at it. His eyes are wide and his lip trembles. He drops his gun and can only stand there. Other than the shaking of his legs, he's motionless. He knows it's the end, as does The Collector.

With a flick of the wrist, the bomb soars back to its sender. All the poor sap can do is scream. The grenade explodes, sending a ball of fire into the air. Flames quickly envelope both the soldier and the unfortunate soul next to him. They howl ear-shattering screams as the flames crackle and pop their skin. The heat is so intense that I think I see their armor melting. Only seconds after the explosion, the struggle is over. They no longer roll on the ground frantically, helplessly. They remain limp. The shrieks that come from their mouths stop. They're dead. In a flash, they've gone from living to simply two burnt bodies on the ground.

Two of the soldiers are dead. Eight remain.

The explosion does have a benefit. It creates enough of a diversion so everyone is distracted, even The Collector... I think. Only one way to find out.

I take the gun that's firmly placed to the right side of my waist out of the holster and quickly aim it at The Collector's head. I'm fairly close, and my gun skills are as good as my yari skills. I'm using a heavier duty hand cannon, so with one good hit, the creature's head will be blown clear off. It'll be easy peasy.

But nothing is so simple with The Collector. There's a soldier to my left. Right before I'm about to fire, The Collector lifts the ground under this soldier's feet. It causes him to fall and stumble right into my line of fire. Things happen so fast and I'm so focused on The Collector that I don't see him coming.

I pull the trigger. As the energy shot flies out, it hits someone's head, but not The Collector's. It pierces the poor soldier who got in my way. At pointblank range, I see his cranium explode into a million pieces. It pops like a balloon that's filled with blood and brains. Some splash on me, some bits fly in other directions. The second after it happens, his headless body slumps to the floor.

Seven left.

I've seen a lot of things in my career as Van Faye's bodyguard, but that was pretty gruesome. Quite frankly, I'm pretty shaken, not because I killed someone, but because his head literally exploded right in front of my face. I replay it in my mind in slow motion. Parts of him are still on my face.

That's why I don't notice two of the soldiers sneaking up from behind The Collector. I really don't know what they're trying to do. They have their guns out, but didn't they just see what happened to the last guy? They're also at pointblank range. Why don't they just shoot? And besides, if they're that close to The Collector, I'm pretty sure the creature knows they're nearby. That's the problem with these guys. They don't know enough about the enemy, and when I told them, they refused to listen. It's because they've never faced one like The Collector before.

I notice another thing about these two soldiers. There are small objects behind them. They don't notice it, as the objects are small and discreet. But they're also long and pointy. I recognize them immediately. It's the spears.

These two poor saps don't have a chance. The spears plunge into their backs with so much force that they easily pierce through the body armor they wear. The needle-like daggers struggle through their flesh, meeting some resistance as they pry through their chests. But after some effort, the pointed ends burst through the front of their torso, completely impaling them. They hit the floor like a bag of bricks.

The Collector is systematically eliminating this team, and it's barely moved a muscle. Only five soldiers remain.

I take a quick glance at Mark Allen. He's crouched under a table, shaking hysterically, panting for breath. His eyes are wide and bloodshot. He's so paralyzed with fear that I'm not sure he even comprehends what's going on.

Yet, on the plus side, he's safe. The Collector hasn't made an attempt on him yet, and I'll be ready once the creature swoops in. Things don't look too good, though, considering the team is getting decimated.

After the success of The Collector's last two kills, the creature has decided to go back to its bread and butter. The spears come out and hover in the air. The soldiers look at them in amazement. I, on the other hand, only see death. I know what happens next.

It doesn't matter what I say at this point, these soldiers are on their own. I grip my yari hard and get ready for what comes ahead.

It starts raining spears. I use my yari to swat them away like I've done so many times before. The other soldiers are not so lucky. The whole lot of them desperately run for cover. Some jump under tables others lunge beneath the beds. Mark Allen ducks his head and remains under his cover but balls up like a baby. As long as they take shelter, they'll be safe from the chaos.

However, two of the soldiers are not so fortunate. As they attempt their dash to safety, they are quickly brought down by The Collector's weapons. Five or six spears plunge into both of their backs. They're killed instantly.

With the spears stuck on the ground, the soldiers see a small window to attack. They quickly emerge from their cover, raise their guns, and start firing. The Collector quickly drops from the air to avoid getting shot and runs toward one of the tables that was overturned from the initial explosion. The creature jumps over it and hides. It's a bit charred but still strong enough to stop the soldiers' blasts.

Two of the soldiers close in. If they concentrate their gunfire enough, the table will be turned to shreds and they can blast away The Collector. However, as they get closer, the table starts to rumble. At first, I think it's shaking from all the impact it takes, but then I realize what it is.

Oh shit, they need to get out of the way.

Too late. The table rockets forward, colliding directly into the two men. It travels across the room at what looks like fifty miles an hour while bulldozing the poor saps. Then it collides into the adjacent wall, essentially pinning the two soldiers caught in its path. A large crash bursts from the collision. Then, silence. All I see is a limp, motionless arm from beyond the table. I'm certain they're dead.

Only one soldier remains. Perhaps he and I can rally forward and take down The Collector.

Or not.

"Fuck this," I hear the soldier say as he runs toward the exit.

The Collector sees him fleeing, lifts up a spear with its mind, and makes short work of him. I simply hear a thud and see him fall lifeless.

It's only me that stands between The Collector and Mark Allen.

"Are you sure you want to do this again?" it says. "The odds have been against you in our last two encounters."

"I have no choice," I say. "I must do as my master commands."

"Then perhaps you need a new master."

I ignore its comments and rush straight toward the creature, yari in hand. The blades come from the creature's gauntlets and it gets ready.

I launch a quick swing overhead, but The Collector blocks it. Thus, I use the handle end of the yari and thrust it forward, knocking the creature in the chest. The being stumbles backward, and I advance with a kick to the stomach, which surprisingly connects. The Collector almost falls backward but catches itself at the last second.

I continue my advance and swing the energy bladed end at the creature's head. I'm hoping it decapitates the creature, but The Collector ducks under it and lunges its right blade toward my stomach. I quickly spin to my left and it narrowly misses impaling me. When I return from rotation, I hit the creature on the back of the head with my handle. It loses balance and clumsily falls forward.

The Collector continues to go headfirst, but it uses the momentum and runs along with it. Now it's going at a full sprint ahead. At first I think the creature is retreating, but then I see where its path is taking it. Right to Mark Allen, who still hides under the table. Shit, I forgot what this mission was all about.

I charge my yari and a ball of energy forms at the tip. I point it at The Collector, whose back is turned to me.

"Dodge this, asshole," I say.

The shot fires and travels to The Collector and connects before the creature reaches Mark Allen. However, The Collector jumps in the air and it hits nothing but ground. Still, I'm happy with the execution, as Mark Allen has narrowly escaped death.

Once in the air, The Collector stays there for a bit. I start to arm another shot, so in response, The Collector jets in my direction. The creature extends its leg and hones in on me with a flying kick.

As the kick is about to connect, I counter by grabbing it in the air and pulling on it toward the ground, hard. The Collector slams down chest first, landing with a thud, and I follow up with a ground stomp. The creature recovers in the nick of time and rolls out of the way of my boot. It then swings at my leg with its gauntlet.

I'm able to react quickly enough and barely dodge the blade. It still hits my armor, though, grazing it and leaving a scratch. I'm fortunate that's it and that my leg wasn't dismembered.

The Collector is still on the ground, so I thrust my yari downward. It's just as ineffective as my boot, as The Collector easily rolls out of the way, and all my yari does is cause a small dent to the floor.

That was part of the plan, though. My power shot is still armed, so while the energized tip is buried into the floor, I fire. The shot is encased by solid ground, and the impact causes a large burst, like a grenade. Pieces of dirt fly at The Collector, temporarily blinding it. I braced for impact, so the small explosion does me no harm.

The Collector gets to its feet and stumbles a bit. It's still stunned from the yari shot. Now is the opening I am looking for. With one mighty charge, I thrust my yari forward. I can see the creature getting impaled in my mind.

Reality sets in. The Collector swings its arm, and the blade from its gauntlet swats my weapon so forcefully that it flies out of my hand and across the room. I'm doomed, completely unarmed other than the pathetic energy blaster I have in my holster. On the other hand, The Collector still has its gauntlet and its spears.

"I've lost," I say.

"Indeed you have," The Collector says. "But you were impressive. Not many can say they fought with me as an equal."

"So are you going to kill me now?"

"What makes you think I'm going to do that?"

"Well, it's the only thing left to do."

The Collector starts shaking its head.

"I wasn't trying to kill you. If I were, you'd be dead right now. No, I was testing you," it says.

"Testing me?" I'm flabbergasted. "For what?"

"You'll see in due time. I can assure you, though, killing you has never been an option. I've only come for my bounty."

"Bounty?"

Without even looking at him, the creature raises its gauntlet and points it at Mark Allen. Before I can even react, I hear a spurt come from it and watch the blade detach from the gauntlet and career at the Allen, right at his neck.

My eyes see where it's going. Mark Allen can only watch the blade coming his way. I try mightily to do something, but it's useless. The only thing I can do is blink. When my eyes reopen, I see the blade slice through his neck, cleanly, like sword. I blink again, and when my eyes open, his head has been decapitated from his body. The blade sticks onto the wall.

The head and body lie on the floor. The Collector then throws a small device and it latches onto Mark Allen's head. A bright flash emits from it upon contact and when the light disappears, so does Mark Allen's head.

"Bounty collected," The Collector says.

I'm too shocked to utter a response.

"Think about what I told you," it says. "This won't be our last meeting."

The creature then lifts its wrist and presses some buttons. The same bright flash that engulfed Mark Allen's head forms behind The Collector.

"You can keep the blade," The Collector says, referring to the one that's stuck on the wall. "Think of it as a souvenir."

And with those words, The Collector gets engulfed in the light as well. A second later, it's completely gone.

I look around at all the bodies that surround me. Countless soldiers are dead on the ground, impaled, exploded, and shot in the head. Mark Allen, the man I was supposed to protect, is dead. We didn't have a chance.

I'm overcome with the death and destruction that fills this room, but then a more sobering realization comes to my mind. I have failed Van Faye's request miserably. Not only that, I have failed the Alliance.

They don't take too kindly to this stuff. It's a trickle effect. They'll punish her, and I will endure the brunt of the blame.

I don't know what to do at this point. Do I dare go back to the Benjamin Plaza Hotel and deliver the bad news to my boss? Should I just leave? Where should I go?

I'm confused and scared. All I know is that I need to get away from here. With once last glance, I make my way to the exit of Sector Six.

Chapter 31 – Iris Lawton

Necessities

September 27, 3071 11:40 PM

"The deed is done," I say to Lucy on my communicator's holoscreen.

I try to keep my voice low. I've teleported far away from Sector Six, but I don't like talking out in the open. I suppose it's paranoia, since I don't know what world surveillance the Alliance has. I'm also a bit antsy because my mask is off. I had to take it off. I felt stuffed in there, and the only cure for that is some fresh air.

I'm perched on a boulder in some remote outskirts in the Wolf's Den. It's a forested area with lots of high trees and woods, and it's far away from any signs of civilization. The time zones match up, so it's still nighttime here, and the blue-and-green glare of the moon shines on me brightly. Somewhere up there Lucy and my daughter hide underground. And I can be with them in a few seconds. That's crazy.

I use this spot in the Wolf's Den as a rally point. Anytime I find myself in danger and in need of teleporting to a remote location, this is the spot I go to. There's no one here, no buildings, not even a cabin. Technology doesn't exist. It's as far away as I can be from my plans, my visions, the necessary evil I must do. It's my personal sanctuary for when I need to clear my head. When the stakes are high and I question every second if I'm doing the right thing, I need a place like this more than ever.

I sit here catching my breath, exhausted from all the combat, all the telekinesis, all the killing. The battle was tough, not physically, but mentally. I just ended more than twenty lives without batting an eye. My righteous side tells me I shouldn't feel guilty. They were Alliance scum and they all deserved it. The logical side of me tells me this is part of the plan. My visions told me they had to die if I was to obtain the GTS. Their deaths were justified. I need to continue with the future I see. If I don't, this whole dream of living free will be gone. It's them or my hybrids, and I will always choose my kind.

There is one side that protests, though—my conscience. I've walked down a dark path from which I cannot return. I have made sacrifices and done reprehensible things all in the name of freedom. Have I grown too powerful for my own good? Some would argue that there is no such thing as having too much power. I hope I'm not like them.

Things may change, though. I used to think people like that were bad. I knew one. He was my brother, Tiago, a hybrid who always believed the ends justified the means. He sacrificed my brothers and sisters because he thought it was for the greater good. When I found out what he did, I hated him. I was angry. My memories of him were clouded by what he did. I didn't see a brother, I saw someone evil.

Yet as I look at myself, I wonder if I've become the same thing. I've tried to rationalize all the bad things I've done in the name of survival. I spin my actions, knowing it is for the future of my species. I also have deflected blame on the Alliance. If they would just let us exist, none of this would happen. My kind wouldn't have to go to war simply to live. They backed us into a corner.

At least that's what I tell myself. With every kill I make, every blow I strike, every spear I impale someone with, I go further down that dark path. And that's when I realize I'm becoming just like the brother I hated so much.

Sometimes I try to think that the clear difference between him and I is that I would never sacrifice the ones I love. I'd rather die than do that. Perhaps my view is skewed, though. Maybe he never loved the brothers and sisters he threw under the bus. He had genuine affection for the ones he cared about, like Alex and Ace. In his mind, he was like me, protecting those who mattered. Now I suppose things have come full circle with me. I won't admit it, but part of me has become like him.

Fighting for survival isn't easy. Eventually, your morals will always go against what needs to be done to stay alive.

It's too late to go back.

"Did you receive the package?" I ask Lucy.

"Yes," she responds. "Mark Allen's head currently in lab."

"Can you get what we need?"

"In time, yes. Have extracting application running and doing records scan on implants within brain. Information housed there. Once download completed, will look through to find data linked to GTS. Confident schematics reside. Will then analyze info and present findings to Iris Lawton."

As usual, Lucy never fails.

"Excellent," I say. "Gather as much as you can. The next phase hinges on the GTS."

"Understood," she says.

There's a brief pause in our conversation as the gravity of our deeds dawn upon us. I quickly shift gears and move on to the next subject.

"How is Ivy?" I ask Lucy.

"Appears fine," she says.

"Where is she right now?"

"With brutes, planning for attack."

"So she is bringing the brutes with her."

Lucy flashes me a curious look.

"Why surprised?" Lucy asks. "Ivy always follows instruction."

"I know," I say. "Ivy has never let me down, but in this case, I was almost expecting her to rebel. I read it on her face when I gave the order. She didn't want the brutes to come with her. Then again, I knew she wouldn't because she didn't go against my orders in my vision."

"Is understandable. Ivy has connection to brutes. But cannot ignore fact that brutes are liability and drain resources. Served purpose as prototype, but now must show new purpose."

We both know what she means.

"Lucy, I've told you what happens to Ivy and the brutes," I say. "Is what I'm doing the right thing?"

"Necessary to overall plan," she says. "One step of many. Futures only play out if acted accordingly. Thus, it is correct action."

"That's not what I meant."

She looks at me, trying to gauge what I'm thinking.

"Asking whether right in terms of morals and ethics?" she says.

"Yes," I respond. "Is this the right thing?"

Lucy pauses. She looks like she's deep in thought, solving a difficult equation where she has an idea of an answer but can't explain it.

"Have never understood morals," Lucy says. "Morals created for altruism, greater good, but always prevent true greater good. Iris Lawton is upset, worried about doing wrong thing. Yet doing wrong thing is actually right. Will help us complete goals that will benefit species. Doing right thing, moral thing, only hinders. Thus, to me, there is no right or wrong. There is only what is beneficial, not to individual, but to us all."

Never have I heard Lucy speak so eloquently. Still, I am unsure of her reasoning.

"I know what you're saying, but sometimes there's more to it than what is the rational choice," I say. "There's this voice inside my head that makes me feel guilt. I've done a lot to get to this point, and many of those things I'm not too proud of."

"Should be," Lucy says. "Without such actions, would never gotten this far. In the end, goal will be realized and sacrifices will prove worthy."

"I don't know sometimes."

The stress from the past few days has left me in a fragile state of mind. Everything comes back to me, not only my recent deeds, but also things that happened long ago. All the people I've killed: Alliance soldiers, Shogun bodyguards, Fang, Fenrir, even Bastion. I remember each hit so clearly. And when I remember, I feel faint remorse.

Lucy senses my doubt.

"Cannot go back now," she says.

I look at her and let out an ambivalent sigh.

"I know, Lucy, I know," I say.

Another long pause comes, this one is more of an awkward silence. Lucy senses the guilt in my words, but these things have always confused her. It's not her fault. It's just the way she is. I know she wants to comfort me, but she simply doesn't know how.

"Coming home now?" she asks, breaking the reprieve in our conversation.

"Not yet," I say.

She looks genuinely confused.

"Thought all actions completed," she says. "Nothing left to do."

"There's still one more person left to deal with," I say. "And this one I feel no guilt for."

She jogs through the possibilities in her mind. Within a few seconds, she knows who.

"Two Van Faye," she says.

"Yes," I say. "I need to meet with the Elephant Queen of Crime one last time."

"Don't believe this visit necessary."

"It is. I've seen it in a vision. And I must say, I'm looking forward to coming face to face with that treacherous waste of mass one last time. She's the one creature I truly believe that deserves to get what's coming to her."

Lucy is about to speak but has some hesitation. She looks concerned.

"Risk unnecessary," she says. "Still have Ash Han to deal with. So far, human has demonstrated she is capable in combat."

"Don't worry," I say. "My vision has shown me how to deal with her too. This risk is necessary. There's much to be gained in this confrontation."

Lucy looks at me skeptically.

"Real gain or personal gain?" she asks.

"What do you mean?" I say in a perplexed manner.

"Do not see any reason for confrontation. Only conclusion is Van Faye visit resolves personal feud. So far, all targets part of Iris Lawton's vendetta, but also have obtained physical resources. Winde and Mark Allen gave leads to GTS. Van Faye offers nothing for cause, only opportunity to punish betrayal to Iris Lawton."

"I'm going to have to disagree. Van Faye is working with the Alliance. I need to cut off all these loose ends."

"Ties with Alliance most likely severed after failure to kill you. Again I state nothing to be gained."

"Well, I guess we'll have to agree to disagree."

We look at each other uncomfortably. We don't say anything to each other for a good minute.

"I have to go get ready," I say to Lucy. "I will check back in to see how things went with Ivy. Take care of her, okay?"

"Will do," Lucy says. "Take care of self."

Chapter 32 – Ivy Lawton

Rage

<u>September 28, 3071 12:06 AM</u>

It's a little past midnight. The excavators should be arriving any minute now. The brutes and I are hiding behind some command consoles near the wall. We patiently wait for those thugs to break through so we can end this.

Until then, I check in with Lucy through my communicator.

"I think the targets are a little late," I say skeptically.

"Should arrive soon," Lucy says. "Are you and brutes prepared?"

"Yes, but I still don't see why we need them here. I can take care of these bozos on my own."

"Iris Lawton has instructed so. Must follow accordingly."

"Fine."

I look over to my brutes to make sure they're okay. The ten of them all have different expressions on their faces. They can't talk, but they don't have to. I can read what they're saying.

Most of them look rather afraid. The cat hybrids, Carrie and Carl, appear anxious. The tiger hybrids, Terry, Tuner, and Tonga, are curious yet also confused as to why they are there. The reptilian and elephant brutes, Croc and Elle, are wide-eyed, unsure of what awaits them in the next minutes. The lion hybrids tend to be the braver ones, and even they are apprehensive. Overall, they just don't understand why they're here and what they've been tasked to do. But I know my brutes well. Once the attacks start, their animalistic instincts will kick in, and they'll be a force to be reckoned with.

At least I hope so.

The thugs are close. The group has tunneled their way and now stand beyond the outer wall. I can hear them talking.

"What the hell is this thing?" one asks.

"Looks like it's a wall to something," another says.

"I wonder what's behind it," a third one says.

"Maybe we should find out," says someone else.

I wish I could tear them apart right now or make their tunnel collapse on them. They'd be wiped out in a single stroke. Unfortunately, though, I don't know if all of them are there. I know there are eleven intruders total, but if I don't kill them all at once and one of them escapes, our secret is exposed.

"It's probably a storage unit. Let's break the wall down to see what's inside," says one more.

"Yeah, get the laser cutter," one of them suggests.

I hear some rummaging and murmuring.

"Okay, it's ready," the initial voice says. "Cut it open."

A sharp crack echoes throughout the pod. Right after, a bright-orange dot appears on the wall where the intruders hide behind. The orange glow expands into a bright dot of light. The synthesized metal quickly begins to melt where the glow is. The dot then starts to move in the pattern of a circle, carving a nice line through the wall. A hole will be cut, and the intruders will have a nice entryway.

I emerge from my hiding place and walk toward where they're cutting. My hands are out, my mind is solid.

"Stay where you are," I tell the brutes.

The intruders have finished their work. A large circle has been outlined on the wall.

"It's done," I hear a member say. "Knock it down!"

"Got it," they respond.

A booming pound comes from the wall. Another one follows. Then, finally, the third one hits, and the wall collapses from the lines they carved. A small cloud of dust erupts from the impact.

After it clears, I get a good look at the invaders. Some have mining tools latched onto their bodies, but all have weapons. Pistols, laser cannons, bombs— they're armed to the teeth. They certainly look like criminal types. I see four pigs and four humans. Strange, there's supposed to be eleven, but I don't see the other three.

I stand in the center. The eight that have made it into the pod stare at me like I'm a freak. I realize that to them, I am one.

"What the hell is that?" one of the humans screams.

The others look on with astonishment.

"Gus, Brad, Dusty, you have to see this!" the other human yells back at the tunnel.

From behind him, still in the tunnel, I see two pigs and one human making their way toward the pod. All eleven are accounted for. Time to attack.

"Lucy, cut the lights!" I yell.

The pod's power is shut off, and everything goes dark. Lucy supplied me with some night vision contacts before I embarked on this task.

"I can't see shit!" one of the humans screams.

"What's going on?" yells a pig.

"Fuck, did that thing do this?" a human exclaims.

The two pigs and one human haven't made it into the pod. They're just outside in the opening. Now's my chance. I raise my hands and point my palms to the tunnel. Then I swiftly close my fist. There's no rumbling, it just closes. Within a few milliseconds, the walls of the tunnel cave in swiftly like a compactor. The collapse crushes the two pigs and human still inside. It happened quickly and cleanly. The poor saps didn't even have a chance to scream.

"What was that noise?" a human asks.

"It sounded like a door slamming shut," a pig says.

"Did you hear that, Gus?" another human asks.

They have no idea their colleagues are dead. I better act quick if I want to keep the element of surprise on my side.

I point my palms at the nearby wall. As I pull my arm back, a large, flat chunk of synthesized metal gets ripped from it. I now hold it steady in the air. *Who should I take out?* The closest enemies to the slab are two humans. They'll do.

With a simple flicking of my wrist, the chunk flies toward the two humans. They have no idea it's coming until it violently slams into their bodies. They get catapulted toward the opposite side with the chunk carrying them. They let out a harrowing scream, but it's too late.

Smash!

It's the sound of two humans getting sandwiched in between a wall and a metal slab that used to be it. The booming noise vibrates the pod upon collision. I don't know if those two saps were dead when they got hit, but they're certainly dead now.

In an instant, the thugs start to panic.

"What the fuck, what the fuck?!" one yells.

"Who got hit? Are you still alive? Answer me!" another screams.

"Quick, get a light in here!" says another.

I see one of the pigs holding something in his teeth. It looks like a small lighting device, which I know can very well illuminate this darkened room. I'll lose my cover. I was so busy with the previous attack I totally missed what this one was up to.

I try to throw something at this pig, but I can't do anything now. He has already flung the portable lantern with his mouth. It lands squarely in the center and once it hits the ground, it activates, shining a bright light that illuminates the entire room.

We're all visible now—me, the brutes, and the intruders. They look at me, but their attention quickly turns to the brutes, who can be seen from their hiding spots.

"What the fuck?" the pigs and humans murmur as they get a good view of the brutes.

Their grotesque appearance differs from mine. I am a unique beauty, aesthetically appealing, while they are malformed beasts. Their physical appearances don't do their gentle nature justice.

"Monsters!" a human yells.

"Kill them!" one pig screams.

My babies never had a chance. The entire group arms their guns and start firing. The brutes' hiding spot helps them take cover, but not all are so fortunate. Errant shots hit the poor souls.

Elle is the first one to go. Her large, elephant-like frame makes her an easy target. She gets shot in the head and a few times in the body, dying instantly. She was so kind, too.

The two cat brutes also get caught in the crossfire. As the shots ring, they try to flee, but the moment they come out from their cover, they are riddled with ammunition. Their legs and hands flail violently, and within a few seconds, their bodies slump to the floor and they lie in nothing but a pool of blood.

Two of the tiger brutes see this and start to panic, making their bodies exposed. A human from the excavation group sees this, raises his rifle, steadies his aim, and takes two shots at their heads. In two seconds, Terry and Tonga are facedown on the ground, skulls blown half apart.

Five are dead already, and only five remain. But now I know my brutes won't go with a whimper. They are what they are, brutish in nature. When threatened, their tender nature quickly morphs into unbridled power. When attacked, they attack back. And now some of their brothers and sisters are dead. It's time to unleash some rage.

Croc, the reptilian brute and more stoic of the pack, surprisingly leads the charge. He quickly emerges from behind the control equipment and makes a dash at the closest enemy he can find, which in this case is a pig.

The pig fires, blasting Croc in the abdomen, but Croc only flinches and continues his run. The pig hits Croc in the arm, but he doesn't stop. The pig fires one last blast at his leg, and while Croc briefly kneels in reaction, he gets back up and continues the assault. I couldn't be prouder. What a warrior.

Croc is now an arm's length away from the pig. The pig tries to fire another shot, but Croc quickly slashes it in the head with his claws. A cut is open, and the pig starts to bleed profusely. Fear quickly rushes onto the poor sap's face because he knows it's the end. Croc then gives a mighty thrust with its hand into the pigs neck and digs in, thrashing its claws at every moment. The pig squeals and shrieks as blood shoots out like a fountain. It tries to do what it can, scrambling its legs, bobbing its head, but it's no use. In a few short seconds, piles of blood have leaked from the pig, and it simply slumps over, dead from the loss.

Unfortunately, Croc's assault has also left him exposed. Another pig sneaks up behind and blasts Croc with a high-powered energy shot. The shot leaves a hole the size of a bowling ball in Croc's abdomen. He's dead even before he hits the ground.

Instinctively, I retaliate by ripping a part of the pod's ceiling and crashing it down on the pig. His head is instantly crushed by the impact. By my count now, five of them are dead, which includes three pigs and two humans.

As I recover from my attack, I see something developing on the opposite side of the pod. Tuner, the tiger brute, and Larry and Lucia, two lion brutes, are cornered against a wall as three pigs swarm them. The three brutes back away slowly, but they're pinned against the wall. These three are much more docile than the other brutes. They don't have a fighter's spirit like Croc. Thus, it's like shooting fish in a barrel for the pigs.

And that's exactly what happens. The pigs let loose and fire away. The three brutes are torn up from head to toe as the ammunition keeps coming. After a good ten seconds, probably over one hundred shots have been fired, and my poor brutes have been ripped up like a piece of paper. Only Leo, a lion brute, and I remain.

The brutes didn't need to come here, they didn't need to die. I could, and still can, wipe the floor with these cronies. Why did my brutes have to get sacrificed like this?

To fit Mother's plans, that's why. But they're dying senseless deaths all in the name of visions. I know my mother is never wrong, I know I should listen to her, but screw it. According to my mother, I'm supposed to use controlled telekinesis to pick the enemy apart, but I can't bottle my emotions. I'm pissed.

I use the same trick I did before, focusing my palms on a part of ceiling that's above the heads of the pigs. But instead of being careful, I exert all my power on it. With one mighty rip, almost a fourth of the ceiling falls down and flattens the three pigs like ants. I then focus my attention on the two humans that remain.

They start firing at me, seeing my power as a bigger threat, but I rip a square of the floor beneath me and position it in front, using it like a shield. Then, using the same move, I lift a chunk of floor from underneath one of the humans. It rises into the air as the human stands on it. I punch the air upward, and as my fist flies toward the ceiling, so does the piece of floor that the human stands on. He helplessly flies into the ceiling and smashes into it headfirst. His limp body falls back to the floor. He's dead.

There's only one left. At this point, he's terrified with the destruction he's seen. He instantly drops his weapon and starts running to the exit. It's rather useless, though, since I closed it off at the beginning of this fight, but I guess his panic has stopped him from thinking clearly.

This should be easy pickings. I prepare for one last telekinetic attack, when suddenly the last brute, the lion hybrid Leo, chases after the human. I'm not sure if he sees this as a game or if he wants to finish the job, but I beckon Leo to stop.

"Leo, come back!" I yell.

He still doesn't listen. He gives full chase to the human, and the human goes in the other direction in a terrified fashion.

While the human is scared out of his mind, he hasn't given up the fight completely. I see him gripping onto something on the side of his hip. It's dark, black, and heavy looking.

As I get a closer look, I realize what it is: a gun in a holster.

"Leo, no!" I scream.

I try to do something to prevent it, but it's inevitable. The human grabs the gun from the holster and spins around, pointing his weapon at Leo. Before Leo can even react, the human shoots three shots. The first two miss, but the last one hits my brute square between the eyes. After it's done, there's nothing but a hole the size of a golf ball in the back of his head. Leo stops running and falls to the floor. He's out before he hits the ground.

"Bastard!" I yell.

The human turns and aims his weapon at me, but I won't even give him a chance. With one stroke, I simultaneously rip several pieces of the wall, all from different directions. I then have them surround the human.

He looks around, horrified by the debris that encircles him. He takes one last glance at me, and I flash him a bitter look.

Then I close my fist and all the debris snaps together with the human in the center. They crush him, encasing him in a tomb. His body quickly collapses to the floor as trickles of blood leak from the cracks of the coffin I've made for him.

Everyone is dead, both intruders and brutes. I'm the only one left alive. I stand, incensed by all this needless death, but I still have one task to do. I activate my communicator.

"Lucy, the deed is done," I say.

"Excellent," she responds. "Use telekinesis to collapse teleportation pod and destroy evidence. Use personal porter to get back here. Good work."

"Yeah, whatever," I say.

My voice gives off a disgusted tone because that's how I truly feel.

Chapter 33 – Falena Snow

Broken

September 28, 3071 4:07 AM

Where am I? It's so cold. Am I outside? I thought I was in a cabin.

Is something burning? It smells like smoke. I can hear my surroundings, smell them, even feel the floor. But I don't see anything. All I see is darkness.

I can't move either. Am I dead? I don't know how I got here or what happened. I'm scared, though. At the same time, I'm a little happy. Maybe I'll be reunited with my mother.

C'mon, Falena, wake up!

I open my eyes. My consciousness is a little hazy. I don't recognize where I am. It looks like I'm inside a cabin of some sort, but there are giant holes in the wall. Debris litters the floor, furniture is turned over, and remnants of ash and smoke surround me. I can feel the cold as a strong breeze flows through the opening. What happened here?

The question, though, is how long was I out? It's dark outside, so it must be nighttime. The moon is starting to fall, and I see streaks of sunlight shining through the sky. It must almost be sunrise.

And then I remember. There was a fight between my pursuer and me, and I lost. The last thing I remember was getting hit in the torso, then his big, hammer-like fists coming down on my head. When we fought, it was reaching the end of the afternoon. I can't believe I've been knocked out cold for almost twelve hours.

My body feels like it's been shot to hell. I'm sore everywhere. My legs are wobbly, like gelatin. My back is stiff and aching. My head is ringing so many different tones. It's a struggle just to blink. I smell traces of blood everywhere—on my fur, on the ground—and I suspect most of it is mine. There's probably plenty of internal bleeding and broken bones. I can barely walk forward without feeling some sort of pain. I'm quite amazed I'm still alive.

The specifics of the battle are a little hazy. I remember getting beaten up, and I remember a lot of explosions and gunfire, but I can't piece together in what order things happened. The details elude me. I recall being up close to my attacker, but his face is blurred in my memories. I recollect he was a large man, muscular, but it's vague.

I start to walk around a bit more and observe the damage that's been done. I scrounge through my belongings to find something I can use as a light. There's a cylinder lantern, and I gently hover my paw over its sensor to activate it. A small bit of light stretches through the room, dimly illuminating it.

Man, this place turned into shit. There are holes in the walls, in the roof, even mini craters on the ground. Everything is stained black. Many of my belongings have been destroyed, though the stash where I got the lantern is still intact.

I step outside to see what else has been destroyed. The landscape has been torn apart by the bombs I set. There's nothing but mounds of dirt and dead plant life everywhere. All of this, and it didn't even stop the guy. He was indestructible.

It's like he was a machine. That's when I remember his arm being stripped of its armor and morphing into a weapon. It was unlike anything I've ever seen. I couldn't tell if it was his suit or his arm itself.

Obviously, the guy had power, way too much power for little old me. What did he want from me anyhow? I can't put my paw on it…

Shit, the data.

I race to find a compcube or scanner. I need to make sure my life's work is intact. I scramble through the pile of undestroyed items to find something I can work with. That's when I see a small two-inch-by-two-inch cube. It's my spare compcube! I quickly boot it up, and by some miracle, it's intact.

Immediately, I attempt to link up to the implant in my brain. Nothing happens. I read the error log. "Damaged receiver. Cannot connect."

"No, no, no, no!" I say.

I hastily log into my cloud to see if the data is at least in my archive.

"No!" I howl.

Everything has been wiped out. Any remnants of my research, Operation Alphas, the proof that my mother was turned into a weapon by the Alliance is all gone. I've lost everything.

Tears start to come down. They trickle on my snout and hit the floor. A part of me wants to think this isn't real, that it's some dream, that I'm still knocked out from the fight. An even deeper part of me wishes I were already dead. I let out a deep howl to express my anger and sadness.

Why, why did this have to happen? I was so close to finding the truth, to getting redemption for my mother, and now everything is lost. I can't even start at square one. My vision, my dream for a justified future is gone.

I lay my body and head on the floor. I'm bruised, battered, and defeated. *What do I do now?*

Perhaps this is a sign that I will never find peace for my mother. I fought the good fight and have been crushed by the authority. Maybe all I can do is simply live my life.

It's too soon to think about anything. I don't know if my pursuer will continue to hunt me down. I don't know if I should pick up the pieces and start over. I'm too tired for that. This fight has taken a lot out of me. I suppose I'll have to slow things down.

But it's not over yet. It may take ten years, it may take twenty, it may take my entire life, but I will obtain the truth once more. And when that happens, no one is going to stop me. No man, no dog, no Alliance. My mother's story will be heard.

Chapter 34 – Two Van Faye

Vendetta

September 28, 3071 4:45 AM

I'm running on empty. I had a tough time falling asleep with everything on my mind. I've had a lot to think about. My deal with the Alliance, The Collector, and who I could trust all kept me up. And when I finally succumbed to sleep, I was awoken a mere few hours later by the worst news possible.

"Wake up, Van Faye," one of those Alliance lackeys told me as he burst through the room. "Your assassin failed. Mark Allen is dead."

"Excuse me?" I asked groggily as I recovered from waking up.

"You heard me. The guy you were supposed to protect was killed by The Collector."

I sat stunned. The words registered in my mind, but it's like I couldn't comprehend them.

"And what about Ash Han?" I asked.

"Gone," the Alliance soldier responded. "There wasn't even a trace of the woman. It appears she fled after it went down. Either that, or she's already history."

That didn't bode well for me either.

"So what happens now?" I asked.

"We're awaiting orders from General Rox," the lion said. "Until then, you'll be waiting here."

"Like hell I will."

"It's not your choice. It's an order from the top. Remember, Van Faye, you're still in cooperation with the Alliance. You'll do as you're told."

I was angry. How dare a lowly Alliance grunt talk to the most powerful crime boss in Fan Zui Bin with such indignity? I wanted him dead!

But I knew I was powerless, and thus, I had to play along.

"All right," I said begrudgingly. "I'll wait until Rox speaks to me."

"Good," the lion said. "We'll be outside in case you need anything."

He then exited the penthouse. That was twenty minutes ago. There's a whole cadre of soldiers just like him. They were sent by Rox to protect me while Ash Han continued her duties, but it's more like they're here to monitor me. And now, after everything has gone to crap, I'm certain Rox doesn't want me slipping away.

I'm stuck in this penthouse under house arrest. My partnership with the Alliance is probably gone. When I go back to Fan Zui Bin, I'll be on my own, and these other crime bosses are probably going to take their stab at a newly defenseless Elephant Queen of Crime.

Of course I won't give up so easily. Without a doubt, a mob war will be coming, and if I go down, I will fight all the way. I will mount my soldiers, my capos, everyone, and turn them into killing machines. No boss will be left alive.

That makes me think of Ash Han. The soldier said she either fled or is dead. I doubt either happened. I'm not aware of a body being found, and Han is too skilled a warrior to be bested by The Collector. I have a gut feeling she's alive.

She's not running away either. She'll be back. I'm her only home. I pay for her expenses. I give her the gear she uses. I train her. I'm practically the closest thing she has to a mother. A relationship like that doesn't simply up and leave into thin air. I will see my bodyguard soon.

But when I do, it won't be a happy reunion. She fucked up big time. That excuse for a human being has probably cost me everything I had with the Alliance. No more implant modifications, no more weaponry, no more resources. It all went downhill because she couldn't complete a simple task. All she had to do was keep one human alive. How hard is that?

And even worse, The Collector is still alive. I'm sure that bastard will come for me one day, and the best chance I have at survival is Ash Han. She may have failed to keep Mark Allen alive, but she better damn well keep me safe. I'm her meal ticket.

Sigh, so many things to worry about when you're at the top. The crown that the Elephant Queen of Crime wears is heavy indeed.

All I can do is wait in this room until Rox addresses me. I'm sure he'll give me the full briefing and deal a complete lashing. Whatever. He better not try anything fishy. I know Rox. He's as ruthless and as shady as I am. When he has no use for his pawns, he gets rid of them.

Wait a minute...

Is he going to do that with me?

He wouldn't dare. I'm the Elephant Queen of Crime, a high profile individual. He wouldn't have his cronies dispose of me. I'm too important.

But I'm not Alliance important. To them, I'm just a criminal. It doesn't matter if I'm a kingpin or a stooge,

I'm someone they can get rid of. In fact, Rox has probably been itching at the opportunity to snuff me out. And I'm the fool who left her fortress to come to Allied city.

Oh shit, is that why he's sent additional guards to patrol the area? Are they really guarding anything? Or are they just a hit squad?

Shit! Ash Han, where are you?

Out of the blue, I hear footsteps coming. I know there were only six guards, but my imagination runs wild. I see twenty lions, twenty humans, twenty crocs, twenty dogs, all lined up, ready to bury me with bombs and bullets. Is this really my last stand?

I quickly dash away from the door and go through my belongings to find a firing baton. I'm a good shot, but my chances of taking down six Alliance soldiers are slim. The adrenaline flows through my body as I nervously stare at the door.

I close my eyes and wait…

…and wait…

…and…

SLAM!

The sound of a giant thud pounds against the door and breaks me from my trance. I stand on edge and wonder what the hell that was.

Another bang comes from the other side, and out of curiosity, I walk slow toward it. *What the hell is going on?*

I'm too scared to open the door, so instead, I stand close to it and listen intensely.

"We need backup!" I hear one soldier yell.

A chorus of gunfire follows his desperate call for help.

"Screw that, just shoot the thing out of the sky!" another guard says.

"Sky?" I ask myself. "What in the world?"

"I think I... Ahhh!" another Alliance lackey screams.

What in blazes is going on over there? Second after second, I hear the soldiers struggling against some unknown enemy. They beg and scream for mercy while the gunfire and thuds continue to echo throughout the air. I carefully lean my head closer to the noise, when a small explosion backs me away. Then the commotion settles down like a blanket of silence has covered the hallway.

I only hear one voice left, and the poor guy sounds like he's on his last limb.

"Please, not the spears!" he pleas.

This is followed by a crisp wooshing sound... and then silence.

"Wait a minute, did he say spears?" I ask myself. "Oh shit."

I turn around and scramble away from the door. Right away, it bursts open and flies forward, slamming into some walls nearby. In the confusion, I clumsily stumble and fall forward. But I get back up and turn around to see The Collector making its entrance.

"We have unfinished business, Van Faye," The Collector says.

I whip out the energy baton and point it at The Collector, but it rushes toward me and swats it away from my trunk. I make a hopeless retreat to the opposite wall. The Collector sees this and throws a chair in my path, causing me to trip over that and land on my head. I'm a little dizzy, but I recover. I look up, and The Collector is right there.

I frantically look around for something I can use to get out of this situation, but there's nothing. It's just The Collector and me. The only weapon I have are my words.

"Please don't," I beg. "You promised you wouldn't kill me."

"What I told you doesn't matter," it says. "Death is the consequence I deal to my enemies."

I watch it take one of those needled blades from its cloak. I've escaped death from The Collector so many times, but I think my luck has run out.

The noise of a gunshot bounces around the penthouse, and The Collector's blade gets knocked out of the air. I hastily look to the right from where the blast came. In the doorway stands Ash Han with a smoking energy pistol.

My bodyguard has one more chance to end this with The Collector. If she fails, we're both dead.

Chapter 35 — Ash Han

Stand

September 28, 3071 5:00 AM

As soon as the destruction had been done in Sector Six, I ran. I had to make my way back to the Benjamin Plaza Hotel. Two Van Faye was the only creature who could protect me. I failed the Alliance and feared their wrath, but at least my boss could talk to Rox and ensure my safety. She may be a horrible individual. She abuses me on a constant basis, treats me less than dirt. She never lets me forget that I'll always be in Sai's shadow. There are times when I wish she were dead. But at least I know she'll have my back when it comes to the Alliance. I think.

I was worried they had gotten to her already. The Alliance is shady like that. After what I've seen while under Two Van Faye's wing, I wouldn't be surprised if they made such hits. That's why I had to hurry back, to make sure she was safe.

When I got out of Sector Six, I had to move stealthily. I refrained from using a teleporter. I did commandeer a hovercar, though, and raced my way to the hotel.

When I got to the penthouse entrance, I was greeted by a disturbing and shocking scene. There were bodies everywhere. They were beaten to pulp, bent and broken on the floor. There were species of different kinds. Bloodied fur, cut skin, broken bones—lions, humans, dogs, the whole lot of them. But they all were brothers that were commanded under the same banner, the Alliance.

These were the guards, the soldiers, assigned to protect Ms. Van Faye. They were my temporary replacements. And now they're dead. I examine one closely, a dog, and see a thin, pointy metal object protruding from its abdomen. I recognize what it is and instantly know who killed these soldiers: The Collector.

I now stand in the middle of the hallway, above of the corpses that litter this hallway. I walk cautiously toward the penthouse entrance and I carefully look around, making sure The Collector isn't hiding anywhere to get the drop on me.

Suddenly, I hear the pleas of my boss.

"Please don't," Ms. Van Faye begs. "You promised you wouldn't kill me."

"What I told you doesn't matter," The Collector says. I recognize its synthesized voice. "Death is the consequence I deal to my enemies."

That's my cue. I grab an energy pistol from one of the slain human guards and rush toward the door. The penthouse is trashed, and there I see The Collector pinning down Ms. Van Faye with one of those trademark spears. I don't have much time, so I quickly point it at the needle-like blade and fire.

It's a direct hit. The spear flies harmlessly across the room, and for once, it seems I've startled The Collector. The creature swiftly shifts its face toward my direction, and I stand defiantly, yari in hand, ready to do this one more time.

"You again," The Collector says. "I thought you'd know better than to pursue me after what I did at Sector Six."

"I wasn't following you," I say. "But now, I have an opportunity to finish this job."

The Collector sounds exasperated. I think I hear a small sigh coming from its voice box.

"Must we do this again?" it asks. "Are you such a slave to this miserable pile of crap that you're willing to risk life and limb and participate in a battle you have no chance at winning?"

"Perhaps you underestimate my skill," I say.

"Trust me, I do not. You are indeed a true warrior. I have battled many foes, but none have matched me until you. I commend you on your abilities. They even surpass mine. But you cannot beat me"

"And why is that?"

"Because I have an edge. I was born with it. I know what you're going to do even before you do. Things only happen because I allow them to. You may think you've gotten the upper hand. You may think you caught me by surprise, but you haven't. I see everything."

At first, I interpret the creature's words as nothing more than bullshit. This is part of its mind games. But at that moment, I start to think about our past battles. I remember the things it's done, and I recall that the creature seemed to have an uncanny ability to anticipate my moves. I thought it was simply instinct, but after this revelation, I start to wonder.

Ms. Van Faye, on the other hand, thinks differently.

"The Collector is just trying to get your guard down," she yells. "Stop stalling, you fucking idiot, and kill the creature!"

"Is this what your life has come down to?" the creature asks me. "Following the orders of this piece of garbage?"

"Shut the fuck up," Ms. Van Faye says confidently. "Han will cut you to ribbons."

Unlike Ms. Van Faye, I'm more restrained in my answer.

"It is all I know," I say sadly. "I live to serve."

"Then looks like you're serving the wrong master," The Collector says.

"Han, you piece of shit, attack!" Ms. Van Faye exclaims.

I do what I'm told. I start my dash at The Collector. The creature follows. The Collector throws three spears my way, but I reflexively jump over them. The Collector is in my range. When I land, I lunge forward with my yari and narrowly miss impaling the creature's stomach. I rear back my weapon and lay a heavy downward slash, but that fails to connect as well.

I try one last time, throwing a horizontal blow, but The Collector catches it and yanks it forward. My hands are gripping the handle, and when The Collector pulls, I go with it. The shift in momentum causes me to lose my balance, and I fall right to The Collector. It's there the creature knocks the wind out of me with a boot to the stomach.

I keel over backward and fall to the floor. The Collector tosses my yari to the side.

"I knew that was going to happen," the creature says.

I'm still on the ground, trying to recover from the painful blow. My palms grip the floor, but I also feel something else. It's small and sharp, and I discreetly grasp it. I take a quick glance to see what I've collected. It's a piece of debris.

"Did you see this?" I ask.

I immediately throw the shard at The Collector's face, but it simply swats it away with its gauntlet.

"I sure did," it says.

"Holy crap, I can't win," I say exasperatedly.

"You're giving up!?" Ms. Van Faye screams. "Pull yourself together, Han! God help me, I won't let you live this down. If The Collector doesn't kill you, I will. I've trained a quitter. Get up."

"Yes... Ms. Van Faye."

I gradually rise to my feet. I don't have my weapon, I simply have my fists. But I clutch them and put them up.

"Are you willing to fight honorably?" I ask.

"Yes," The Collector says.

The creature drops its cloak. The moment it drops, I hear the sound of dozens of spears clanging on the floor. The creature has disarmed itself. It's just the two of us, human and freak.

I start off with a strong right hook, but The Collector blocks it with its arm and counters with a punch to my stomach. I feel the full force of the blow and get on one knee.

Though dazed, I quickly get back up and once again get in my stance. This time, I unleash a devastating front boot kick, but The Collector catches it and slams me to the ground. I'm on my back, but I recover with a roll and put my fists back up. I expect a counter blow, but The Collector does nothing.

I'm a bit baffled at this point. I can't get anything past The Collector. I know if I launch another attack, I'll just be countered. I have no doubt that what The

Creature said earlier is true. Somehow, it's able to
know what I'm going to do.

I try one more attack, a punch to the face. Without
hesitation, The Collector simply catches my fist, holds
it for a few seconds, and then lets go. I back away,
stunned and confused.

I don't know how to continue. Whatever I do, it'll
fail. I feel useless. So all I can do is let my guard
down. I drop my hands to my sides and stand there in
awe at an undefeatable opponent.

The strange thing is The Collector does nothing. It
doesn't take advantage, it doesn't attack. Throughout
this whole time, it hasn't thrown one punch. It's as if it
didn't want to, and I'm kind of confused as to why.
We've had some great battles. I am the enemy. The
creature has no reason to spare me. Yet here we stand,
staring at each other with odd respect.

Of course, this pisses off Ms. Van Faye to no end.

"Why are you standing around like a damned
idiot?" she scolds me.

I say nothing. I don't even look at Ms. Van Faye. I
just look at The Collector, who doesn't even react to
her words.

"Are you retarded and deaf?" she continues. "I'm
asking you a question!"

I continue to disregard her.

"You ungrateful little fuck up!" she screams.
"You're in no position to ignore me. You've failed the
Alliance. You've failed me. You've been a failure all
your life. First you were a street rat, a filthy human
child that should be dead. And you dare show me
disrespect?! If it weren't for me, you'd still be rotting
away in that orphanage. Yet what quality can I expect
from the sludge that came out of a whore's belly? You

disgust me. I wash my hands of this. This freak could kill you for all I care. It'd be a better fate than the one dealt to my poor Sai."

I've taken a lot of verbal abuse. Every day practically. And I've always taken it. Yet, as I endure this one, I can't help but feel the anger boil up inside me. All my life, I've been bred to feel worthless. It's what Ms. Van Faye has been doing since childhood. But this past week, I've been feeling different. My battles with The Collector have proved to me that I have the potential, that my skills are worthy. As odd as it sounds, my enemy has shown me this.

And it appears the creature knows.

"Like I said before, you are serving the wrong master," The Collector says.

"And who should I be serving?" I say. "You?"

I'm not sure if it's trying to manipulate me. I try to keep my guard up.

"No," The Collector says. "I do not enslave. I simply lead. You are free to do what you want. I can see the future, but your future belongs to you. Take charge. Control it."

I look at The Collector and I look at Van Faye.

"I've lost the ability to control from the day I was born," I say hopelessly.

With that last statement, I wind my fist up and let out a mighty punch. I'm fully expecting The Collector will block it, but I had no choice.

To my utter amazement, this one actually connects. My fist rams The Collector's face, and the creature stumbles backward. It's not a knockout, but it's enough to stun the creature.

Something else happens, though. Immediately after the punch connects, something flies from The

Collector's head. It's a black object, flat, no bigger than The Collector's face. I take a quick glance and realize it's actually something that the creature wears. It's a mask!

I swiftly turn my focus back to The Collector and my jaw drops in disbelief. I look at Ms. Van Faye, and she is equally astounded.

All this time, I thought she was a human, but her face is something I've never seen before. She has the facial structure of a cat with some human elements mixed in. Her ears are pointed and some light fur covers her face. Her eyes are large with a yellowish hue, much like a cat. I don't see whiskers, but I see a small, soft nose.

The odd thing is everything else looks human. She has hands, legs, is bipedal, and stands upright like a human. Then again, the only thing that's exposed is her face. Who knows what's lurking underneath all that body armor? My imagination starts to run wild. She's half human and half cat, something that I only thought existed in science fiction.

Van Faye and I continue to stare while she looks at us stoically. I mean, I think it's a she. She certainly looks feminine enough.

"What the hell are you?" Van Faye finally blurts out.

"I am not a human, I am not a cat. I am a new species created long ago, and since then, I've been hunted, brought into hiding. I know what it's like to fear authority, live in terror. I've seen my loved ones fall, but I've also seen the helpless rise into power," she says. She then looks at me. "I'm an outcast, just like you."

Her voice is much different when the mask is off. It's soft, gentle, something I would have never expected from such a powerful enemy. Her words come out with comfort and peace.

"An outcast?" Ms. Van Faye scoffs. "Don't give me that garbage. Outcasts are just another way to say unwanted. Am I supposed to feel sorry for creatures like you? Hardly. Outcasts like you deserve your lot and should be eradicated."

"But she's right," I argue with Ms. Van Faye.

The Collector's words have hit my emotional core.

"I am an outcast just like her," I say. "I'm a human that lives in a country where we are the minority. I've been bullied, stomped, and put into a corner by everyone I know. I am an outcast. Do I deserve to die?"

I think about my childhood and being under her tutelage. All those years spent training and following orders, half out of fear, half out of duty. Despite all the abuses, all the putdowns, all the verbal lashings, I strangely looked up to her. And now I'm on pins and needles hoping for a response that validates all the time I've wasted.

Without any remorse or guilt, Ms. Van Faye simply flashes a smirk.

"I stand by my words, you grunt," she says. "You mean nothing."

I can't take it anymore. In an act of pure emotion, I run to my yari, which is a few feet away. The Collector doesn't get in my way. Instead, it simply observes.

Once I get it, I grasp it tightly and look over at Ms. Van Faye, who still has that condescending look on her face. We meet eye to eye, and even now, she only sees me as a bug she can crush.

Not anymore.

With all my might, I throw the yari like a javelin. It zooms through the air and lands directly between Ms. Van Faye's eyes. It slices her skull and enters her brain. Blood spurts out and continues to pump out of the newly formed hole.

The smirk on her face is gone. It's been replaced with a before-death look of shock. She didn't expect I would finally rebel. Hell, I don't think she even knew she was going to die until she felt my yari plunge into her skull.

After it's done, The Collector slowly walks to Ms. Van Faye's corpse.

"I told you I wouldn't kill you," it says.

The creature then turns to me.

"Did you know that was going to happen?" I ask The Collector.

"In a sense, yes," she responds. "But as I said before, you are in control of your own fate. All I can do is simply watch it unfold."

I look over at Two Van Faye's corpse. Her dead eyes are still open, and blood continues to trickle out of the gash in her head.

"So what happens now?" I say. "I have nowhere to go. Ms. Van Faye was my only source of income. I have no home to return to."

"You are an outcast now," she says. "But know that you are like me. We are both shunned members of society, living in a world that hates us. That is why we must stick together."

She reaches in one of her pockets and takes something out.

"This is a communicator," she says. "When the time is right, use it. I will be waiting on the other line.

If you ever wish to join me, know that you are welcome. We are no longer enemies. I respect your skills, and I hope it is mutual."

I look at the communicator. At first, I'm skeptical, scared that this might be a trap of some sort. But my instinct tells me to trust her. I cautiously take the small device from her hand.

"I'll need some time to think about this," I say. "Until then, I'll find somewhere to go."

"Take as much time as you need," The Collector says. "We will be waiting."

She starts to press some buttons on her armor and that bright ball of light I've seen so many times forms behind her.

"Wait. Before you go, what is your name?" I say. "Your real name."

She looks at me and flashes a soft smile.

"My name is Iris Lawton," she says. "And I am a hybrid."

She walks into the light, and moments later, it disappears, taking her with it.

Chapter 36 — Ivy Lawton

Understandings

September 28, 3071 10:20 AM

When Mom finally got back from her mission, I wanted to tell her about last night. I wanted to pour my emotions and vent out my anger. I wanted to tell her that I love her, but she broke my heart.

I was ready to unleash it all. But she looked tired, haggard, and battle torn. She's been through a lot the past few days. From what Lucy's told me, she's gone up against assassins, crime bosses, and slew after slew of Alliance flunkies. After all of that, she got what she needed, the GTS schematics, the key to our plans, the key to a chance at hybrid freedom. I didn't want to take that moment away from her, so I refrained from confronting her.

However, a few hours have passed, and my mother has had time to rest her weary body. My mind, on the other hand, is still restless. All I can think about is the slaughter that took place in that teleportation pod. All of the brutes are dead. They never really had a chance. They were strong and brave, but they were against a team of criminals armed with weapons. Only I was left standing. I got the job done, but at what price?

The thing that gets to me is my mom knew it would happen. She said the mission would only be won if the brutes were there with me. I suppose she was right. I mean, the intruders are dead. But why the brutes? That same vision told my mother the outcome. That means she knew the brutes would be killed. Yet she sent them willingly to their deaths.

How could she do that to me? She knew they were my babies. She knew I cared for them and held them dearly. She knew they gave me hope in a time that is hopeless. My mother loves me, but if she truly did, she wouldn't have put me in that position. She wouldn't cause me such pain through the loss of the brutes.

Sometimes, I don't know about her. She is my mother, but she is also a ruthless leader willing to do whatever it takes for her goals. I used to be able to separate the two personalities. When she took off her black armor and shed the role of The Collector, I knew I was speaking to my mom. The moment she put it on, I knew it was time for business. But moments like these make me think the lines have blurred.

I have to be honest with myself: she never liked the brutes. Like Lucy, she saw them as a liability, more mouths to feed, a drain on resources that would never be able to contribute. Yet while Lucy was very upfront about her reasons, my mother was always more restrained. I think it's because she wanted to be sensitive to me since she knew my connection to them. She didn't want to say anything about them that would upset me.

I think about the past days, though, and wonder if she hated them. It's the only reason she would make me bring them to the mission. She knew they would die, so what better way to get rid of useless creatures than to have the enemy stamp them out? She could never kill them herself, not without making me hate her. So perhaps this was the perfect opportunity for her to do so.

That makes me furious. It makes me feel less loved, that I am simply another one of her pawns in her plans. She tells me about how she needs to make sacrifices, how everything is for the greater good. But is there no limit?

I have to ask her these questions. I have to find out what she's thinking. She's taking a break in her quarters, but I march there, ready to demand the answers I deserve. The door opens, and I see her leisurely lying on her bed.

"Ivy," she says. "I'm so happy to see you. It's been a long week."

She looks just as tired as she did when she first arrived back. Her eyes are discolored, the light fur that adorns her face appears ragged, and her posture is slumped and fatigued. I feel a little bad bringing this up to her while she's still recovering.

But then I think of the brutes, their mangled corpses, and the times I've had with them. It fuels my emotions and makes me stay strong.

"Why did you do it?" I skip all the small talk. I speak in a tone that's desperate and heated.

My mother looks at me blankly. It appears she's confused by the sudden and unexpected outburst of rage I'm showing. It's an act, though. I know she knows why I've come to confront her. My mother knows everything.

"What did I do?" she says unconvincingly.

"You sent the brutes to their deaths," I say as my voice rises. "Why? You knew they were practically my children."

She doesn't respond. She simply stares at me with a hint of shame in her eyes.

"Answer me! Why did you do it?" I ask.

She takes some time to think of her answer and then, finally, she speaks.

"Ivy, sometimes things aren't so simple," she says. "Sometimes I have to make decisions that are difficult, but in the long run, they're the right ones."

"Right ones?" I scoff. "You think sending a group of innocent creatures to their deaths is the right decision?"

She hesitates, then answers.

"Yes," she says.

"Oh, I get it. It was the right decision because you hated them, right?" I say. "You saw them as liabilities, so you needed a way to get rid of them. In the long run, that was the best decision, wasn't it? No more useless mouths to feed? No more resources drained? Yeah, I can see how it was better for us, huh?"

My words come out sharp and are filled with spite.

"You knew how much they meant to me," I say with tears in my eyes. "Yet this is the choice you made, a willing one to hurt me. Sometimes I wonder if your plans, your sacrifices have no boundaries. Sometimes I wonder if I even matter, when it comes down to me or your plans, which will you choose?"

I quickly wipe the tears with my hand. When I can see again, I'm shocked by what I see. My mother looks wounded by what I've said. Her eyes are slumped and start to form tears. My words have broken her heart. She's the strongest creature I know, but at the same time, she's fragile.

"How could you think that?" she asks me. "How could you question my love for you?"

I don't answer. Now I'm the one who's ashamed of my actions.

"Yes, it's true," she says. "I knew how much they meant to you. And I knew that the brutes would die in your attack. I saw it in my visions. I sent them to their deaths willingly."

"But why?" I ask.

"Because, if they hadn't gone, then you wouldn't have made it out alive."

"That's bullshit. The brutes didn't even put up a fight. I took out those thugs on my own. I could have done the job with or without them. The brutes' presence was needless."

"That's not true. When I looked into my visions, the first one I saw was you taking on those thugs by yourself. You put up a valiant fight, but eventually, they killed you."

I'm stunned.

"No, I don't believe it," I say. "I killed those criminals on my own. It was easy. I can't see how they killed me."

"They did," she says. "It was easy because the brutes distracted the enemy. Their focus was scattered. Instead of going after one target, they had to go after many. You may not realize it, but the brutes did help you. They provided the enemy with more targets than they could handle. And while their focus was shifted, you attacked them."

I think about what my mother says, and it makes sense. As much as I don't want to realize it, what took place tells the story.

"There had to be another way," I say.

"There wasn't, not if you were to live. I saw many visions, and the result was always the same if the brutes weren't involved," she says remorsefully. "And I would never let anything happen to you. It was painful to see you die so many times, in so many other realities. So in my eyes, the brutes were a worthy price to pay if it meant keeping you alive."

"Why did we even fight these thugs? Why couldn't we have left them alone?"

"If we did, all would be lost, and we'd all be dead. I've foreseen that future as well."

I start to come to the realization that seeing the future never makes anything so simple. My mother had nothing but tough choices to make. Every future she saw was a fatal one. In the end, she had to make the one that hurt the least. Now I start to understand.

"Why didn't you just tell me?" I ask her.

"Because if I did, you wouldn't have agreed to it."

I don't say anything in response.

"I'm guessing I'm right," she says.

I simply nod my head.

"Ivy, life isn't always so simple," she says. "You of all creatures should know this. Look at our existence. It's been one of controversy and hardships that no other being could compare to. We live underground. We fear the world. It's not by choice it's by reality. I dream of a day when we will be free, living amongst others. No more hiding, no more plans, simply that our kind can live within the masses without fear of repercussions. But the road to that dream is never easy, and only through sacrifice can we get there."

She looks away from me as she fights the tears.

"There are times when I look at myself in the mirror and wonder what I've become," she says. "I've seen so much death. I've dealt it too. A long time ago, I would have never thought myself capable of such acts. There will be regret with every decision I make. But it's what I must endure for the future. If you are upset, if you hate what I've become, tell me, and I will understand. But I hope you understand as well."

My rage is gone. I can't stay angry with her. She's gone through so much in her life and has fought so hard, not only for independence, not only for herself, but for all of us.

I walk next to her bed and grasp her hand.

"I'm sorry, Mother," I say.

"And I am sorry too," she replies.

Time freezes. Down the road, we may have more clashes. I may disagree with the things she will do, but she is my mother, and I would follow her anywhere. Now I understand.

Chapter 37 – Maya Lawton

Mothers

October 30, 3040 1:01 PM
"Tiago is right," Iris says to me.

We've just had lunch. The whole family wasn't here, but Tiago and Iris were. And once again, when Tiago is involved, sparks are bound to fly. We had an argument, one of many, about why he has to stay at Chakming Drive. Like all the other times, I've told him my reasons, and he's not happy with the answers.

After the war of words was over, he stormed out of the kitchen, leaving only Iris and I to our soup. He's becoming much more difficult to control. I guess he's no longer a child, but rather, an adult. My mothering has no effect on him.

He's going to leave soon, I can feel it. I've tried countless times to warn him of the dangers out there. I've told him he'd be discriminated against, that the Alliance wouldn't even give him a chance. Naturally, he ignores everything I say. He thinks I'm the enemy, not them.

Of course I don't want him to go. He is my son, and I love him. We've had our differences, but I will always look past that. I remember when he was small, such a cute little guy. I'm worried that if he ventures off, he will expose and endanger the rest of us. Not all of my children have as strong as a desire for leaving as he does. Leonard, Maddie, and some of the others are perfectly content here. If he leaves and gets found out, he'll be taking his brothers and sisters, and me, down with him.

Some of the other children are supportive of him. Alex and Ace want to leave too, and they'd follow him to the ends of the Earth. There are some in the middle ground like Lombardi, Isaac, and Oscar.

And then there's my special little girl, Iris. She's so difficult to read. I always thought she agreed with me. As Tiago and I argued, she gave no sign that she was on his side. Yet when the shouting match was over, she started to speak, and I'm shocked to hear the words coming from her mouth.

"Tiago was right?" I say, repeating her question. I speak in a confused manner.

"Yes," she responds. "We can't stay in this house forever, we have to leave one day."

"Iris, I'd expect this out of Alex or Ace, but I'm surprised that you're saying this."

Iris appears to have shame in her eyes.

"I don't know," she says. "I'm tired of being cooped up in this home."

"I know but I can't stress enough why it's important for us to stay hidden," I say.

"Does that mean we're just going to live here forever?"

Hesitation shows on my face. I don't answer, but my expression gives it away.

"So we are?" Iris says in astonishment.

She's shocked, disgusted, and horrified.

"You can't do this to us!" she begs.

"I know it's difficult to understand," I say. "I know that this house might seem like a jail. I know that what

I'm doing is cruel. But what am I supposed to do? I know what will happen when the world finds out about you. I'm the only one who has seen things first hand. The Alliance, they'll rip you apart."

"That's not true. Just give them a chance."

"It is true. As much as we don't like to believe it sometimes, the truth is the truth."

She's enraged.

"You think you know everything," she says. "You're wrong. One day, we're going to leave, with or without your permission. The world will know of our existence. And when that day comes, we will be living among them, free."

"Free?" I ask. "Is that the word you use to describe it? So what does it make this place, a prison? Am I your warden?"

She doesn't respond, but she continues to stand defiantly. We look at each other, my heart broken by what she's said, her eyes glaring in anger.

"I have nothing else to say," she says. "May I go back downstairs to my room?"

"You... you may," I say.

She angrily storms out of the kitchen and leaves me alone with my lunch.

I'm hurt. I've had these kind of conversations with Tiago before. There are times when he's cursed at me, told me that he wish I wasn't his mother. I could always take it from him because it was expected.

With Iris it's different. She's usually so kind, so cheery. For her to lash out like this is completely out of the blue. I never knew she wanted to leave so badly. Maybe the signs were there and I never noticed.

Now I'm here, eating lunch alone. It's gotten cold. I have eleven children, but I feel incredibly lonely. All the decisions I've made, the rules I've imposed, it's been for them. I know it makes me unpopular, I know that they will always disagree with the restrictions, but in the end, it's for their own good. Every sacrifice I make and tough choice is always for them.

Hopefully, one day they will see this, and if they don't, at least they will understand what it means to make tough choices. The right decisions don't always seem right, but once you realize they are, then it's worth it.

Chapter 38 – Iris Lawton

Targets

September 29, 3071 8:02 AM

I've finally gotten a full day's rest. Thank goodness. I needed it.

I thought I'd have yesterday to relax, but it turned out to be mentally and emotionally draining. I hope my relationship with Ivy hasn't faltered. She is my daughter and I am so proud of her.

I've been thinking about our conversation and the things I've done the past decade. When I first started this journey, I was so naïve, so unsure about my powers. Then I got older, and I realized how powerful I was. I could see that my goals were within my grasp, all I had to do was reach for them.

Unfortunately, the road there wasn't a clean one. I've had to do plenty of things, immoral things. I've killed many, and I'm sure I'll have to kill more. I try to tell myself that it's just what I have to do. In order to be a leader, sacrifices have to be made, hands have to be dirty. But how far will I have to go? And how far am I willing to go?

I'd like to think there's a limit, but that ceiling is slowly rising. I used to feel guilt every time I had to kill an Alliance soldier. Now, I'm not so sure. All I can see is that chance at freedom. Everything else is secondary. Is that the right way to think, though? Will I be losing myself the deeper in I get?

I'm not sure. There are days when I wonder if I really choose to live this life, or am I too bound by my desire for a better future? I suppose I was thrust into this path unwillingly. If Lionel Changer never had Bastion kidnap me, I could have been living a different life, one that would be peaceful, one where I was truly happy. I would have been with Fenrir.

Some days I rewatch those last moments I had with him. The Alliance had turned him into my enemy, a shadow of what he used to be. He became a beast with a mechanical soul, and his first task was to kill me. We fought to the death, and I came out the victor, but as he lay there, dying in my arms, I saw a hint of the Fenrir I knew. He didn't speak, he simply looked into my eyes and I saw the wolf trapped in a body he could no longer control. It was the hardest kill I ever had to do, but I did it. I granted him mercy.

I have that last recording, those last moments of his life. We harvested it out of his video feed, straight from his armor. We could have used his body to advance our technology, but we had Fang for that. There was no need to desecrate my love even further. Then we buried him. I hold on to the feed so I can always remember the last seconds I spent with my wolf warrior.

We could have been together, living out in the woods. This chaos that is my life would have never existed. If only Lionel Changer never had sent Bastion to abduct me.

Then again, if I had never been captured, I wouldn't have had Ivy, and the hybrid species would be extinct. I'd be the last of my kind. There would be no hope for the future, no plans for a world where hybrids live free. That's heartbreaking.

I suppose I shouldn't lament on it too much. Sometimes, we can't choose the destiny given to us, no matter how hard we try. We can only play the hand given to us to the best of our ability. So that's why I choose to live on and continue my quest. It's the only thing I can do.

I walk into the research room. There, Lucy is busy working on her compcube. I come up behind her and almost startle her.

"Iris Lawton," she says. "Was not expecting you to recover so soon. How is condition? No longer exhausted? Healed?"

"Yes, I'm feeling better," I say. "Still a little tired, though. How is it on your end?"

"Well."

She has the GTS schematics up on her holoscreen. She's been studying the design since I handed her Mark Allen's head.

"You're working quite quickly," I say to Lucy in an amused tone.

"Was excited to get information on GTS," she says. "Always eager to work on new project. This one has great potential."

"How did you extract the information?"

"Mark Allen had data implants within brain. Simply had to dissect, take out implants, and download data directly from source. Implants very advanced, much more advanced than what we have on record. But still got the job done."

I pat her on the back.

"You never cease to amaze me," I say in a warm voice.

"Thank you," Lucy says. "Will also be able to use cranial implants for future designs."

"We might need those in the future. But back to the main topic, what can you tell me about the GTS?"

Lucy turns her attention away from her holoscreens and looks at me.

"The GTS, also known as Genetic Targeting System, was underground Alliance project developed during Eli Winde's era," she says. "Goal of project was to act as insurance policy in case any certain species started uprising. GTS device has capability to target and destroy specific species and only those species based on genetic pattern. Thus, weapon could be used to harm only one species while other species are safe from harm."

"And how would it do that, exactly?" I ask.

"Chemical compound. User codes structure of target into the GTS operating system, then gaseous compound created on spot, capable of killing such targeted species."

"So it's essentially a deadly gas that's only deadly to the species you want dead. And you can change whatever species the gas is deadly to on the fly?"

"Simple explanation, but yes, that is what Genetic Targeting System does."

"And what radius could the dispersal unit reach?"

"Up to one hundred-mile radius, minimum."

I stop to think for a bit.

"I can see why the Alliance developed such a weapon," I say. "This would squash any threat an individual species would pose. If the gorillas get too powerful, the GTS is there to equalize them. If the cows start to rise, the GTS would even the playing field. It's essentially a weapon to keep everything in control, a weapon of mass destruction in an age where there are none."

"True, but project was never completed," Lucy says.

"The Alliance most likely realized what they had created and saw this would simply add to the problem. That's why they abandoned the project and classified it."

I look at the holoscreen.

"So do you think you can recreate it?" I ask Lucy.

"With enough time, yes," she replies.

"Good. I've already explained to you the long-term plan. Many centuries ago, the world only belonged to humans. Once the other species became just as intelligent, they had to fight for their place in the world. Their trump card, though, was the weapon of mass destruction they created. They used it to win their war and stake their claim in the world."

I point to the GTS schematics on the screen.

"Our army will be built and our rebellion will happen. But this will be our trump card. We will use it to wipe out our enemies while ensuring we survive. And then, we will finally gain the freedom our kind deserves," I say.

Lucy looks at me but says nothing.

"A long time ago, when the animals fired off their WMD, they called it the Event," I say. "Now, we will have an Event of our own. It won't happen overnight, but I envision a future where it will happen. We'll have to get to work soon. It's time to get our hands dirty."

Chapter 39 – General Rox

Unfinished

October 3, 3071 11:01 AM

"Your pre-lunch meeting has arrived," my secretary, Jo, says to me.

"Ah, of course, send him in," I say.

I'm in my office, resting after back-to-back meetings with my superiors. They aren't happy. It's been a horrible week. Mark Allen is dead. He was the head of my covert science team, the leader of the Implant Program. He was handpicked to succeed Eli Winde in his work, one of the original team members that has made my soldiers so strong. My future plans were riding on him, and now I have to worry about what happens next.

The shitty thing is I knew it was coming. The moment Eli Winde was murdered, we were ready to take on The Collector. I had a cadre of guards protecting Allen round the clock. We made sure he stayed only within the facility. We took every precaution possible.

And he's still dead.

I suppose my greatest folly was that I trusted that damn rat, Two Van Faye. I had reason to. Her bodyguard, Ash Han, had skill and was the only creature able to go toe to toe with The Collector. They fought several battles, and Han was able to come out alive in each one. Not even my most elite soldiers could make that claim.

Yet, in the end, it all went to hell. Ash Han failed her mission. Mark Allen was decapitated, his head never found. It's probable that The Collector... well, collected it.

I was ready to rain fire on Two Van Faye. Our partnership was over. Then I found out she was dead too, and Ash Han was nowhere to be found. And that's how things ended.

It's kind of a shame. In many ways, Van Faye was an excellent informant. Through her, the Alliance was able to infiltrate Fan Zui Bin and learn its mysteries. We accomplished something we always aimed for, but never could do.

Then again, she won't be missed. She was a pain to deal with, always bitching about something. And she thought she was bigger than she really was. She never realized how replaceable scum like her are, and that's exactly what we plan to do. We'll find someone else to be our contact in no time.

Personally, I think I'm done with Fan Zui Bin. Some other Alliance top dog can take care of it. I never enjoyed dealing with Van Faye, and I certainly don't look forward to working with the next one. Those Fan Zui Bin thugs are all scum.

Suddenly, the door opens, and in walks my next appointment. It's a large, stocky, Caucasian man, one I've worked with for many years now. He's my top agent, the one I wish I sent to protect Mark Allen. I couldn't, though, he was occupied with another mission before the Allen crisis started.

"Sir," he says, saluting me.

He has one hand touching his forehead. It's all serious business with him.

"At ease," I say. He lowers his arm. "How did things go in the Wolf's Den?"

"Excellent," he says. "The mission was completed efficiently."

"And the data?"

"It's no longer in the head of the wolf who stole it. I did a total mind wipe. Everything is cleared out and cleaned."

"Did she cause much trouble for you?"

He scoffs at my statement.

"Hardly," he says. "C'mon, look who that rookie was up against."

I simply chuckle at his statement. But then I get back to my serious self.

"Good work obtaining the data," I say. "Who knows what that wolf was planning to do with it, but if it had gotten out, we could have had a wolf rebellion on our hands. I don't think they would take kindly to the experiments we did on their kind in the initial stages of the Implant Program. You have helped avert a worldwide crisis."

"All in a day's work," he says.

"So what did you end up doing with the wolf herself, this Falena Snow?"

"I had to knock her out to erase the data, but she's still alive."

"You let her live?"

"You never told me to kill her."

I flash him a glare of mild annoyance.

"I thought you would have taken the initiative," I say in an irritated tone.

"Look, I do what I'm told," he says. "I wasn't told to do that."

"Very well. But just know that one day, you'll have to sweep up that mess."

"Should I do it now?"

"No, there's something much more pressing that I'm assigning you."

"A new mission?"

"An old one."

I activate my compcube and use it to play a holographic video.

"This is the penthouse of Two Van Faye," I say. "She didn't know it, but I had it rigged with surveillance equipment. You have to be extra careful around these criminal types. Now watch."

My agent looks at the holoscreen intensely. On it is the last confrontation between Ash Han and The Collector.

"You want me to kill this target?" he asks. "Find The Collector because everyone else has failed?"

"Yes, but as I said before, this isn't a new mission. It's an old one," I say.

"I've never been assigned to kill The Collector."

"Perhaps you have. Continue watching."

Han and The Collector are engaged in a furious battle. Just when it looks like it's over, Han throws a desperate punch. The Collector's mask flies off and reveals what lies underneath, not only to Han and Van Faye, but to my cameras as well.

"Look familiar?" I ask my agent.

His mouth drops in shock. He's speechless, completely stunned with what he sees on the holoscreen.

"Halfkinds," he utters.

"Yes," I say. "Many, many years ago, I sent you on a mission to eliminate their kind. It was called Operation HORUS. When it was over, we thought we wiped them all out. The mission was a success. Yet it looks like we were wrong. They still exist, and all this time they were right under our noses."

My agent remains stunned.

"Judging from my dealings with The Collector, they've grown powerful," I say. "And now they have all that sensitive information stuck in Mark Allen's head. The GTS project was never fully developed, but if these halfkinds are somehow able to recreate it, the damage could be catastrophic. I need them eliminated. That's why I'm entrusting you. I'm already in hot water with my superiors over all this, so I need it handled. I'm not sure if The Collector is the only one left or if there are more. I understand it may be a long search, but eventually, you will find them. You will destroy them. You're my best shot."

I look him straight in the eyes. He's no longer stunned, just ready to get into action.

"Agent Brock West," I say. "You have a mission to complete."

About The Author

Andrew Vu is a novelist who was born in San Jose, CA. He graduated from UC Berkeley in 2007 and currently resides in Oakland, CA. During his spare time, he enjoys movies, video games, and watching sports. He roots for his California Golden Bears, the Kansas City Chiefs, the Golden State Warriors, and the Oakland A's.

If you enjoyed the book, feel free to leave a review! The author greatly appreciates and welcomes any kind of feedback.

Now available:
Halfkinds Volume 1: Contact
http://www.amazon.com/Halfkinds-Volume-1-Contact-ebook/dp/B009RG6AUM/

Halfkinds Volume 2: Horus
http://www.amazon.com/Halfkinds-Volume-2-Horus-ebook/dp/B00BIR36QO/

Halfkinds Volume 3: Alphas
http://www.amazon.com/Halfkinds-3-Alphas-Andrew-Vu-ebook/dp/B00GB8KUWI/

Also check out the Halfkinds online encyclopedia at http://halfkinds.wikia.com!